Marissa Monteilh

SOMETHING
he can feel

A Life Changing Book *in conjunction with* Power Play Media

Published by
Life Changing Books
P.O. Box 423
Brandywine, MD 20613

www.lifechangingbooks.net

This novel is a work of fiction. Any references to real people, events, establishments, or locales are intended only to give the fiction a sense of reality and authenticity. Other names, characters, and incidents occurring in the work are either the product of the author's imagination or are used fictitiously, as are those fictionalized events and incidents that involve real persons. Any character that happens to share the name of a person who is an acquaintance of the author, past or present, is purely coincidental and is in no way intended to be an actual account involving that person.

Library of Congress Cataloging-in-Publication Data;

ISBN 978-1-934230862

Also by Marissa Monteilh

May December Souls
The Chocolate Ship
Hot Boyz
Make Me Hot
Dr. Feelgood
As Fate Would Have It

Preface

Each year, domestic assault affects more than six-million women. Domestic abuse has plagued marriages for centuries. And even though it is strongly looked down upon, and women have gained equality, intimate abuse is still a growing problem.

Though there is no excuse for violence, part of the reason might be that nineteenth century religious beliefs often encouraged women's subordination in the household. Some men incorrectly felt justified to use violence. The husband was seen as superior, and she, the wife, was seen as his property. He was the owner and it was his duty to protect her and limit her behavior. Unfortunately, marital cruelty spelled male domination.

If wife beating was perceived as a man's legal right of power over his wife, what about husband-beating? What are the true numbers of men who are beaten by women? What about marital cruelty that spells female domination? Even though there are patriarchal views of women being subordinate to men, what would make a man subordinate to a woman from a matriarchal standpoint? What would cause a woman to take on the superior role over her husband and take control over his actions through violence?

Something He Can Feel flips the script on spousal abuse. It is the story of a wife who deals with extreme issues of anger and rage, and her fervent battle with control. Not knowing how to channel her feelings, nor understanding the root of the anger, the wife takes out her frustrations on the closest person to her, the person she's promised to love, honor and respect…her man, verbally and physically attacking him as a release from her internal pain whenever the green-eyed monster comes to visit. All because of her fear of losing him.

The main character in *Something He Can Feel* is playing a man's game by making sure her husband can feel her pain in exact measure, or so she thinks. But when she's forced to come to terms with her past, her present, and her future, and make some serious decisions about herself, can she break her long pattern of behavior and save herself, when her first impulse is to be a husband-beater?

Ack-dedi-note

As opposed to an acknowledgement section the way I usually write one, I'd like this section to be sort of an acknowledgement, dedication, and author's note, all in one. I call it an Ack-dedi-note! ☺

First of all, as usual, I thank God for my gift. I have found my passion and my professional purpose, and I am grateful each and every day of my life for that discovery. The word of God plays a major part in this story and I don't believe it could have been written as vividly without those scenes.

I'm thankful for my family and friends who understand my career, who allow me the times of isolation when I must go under-ground, and who support me unconditionally. I love you one and all!

A big hug of appreciation to authors Mary B. Morrison and Victoria Christopher Murray.

And I offer deep and personal thanks to Nakea Murray, Tressa Smallwood, Leslie Allen, Aschundria Fisher and everyone connected with Life Changing Books and Power Play Media, for believing in this unusual story when some were afraid of it. A broken, abusive female character–oh my! A story about a flawed female protagonist, told in third person while keeping close eye on all of her dysfunctions, yet striving to keep her three-dimensional. I knew this story had to be and would be told. It is definitely my most challenging book to date.

I also knew that even though I had a couple of options as far as who to contract with, the right home for this story was Life Changing Books. It was Nakea and Tressa, along with Leslie, who have all allowed me the freedom to write this novel the way I wanted to write it, and who encouraged me through phenomenal, detailed copyedits to really dig in and get to the heart of Marina Maxwell Baskerville. Thank you Life Changing Books for being brave enough to nontraditionally change lives through the book you publish whether it be the lives of authors or the lives of readers. I'm proud to be a part of the LCB family!

I want to also say that I wrote this story because I believe it needed to be told. I'm speaking of this particular story, not some other story. In society today, we have many versions of books, movies, plays, documenttaries, television shows, etc., told about women who are physically and verbally abused by men. And I acknowledge that each story is different, and each story is necessary, told just the way the writers meant for them to be told.

I've written *Something He Can Feel* to tell the other side of intimate abuse. The countless numbers of men who are abused at the hands of women need their side told as well. There are men who are ashamed and who suffer in silence in vast numbers, partially because they don't want to be seen as wimps, as punks, or as soft. They feel the pressure to be something they're really not, and their egos can't handle the criticism. While women hide in shame, suffer in silence and keep the abuse that's brought upon them a dirty little secret, men, as well, haven't learned yet that it's okay to tell, maybe even more so. They get caught up in society's standard of what a real man should be, and so they, too, suffer in silence.

I did not write this book so much for the male victims of partner abuse. I wrote this story for the female perpetrators of the abuse. Because more often than not, in one way or another, they've been victims themselves. I do hope that men read this story, don't get me wrong. But, if there is one woman who reads this story and it reminds her of a woman she knows, or better yet, if it reminds her of herself…if there's one woman who can recall a moment when she too felt rage…if there's one woman who can remember what it felt like to not be understood by a man so they swung…if there's one woman who can remember feeling so jealous that she felt her only option was to throw something…if there's one woman who believed that she just plain old wasn't being heard, so she raised her voice because she needed to get someone's attention, then this story was worth the labor. Therefore, *Something He Can Feel* is dedicated to all of us women.

Abuse is about control. It is wrong, it is demoralizing, and it scars for life. And yes, it is abuse even if it is a slap, a kick, a punch, or an object is thrown.

If you or someone you know is an abuser or an abusee, I beg you to seek help. Contact the National Domestic Violence Hotline at 800.799.SAFE, www.ndvh.org, or discretely tell someone at work, or at church, or someone else you can truly trust. But reach out. Don't suffer in silence any longer, whether you are on the receiving end, or the giving end. Don't let the shackles of shame keep you a slave to anger. Give yourself something you can feel…peace.

With much love and appreciation,
Marissa Monteilh
a.k.a. The Diva Writer
www.marissamonteilh.com
www.myspace.com/divawriter

Introduction

“...the agony and the ecstasy.”

The make-up sex was powerful insanity. She literally fucked the shit out of him.

Aretha’s song *Something He Can Feel* serenaded their frenzied bumps and heated grinds, permeating their audible senses. It was as though each note was being poured into their bodies like thick, sweet molasses, guiding their interlocked silhouettes into a sticky, sensual, soulful, sensational frenzy.

He allowed the aroma of her familiar Tahitian vanilla body oil to travel up his nostrils. "You promise to cut that shit out?" he yelled while vigorously pounding her hot, shapely frame with intense, repeated, rhythmic strokes.

It, the make-up sex, was a noun.

It really was a person, place, and thing.

It had a life of its own.

It screwed him back with all five senses.

It could be seen, tasted, touched, heard, and sniffed.

The stimulating three-letter word was commanding enough to unmistakably wash away all of the punches, the slaps, the words, the lies, the yelling, the door slamming, the hang-ups, the threats, the denial, the therapy, the accusations, and the jealousy. The make-up sex made up yet another reason to try and forget the violent past and the heartbreaking emotional pain.

She grinded fiercely.

It was carnal.

The lustful chemicals from the gyrating strokes and strong orgasms and wet kisses and flowing tears and whispered pillow-spoken promises were authoritative enough to make him believe she'd never go there again. She would never, ever, ever, ever, ever…go off on him again. But it was like a chain smoker who doesn’t realize she keeps lighting up. It was a conditional reflex. For her, it was a cerebral dance.

His name is Mangus.

Her name is Marina.

Marina Maxwell Baskerville.

He is her husband.

She is his wife.

She is his wife and his life.

She is his life and his psycho passionate mate who did everything to the max.

She did everything to the max from cursing him out to riding him through his robust throbbing ejaculations.

Riding him through his ejaculations while talking shit either way.

Talking shit, and yelling either way.

Driving him abso-fuckin-lutely crazy.

He stroked her madly with the animalistic intensity of his frustrations, still erect like a stone column, after releasing his love once, twice, almost three times.

How could he break away from her one-two punch when the reality was that Marina Maxwell Baskerville was his love and his lover?

Yet she was a husband-beater.

"I promise," she said, looking smack dab into his gorgeous, forgiving, cocoa brown eyes. "I'll never do it again."

She hoped that the depth of her commanding hips spoke louder than her usual predictable words as he continued to lose himself inside of her receiving body, deep inside the depths of her very being, hitting his fast approaching third burst harder than he'd ever been hit in the face.

Inch-by-inch.

He was lost.

Caught between the agony and the ecstasy.

The ecstasy being the vagina.

The agony being the fist.

He had it bad. Pussy whipped, bad!

Prologue

1990

"...in hell where I belonged?"

My name is Marina.

It was July 12th.

From what I recall, it was my very first memory of what it was like to feel absolute anger…and take it out on someone you love.

I remember it was one of those muggy and heated afternoons in the Southwest area of what we call Hotlanta. It was the kind of heat that made sweat bead-up on your forehead, almost like tiny raindrops.

It was two-years after my father died.

I had a summer job at a little dress shop and I was a sophomore at Westlake High School where I was on the track team.

It was a moment when I had an absolute out-of-body experience.

I actually saw my body from the outside in.

And it scared even me.

His license plate read *Loose Goose*, which was also his CB radio handle. How appropriate.

"Stop this fuckin car, now," I screamed with an high-pitched intensity that matched the speed of his souped-up, banana-yellow Camaro. With wide tires and a radio antenna sprouting from the center of his rear spoiler like a beanstalk, his car was just as fast and flashy as he was. "Punk ass mothafucka." My voice pierced even my own ears.

Applying a forceful, neck-jolting slam on the brakes, my lanky basketball jock, high-school senior boyfriend, held tight to the steering wheel as his pride-and-joy screeched into a circular spin and then came to an abrupt stop. The oversized speakers belted "*Kiss*" by Prince.

Burnt rubber was the smell.

Smoke from the Pirelli tires filled the air.

My teenaged heart went thump, thump, thump, in the same quick intensity as the heat of my puberty-filled anger.

I pulled on the chrome door handle with force. "Let me the hell out of here," I yelled as I kicked the door squarely. The handle would not cooperate so I pushed with all of my body weight, which was about a buck-oh-five worth back then.

He turned off the ignition and yanked the key. "You know you can't just get out of this car in the middle of the street. You're miles from home."

"Home will be anywhere you're not," I hollered as the heavy door suddenly flew open.

"Marina, get back in here," he shouted through clenched teeth, reaching toward my slender fleeing body, just barely grazing my bony left elbow.

I hopped out wearing tight blue jeans and slammed the door as he simultaneously opened the driver side door.

"Get back in here so I can take you home." He jumped out high-stepping with his long legs. He wore a dark blue, nylon-jogging suit.

I began sprinting down Cascade Road onto Danforth, into a little subdivision with big homes. It was unusually quiet and no one walked the streets. "Leave me the hell alone."

"No. I won't leave you alone out here by yourself. Now you get back here." He grabbed my arm and pulled my blouse from behind. I snatched my lean body away. My cotton sleeve ripped like paper. He moved his hand back and up toward the sky.

I made an abrupt stop and an instant about-face, bracing my feet in a balanced straddle, pulling my leather purse strap up my arm with my left hand.

He looked willing to retreat. "Sorry about that."

I balled up my right hand and pulled it back toward my shoulder, inhaling and exhaling in waves. I gave him a side-angled look. My face was blood red. "Did you just rip my blouse? You don't want to fuck with me. I promise you. But you know what? Try me." My eyes dared him. They begged him. They pleaded with him.

He held both hands up in surrender. "Marina. Calm down."

"Oh, hell no. You do some shit like fuck around on me like that and then wanna tell me to calm down? You risked me and my feelings just so you could fuck around by pulling that tired ass move."

"I didn't mean to hurt you."

I stayed in pre-jab position. My tennis shoes were positioned one in front of the other. Laila Ali's best fighting stance had nothin on me. "You just didn't mean for me to find out."

Looking puzzled, he shook his head while lowering his arms to his side. "Why are you acting like this? This is not like you. Are you about to start your period?"

Oh no he didn't. "How dare you blame your behavior on my damn menstrual cycle? I'm acting like this because I fell in love with you, that's why. The question is…why did you fuck a tramp like Clydra Champion, of all the girls in school?"

"I didn't."

"You did."

"I didn't."

"You did."

"I did not."

"Howard, you sure as hell did. I heard you."

"What are you talking about?"

"I was at her house."

He blinked a mile a minute.

My breaths slowed a bit. I dropped my hand but still kept my fist clenched. "You were set up. What happened was, we called you to see if you would take the bait. I should have known that your weak little dick would jump at the chance. I was on the other phone in her mother's room when you accepted her invitation to meet you at the *Motel 6* on Old National."

I sniffled like I wanted to cry but my anger chased away my tears.

I kept yelling, "And then, you had the nerve to stop by my job to pick me up afterwards, wearing the same damn pants you pulled down to fuck her nasty stank behind. The sweat pants I bought you for Christmas. I know you two just left the motel. It was all I could do to wait to confront your ass." Another tear traveled right into my mouth. I pressed my lips together to catch it and tasted its warm saltiness. My throat tightened as I fought to swallow my own saliva that in actuality, I wanted to spit right in his cheating ass face. My breathing again sped up. I could feel the redness of my squinted eyes as I spoke through gritted teeth. "You're just a typical man. And that bitch went on ahead and let you fuck her. I can't believe you both betrayed me."

He stood tall with an expression that said his mind was racing to grasp one last bit of denial. "I don't know what you're talking about. I'm telling you, I went to take my mom to look for a new Cadillac this afternoon and that's it. You've gotta believe me."

I opened my hand and raised it high to meet to his face, flexing it within one inch of his nose. I wanted to smash my palm right up against his wide nostrils. I never did like his nose. "You went to fuck Clydra. So fuck you." I began to turn around but his voice placed stop signs in my path.

"Marina."

I looked back and he took a half step toward me. I said, "If you take another step, I will beat you down."

He pointed back in the direction of his Camaro. "You will get your ass in this car. Now."

I pointed back in the direction of his Camaro. "You will get the hell out of here and leave me alone. Now."

"Marina, I'm telling you. We didn't do anything."

"You are such a dog and a liar. I hate you." I shook my head in pity.

"Fine, then, hate me. But I know one thing...you can be as mad and as hateful as you wanna be, but I'm not going anywhere. And I won't hit you. My mom raised me better than that. Plus, I won't risk going to jail or getting kicked off the team. So, I'll just follow you all the way home, or wherever you go, no matter how long it takes." He folded his arms.

"And I'll scream and tell the first person I see that you're following me. I'll swear I don't know you."

Through his eyes I could see the words *fed up* flash into view. As quick as the flick of a light switch, he waved his hand at me. "You know what? Forget it. You'll be sorry because nothing happened."

"As long as I'm no longer fuckin your cheating ass I don't care."

"Goodbye. And good luck with your temper problems." He excused me with a cutting glance.

"Good luck with your dick problems."

"Psycho."

"Loose Goose."

"Now I will be."

I again raised my flat hand to him like a valley girl. "Whatever."

"Go to hell."

"Asshole." I headed in the other direction. The wind was non-existent. The bright rays of the sun stung my face. I was heated. I was literally as hot as hell. I was hot blooded. I was hot and bothered. I was fuming. I took two steps. He said one word.

"Bitch."

Oh no. Did the world just stop? I ask you, did the world just stop? Somebody please tell me the world did not just stop. I turned back in his direction and cocked my head to the side. "What did you fuckin call me?"

He had the nerve to simply turn around and walk away.

My loudness shifted into another level. Whatever tinge of valley girl I had in me before was now chased away by a neck rollin, one-hundred percent ghetto chick. "Get your ass back here. What did you call me?"

His feet were moving extra swiftly. He spoke his words while still giving me his back. "You have a real problem."

"Did you just call me a bitch?"

"Yes. Yes, I did. Because you are." His steps quickened even more. Even with a view of his cowardly back, I could clearly see his denial. I could smell his dogism.

"Mothafucka. Get your ass back here." I screamed my words and shifted into a fast jog, staying right on his heels at all times. I managed to pull the material of his sweat jacket from behind. He jerked away and then stopped. So did I. He turned around and faced me. Cockiness resided in his gigolo-laced brown eyes, and it pissed me the fuck off.

The words *beat his ass* flashed before me and that was all I saw as I welled up with even more anger and just started swinging. Swinging like he was the baseball and I was the bat, about to hit a ninth-inning home run out of the ballpark. In a flurry of fast paced moves, I stood on the tips of my toes and took his nose into my furious hand and bent it upward like I was turning a damn door handle, squeezing his flesh like silly putty. He reached for my arms, trying to pull me away, but I dug my fingers into his face and pressed as deep as I could and began scratching his eyes out. He held on to one of my hands, but with my other hand I kept hitting him in the mouth like I wanted to put his ignorant ass in a coma.

He released my hand and spun away, stumbling slightly from the uneven ground. He fought to keep his footing and jumped back in a fighter's stance, leading with his right leg.

I stood firm. "Dumb ass bastard." My chest rose and fell quickly.

He rubbed his mouth and his face and then looked down at his hand. The cowardly blood of a liar dripped from a deep cut on his cheek, and his nose looked like it was actually throbbing. His eyelids were red.

He squinted as though the sun was blinding, but in a desperate counter attack move of his own, he clenched his hand and drew his arm back, sending his fist surging into my jaw just as I tried to lower my head and duck, but he caught me with a right hook.

My head darted back and I swear I saw stars. My vision was blurred and I struggled to focus. My jaw felt like it was on fire. I squeezed my eyes shut and then opened them and a tear fell from my eye just as the sight of him cleared up and I saw him standing there, with his head low and his chin down, looking at me like he was yearning to fuck me up.

His hateful look said I needed to get a grip, like he couldn't believe I was still standing toe-to-toe with him.

He asked loudly, "Now are you ready to listen?"

I shook my head. "You called me a bitch, so bring it on. Standing there like you wanna box. I'm ready for your ass."

He looked amazed and leaned toward me while I stood firm again. He took one step my way.

And then two.

And then he was within six-inches of my face. I counted to ten while he blinked on each count.

He had the nerve to yell each word. "I did not sleep with Clydra."

Just what I hate. A fuckin liar.

I shifted into a kicking whatever part of his lanky body I could connect with, mainly to his ribs and to his measly little penis. He covered his nuts with his hands and then he saw a passing car slow down. He began to run backwards toward his car, trying to act like he was retreating.

With the side of my face stinging, I fought to run as fast as I could. "You fuck around on me and then when I call you on it, I'm the bitch? You need to be proud of your player status. Don't lie about it. If more women went off on you assholes, maybe you'd think twice before you went pussy diving with someone's best friend. This is for every woman who you have fucked around on, or ever will fuck around on in your entire tired ass life."

"You know what? You need to be locked up. You…"

"Call me a bitch again. Go ahead."

He looked like he just wanted to be gone and pivoted the other way like he was running the forty-yard dash. I still gave chase to his every stride.

"Get your ass back here."

With each breath and each step, he kept getting further and further away. My mind wanted to connect with his back so badly, but my fatigued body wouldn't allow it. Still, I ran and ran, and before I knew it, he was opening his car door, starting it up, and putting it in gear all at once.

One quick second unfolded in complete slow motion. As hard as I tried, I couldn't manage to leap across the ten or so feet toward the tail end of his car fast enough. I wished I could have gone air-bound like Mike. I wanted to fly.

He put the pedal to the medal and all I wanted to do was get my fingertips within reach of his fleeting, shiny, silver radio antenna.

He took off just as I…just as I realized that his antenna was in my hand. Without even noticing that I really wanted to, I took the antenna into both hands and broke it in half with a jolt, as the fumes from his exhaust crept up toward my face.

It was then that in the distance I heard a police car's siren.

I stood breathing hard as hell with sweat running down my face. I exhaled.

And then I noticed a young girl, maybe five years old. She had dark, curly hair and she stood on the front porch of a large, redbrick house, looking over at me with her mouth as wide as her enormous dark eyes. Her youthful mother stood behind her, with her hands on her daughter's shoulders, making a point of turning her child around to escort her away from my questionable sanity and back into the safety and normalcy of their home.

There I stood in the bright daylight, exhausted, blinking with shame as I looked away from them in humiliation. I wore my indignity like a badge, along with the tiny splatters of blood on my forearms.

The sirens sounded closer.

Then I noticed an elderly man standing on the corner watching me. He shook his head. Even from where I stood, I could see his shame for me in his eyes. My shame for myself was the same.

I stood with each half of the broken antenna in each hand. I relaxed my swollen hands and dropped the pieces in the street. As the slender metal met the gray pavement with a bounce and a thud, I turned around, walking while eyeing the sidewalk. I could feel my jaw pulsating. And I could feel my tail between my legs. I made a point to not step on a crack. What if I fell straight through one and ended up in hell where I belonged?

After a few blocks, I found my purse, but not my pride. Where had I been for the past fifteen minutes? Who was that crazy ass girl? And how could I ever make sure she would never, ever…come back again?

The sound of the sirens stopped.

Chapter One

Summer 2007

"...a waist twenty inches smaller than her hips..."

Her posture was grand. She always sat up straight with her shoulders back and her forever legs crossed. Perhaps it was from her brief year of ballet training as a child. Her elongated neck and stature were the epitome of regality and grace. On the outside, she had it all together.

And in the news business, it was her outsides that had gotten her so far in her career, along with her gift for telling a story, and her exceptional level of intelligence. She had always been on the honor roll in high school, and graduated at the top of her class from Kennesaw State University with a degree in communications. She was a hard working, liberated woman who aside from her fame and success in the world, was finally proud to be able to say that she had found the man of her dreams. And she was about to be married.

"And that's our four-o'clock newscast for today, the 1st day of June. From Bob, Jim, and Ann, and everyone here at First Witness News, I'm Marina Maxwell wishing you a good afternoon. We'll be back at six-o'clock. We hope you can join us. Until then, keep the faith."

After Marina's usual closing wink to her adoring viewing audience of the number-one rated newscast in Atlanta, a smile of beauty grew across her face. She ran her French-manicured fingernails across the back of her cherry wine, conservative bob-hairstyle, fingering her soft curls.

With the station's crested ink pen in her left hand, the very hand that adorned her multi-carat, platinum engagement ring, confident and curvy Marina sported her tailored, coal-black and yellow St. John suit as she ended the program while the closing credits rolled. She shuffled multi-colored teleprompter pages and made small talk with her conservative looking male co-anchor named Bob Hill.

"Clear," yelled the young floor director.

"Good show," Marina told her partner, as they stood simultaneously and then stepped down from the state-of-the-art set, removing their earpieces. She placed her supportive hand on her co-anchor's back.

Blonde and tanned, Bob Hill motioned for her to proceed first. "Good energy, Marina. Your upcoming nuptials must be coming along nicely. I think marriage will do you good. I've never seen you look so happy."

Marina's warm grin spread. "I am pretty happy, Bob. Life is good." She was in her usual post-anchorwoman fifth-gear. "Are you and Jennifer gonna be able to make it?"

"I believe she RSVP'd a positive response. At least I think she did."

"Oh good. I'm sure she did. I've been a little busy lately, just piling up the reply cards without even opening them. I've got to work on up-dating our confirmation list as soon as possible."

"I'll bet you have a lot of people coming."

"We're planning on about a-hundred. It's been tough narrowing it down."

The assignment desk editor spoke as they approached him. "Marina, line two is for you."

"Okay, thanks. I'll see you in an hour Bob."

"Sure thing," he said as he nodded, stopping at the assignment editor's desk.

Marina headed in the direction of her cubicle, wearing a happy face along the way. She had big Maybelline eyes and a waist twenty inches smaller than her hips, mainly due to her backside.

She grabbed the phone just as she took her seat, slipped off her black leather pumps, removed her tiny hoop earrings, and maneuvered the wireless mouse while glancing at her flat screen monitor at the same time. "This is Marina." She listened intently and then spoke softly. "Hi Mabel. I'm sorry but I can't get by there today."

"Why not?" Marina's mother asked.

Marina flexed her jaw. "First of all, I'm on the air later, and I have an in-studio interview in about one-half hour, and the Make-A-Wish Foundation is coming by so I can meet a young lady as a part of their mentor program. Plus, I'm filling in for Pam Sykes who's out for a couple of days, so I have to do the late news. That means it'll be about midnight before I get out of here. This is one of my nearly twelve-hour days."

Her mother sighed deeply. "What am I supposed to do, Marina?"

"Mabel, I don't know."

"I don't have anyone else but you."

"Yeah, well you should."

"What does that mean?"

Marina split her focus, checking out her many awaiting emails. She clicked her mouse twice. "Look, I've really gotta go."

"What about Mangus?"

Marina's eyebrows dipped. "What about him?"

"Do you think he can come by and take me to my check up? He offered to before, and I know he lives not too far from here."

"Mangus is at work, too." Marina opened an email from a cancer organization announcing that she'd been nominated for their community support award. She spoke as she scanned the words. "You need to get one of those services that pick-up seniors. I think that would be a convenient resource at times like this."

"I'm hardly a senior. I'm not even sixty."

"Well then see if you can network with someone at the singles meetings you attend every week. Have you even tried to make any friends over there?"

"Not really."

"Plus, I think it would be good if you could let us know way beforehand when you have appointments. You always call just before, always in a panic."

"You're getting too big for your britches, young lady. And those old foggies at that center bored me to death. I haven't been there in weeks."

Marina again scrolled through her in-box for priority messages. "Anyway. I don't have the same hours now so I can't help you out late afternoons and early evenings like I did before."

"I'm calling Mangus. I'm calling Mangus. I'm calling Mangus."

Marina took a long pregnant pause. She wondered if her mother actually said those words three times, or if it just sounded three times as annoying.

While turning away from her computer, an instant light-bulb moment flashed across the screen of her mind. Marina realized suddenly that it wasn't so much her mother's words, but it was her mother's deep, slow,

low volume of a voice, nearly a seductive tone, that made goose bumps gather along her skin.

She closed down her email and pushed aside the mouse. "I told you, he's at…you know what? Go right ahead. Call Mangus." Marina promptly jumped to her feet, slipped on her shoes and grabbed a beta-tape from her desk.

Mabel spoke one level above under her breath. "Your own fiancé treats me better than you do."

Marina lifted her hair along the back of her neck and rubbed her moist skin. "Like I said, I've gotta go. Keep the faith. Goodbye."

Marina immediately placed the receiver to the hook and stepped away toward the editing bay, shaking her head yet managing to give a major grin that exposed every one of her bleached teeth as she strolled along. All eyes in the newsroom were on her. "How's the number-one rated news team doing? Okay?" She spoke like a cheerleading captain.

"Yes, Marina," her coworkers replied in song-like unison.

She flashed an A-okay sign with her thumb and index finger. "Good. Let's make this next newscast the best one ever. Excellence is our goal." She ended her sentences with exclamatory nods.

Excellence had not eluded her when it came to work.

But excellence was not her friend when it came to men, or when it came to her mother.

Mabel was an irritating reminder to Marina of why things were the way they were.

She was a reminder of the root of it all.

A reminder that nightmares really do come true.

A reminder of where Marina came from and why, when she was younger, she had no choice but to leave home and get away.

Chapter Two

"Her bark is bigger than her bite."

Even at the age of fifty-six, Mabel Maxwell, Marina's mother, was still able to turn heads. Back in the day, she had been sought after by men of all ages and men of all races.

When she was in her twenties, she was known for having the body-of-life. Her rear end was her calling card, her attention-getter, and her claim to fame. And she had passed it on to her only child, Marina. Mabel was tall, dark, and now a little bit more full-figured, but her hips still swelled gracefully out of her waist. Her silhouette was womanly sexy.

An hour after her phone call to Marina, Mabel rushed around her small one-bedroom apartment in Lithonia, trying to get herself ready just in case she could get a ride. After her tuna fish sandwich on wheat, she placed her late lunch dishes in the dishwasher, and cleaned off the laminate counter.

On a regular basis over the past year or so, she used her at-home auto monitor to check her blood pressure, now needing to take meds every day and see a doctor monthly. She'd been dizzy lately, short of breath at times, and extremely tired. Her hands felt numb every now and then. Also, her joints seemed to ache but she hadn't yet decided to tell her daughter.

She left word for one of the young ladies who ran the weekly singles meeting, even though deep down she didn't want to bother her. And she also left a message for her future son-in-law, Mangus.

Mabel didn't drive since she'd gotten in a car accident years ago that traumatized her to the point where she never got behind the wheel again. She'd been hit head-on by a man she was dating. And though she walked away with only a small break to her collarbone, he lost his life. Marina, who was also in the car, was released after a minor blow to her forehead. She'd jerked forward into the dashboard.

Mabel had banked the money the insurance company paid her but it didn't take long to run through it. She now lived solely on social security.

She plopped her long body onto her soft, green leather recliner after pulling out the yellow pages to call a taxi as a last resort. She spoke out loud. "Keep the faith? You've gotta have some faith in order to keep it." Mabel ran her hand through her short hair. The strands were dark gray like an overcast sky. And that's just the way she let it be.

She grabbed the cream-colored old-school phone upon the first ring.

"Hello."

"Hello Mabel. How are you?"

A smile took over and her lips spread like butter to expose her semi-crooked capped teeth. "Mangus. Oh, I'm fine, honey. Thanks for returning my call. It's good to hear your voice."

"Good to hear your voice, too."

She sat back and pressed the TV remote. Instantly, the image of her newscaster daughter appeared. She was reporting on a bank robbery in progress.

"Mangus. Your future wife is on television."

"I know. I'm watching her right now."

"She looks so good."

"She got it from you."

Mabel blushed like a teenager. "You are the sweetest, Mangus. I'm glad you're not out on that call. I think about you being out there protecting the streets all the time."

"No need to worry about me."

"Well, I do. And how are your mom and dad doing anyway?"

"They're well, thanks."

"Good. You know what? I don't want to be a bother but I need to know…"

"Mabel, Marina already called me."

"She did?"

"Yes. And of course I can pick you up. I'll be there shortly."

Mabel raised her eyebrows and crossed her legs. "Are you sure? I don't want to interfere. I know it's late but I tried to get the last appointment of the day."

"No problem."

"You're not picking me up in a patrol car are you?"

Mangus let out a hearty laugh. "No, Mabel. I'm off today."

"You are? Marina said you were at work."

"I know. She thought I was. She let me have it about that."

She shifted the receiver to her other ear. "About what?"

"Because I forgot to tell her I had the department's annual test at the shooting range, so I didn't have to actually go in."

"Oh, surely she understood that."

"Yeah, but she was right. I should have told her. I forgot."

Mabel clicked her tongue. She glanced again at her daughter's image. "Oh, don't you let Marina boss you around now. Her bark is bigger than her bite."

"It's all about making the woman happy, that's what my dad always said. And that's why I'm headed in your direction now. See you shortly."

"Thanks Mangus. Thanks so much. Marina doesn't deserve you."

* * *

The sky had long turned into late evening but the temperature had only cooled slightly.

A little bit after the final day's news report, Marina was on her way home in the darkness. She pressed her bare foot to the accelerator and cruised the deserted highway in her sterling silver Acura TL. She adjusted her earpiece after instructing her phone to dial Mangus.

"Hi, honey. Now I just know Mabel had something negative to say about me for not taking her to her appointment."

"She did not. How was your day?" Mangus asked casually.

"It was okay. You mean she didn't mention it? I'm telling you I would have done it if I'd had the time. But, oh well. That woman just gets to me." She inserted her favorite Mary J. CD, *Growing Pains* and selected the *Work in Progress* track.

"Baby, you already told me you were busy and couldn't get away. No worries."

She sang along, tapping her fingers on the steering wheel, *And just like me, tryna be complete*. "No worries, huh? Okay, no worries. Listen, Mangus, did you get an RSVP from Bob Hill and his wife?"

"Yes. I gave it to you."

Marina turned down the volume of the music. "When was that?"

"Last weekend. I handed it to you when you came over."

"Oh really? I don't remember."

"I handed it to you with some other mail addressed to you."

She gave a semi-neck roll as though he was in the car. "But you noticed that an RSVP was with the stack and didn't tell me?"

"Yes, I noticed. Why?"

"Well, Bob told me they replied and I felt stupid."

"We can go over all that this weekend and get it organized."

Marina signaled to turn as she was behind a car at a four-way stop. The driver hesitated as a car to their left gave them the right-of-way. Marina said to the car in front of her, "Go ahead. Dang." As they proceeded she continued, "Okay, but next time, please keep those responses separate, maybe in a specific place, and let me know right away."

"Okay."

"We probably shouldn't have used your address for those anyway. Or, like your mom said, we should have let her handle it."

"You're at my place more than your place. We're fine."

She proceeded down the street, shifting into second gear. "Okay. If you say so."

Mangus paused. "How are you anyway?"

"I'm fine. Are you on your way? I wanted to go over the confirmation lists, and I need you to help me decide which furniture to list for sale." She shifted into third.

"I'll be by soon. I just need to return a couple of phone calls."

"Oh, Mangus. Can't you meet me there?" Fourth gear was next.

"I'll see you soon, sweetheart."

Marina swallowed and released her exhale abruptly through her nose. She focused. She counted to three. "Mangus, thanks for taking my mother to her appointment. But please, don't give her the impression that calling you at the last minute is okay." She shifted into fifth gear.

"She was no problem."

"But next time…"

"Next time, what?" His sentence sounded as though two question marks were attached.

Marina approached a red light and downshifted. "Nothing, honey."

"I love you," he told her.

"I love you, too." She shifted into neutral and peeked into the rear view mirror, examining the vertical line between her eyes. She tried to smooth it away by raising her eyebrows but it didn't work. She looked forward.

"Bye." Mangus waited.

As the green light shone and she again proceeded, Marina took the onramp to the freeway and tried to be…good. She simply said, "Okay," even though it felt as though something else needed to be said. Something firm. Something to let him know that she was unhappy with his refusal.

Mangus spoke without a beat being missed. "Hold up. If you really want me to head that way now, I will."

Her words were casual, yet her mind was anything but. "No, that's okay. Take your time."

"Okay."

They disconnected.

Marina did it. She let it go. She wondered if a part of her really wanted him to stick to his refusal. But she knew that it was just part of Mangus' nature to make concessions for his woman. It was the number one thing that she loved about him.

It was also the same thing that bothered her the most.

Chapter Three

"He's just too damn nice."

"Dial Leah," Marina said out loud as she continued home along 285 in the dark of night toward her place in Powder Springs. She heard Leah's one word greeting. The wild and wonderful Leah Hyatt-Mitchell was her old college roommate while they attended Kennesaw State. "I should have known you'd be up."

The sound of Leah's television blasted in the background. "Please, I'll be a night owl for the rest of my days, you know that."

"Yes, you will, girl."

"How are you doin? How'd your broadcasts go today?"

Marina spoke slowly. "Good, good. Work is cool. You know what though? I've just had a lot on my mind lately. And I've been doing a lot of thinking."

"I'm sure you have considering that the wedding is coming up so soon."

"No, it's not that. It's just that I'm trying my best to deal with Mangus."

"What do you mean deal with? What's there to deal with? That man is perfect. He proposed and you accepted so you need to be working toward spending the rest of your life with him. And he's fine as hell. Don't mess this shit up now, Marina."

"Excuse me? Don't mess it up? I am not gonna mess anything up. But, you know it's just like I told you before, Mangus can be very passive." Marina shook her head. "He's just too damn nice."

"Too nice? And that's a bad thing? At least he's not some loser, or some chauvinistic, domineering asshole. You want him to kick your butt and treat you like shit?"

"Of course not. Like I said, my one and only complaint is that he's just plain old nice. And not just to me, but to everyone. He's almost a pushover."

"Marina, from what you've told me, I still say he's perfect. And believe me, I know men. Being nice is how he charmed you in the first place. You weren't meeting too many nice guys, remember? And I know he's really nice in the bedroom. I mean, you did say he can work it, everywhere from the bedroom to the back porch."

"Yes, I did say that. Feels like I never should have though. You know what Leah? I don't expect you to ever get what I'm saying." Marina took the off-ramp and headed toward the traffic light. "Anyway, how's D.J. treating you?"

"D.J.? Please. Now there's a man who's trippin. He'll call and ask me out and then he'll be an hour late after not answering his cell, even after I've left message after message asking where the hell he is. My final message is always one where I finally tell him to turn back around and go straight the fuck home. He still shows up and talks me into letting him come inside so he can apologize, which he usually does with his face between my legs."

"Damn, D.J.," Marina said with a quick chuckle.

"Oh, the man knows how to make up, I'll give him that. But, we always end up ordering in, like pizza or Chinese, and then we end up screwing all night long. D.J. never takes me anywhere. So girl, be happy and quit complaining. You could be with a man who's late, cheap, boring, and can't fuck. I'd take Mangus over D.J. any day of the week."

"Yeah, well you can't have him. Anyway, where have you been? I've left you three messages over the past two days and you never return my calls. What's your problem?"

"Shoot, I'm usually busy trying to get this financial planning business off the ground. Working nine-to-five at Washington Mutual is wearing on me but good. Plus, I admit that I do get a little depressed over how D.J. flakes out on me. I've bonded to the man's damn penis and can't fuckin think straight. After two years of dealing with him, I thought things would be different by now. I just need a good man like Mangus."

"Leah, I told you, you need to put your foot down. You did the same thing with Ricky and Tyson, always taking their shit. You have to show D.J. that you have boundaries. It seems to me he thinks you don't have any rules whatsoever."

"I did set the tone with him early on. But, unfortunately, what I said and did were two different things. Shit, I just can't help myself. I let him come by and we always end up staying in. I just get weak when it comes to him. Not everyone can have a relationship like you and Mangus."

Marina headed down her street, Sweetwater Lane. "Well, I know one thing. D.J. will surely straighten up if you kick his tired butt to the curb. You always let guys off easy. Your actions have to match your words."

"I do get on him now, so don't get it twisted. He knows I am not one to mess with."

She signaled to pull into the driveway to her three-bedroom condo and pressed the garage remote. "Oh yeah, big, bad Leah. Girl, please. Anyway, have you gone back to that bridal salon in Dunwoody to choose your dress from the three we narrowed it down to yet? The wedding is only one month away you know."

"Yes, Marina. I did that yesterday. I'm excited for you, girl. And I know you're extra excited."

Marina pulled into her single car garage and stopped, put the car in park and set the brake. "I will be. I'm still kinda stuck in planning mode right now to feel too much excitement."

"Well, I've handled all that's on my to-do list so I'm cool."

Marina inquired, "And you called the chapel to change the time of the ceremony to noon."

"I did."

"Thanks. Well, have a goodnight, my maid of honor." Marina turned off the ignition and took her purse in hand at the same time she stuck her foot back in her high heel shoe.

"You too, soon-to-be Mrs. Mangus Baskerville. Ooooh, girl, I was thinking about that this morning. That's one last name you can have."

Marina opened the car door and paused before stepping out. "What?"

"I mean…I know his dad is a political figure and all, but dang. I just know you're keeping your on-air name. Are you sure you're gonna want to own that name for the rest of your life? That is, if this does end up being the man you end up with until death do you part."

"Unlike you, the marrying woman, of course I will. Why else would I be marrying him?"

"Okay, fine, throw that in my face. I'm just saying, you know how your ass can be, drama queen. To coin your very own phrase, I'll just keep the faith."

"For your information, that's not faith. That's a fact."

"You know I'm just kidding. I know you've changed and I'm happy for you. And no matter what, I love you."

"I love you back. And thanks again for everything."

"You're my girl," Leah said.

"And you're mine. Goodbye." Marina disconnected the phone, closed the driver side door, and took a few steps to reach for the doorknob that led from the garage to the kitchen.

"What do you mean why else would you be marrying me?"

In a snap, Marina jumped and threw her head back. "What? Oh my God, you scared the hell out of me. What are you doing here?" With bugged eyes, she gazed at her man standing before her.

"You asked me to meet you here, and so here I am." As she stepped inside of her large, gourmet kitchen, Mangus spread out his arms and leaned in toward her face, slipped his hand behind her neck and planted a peck on her cheek.

She could see reflections of candlelight flickering behind him. Her hand found her chest. "How'd you beat me here?"

He closed the door behind them. "I wasn't far away when you called. I'd planned on coming the whole time."

Marina placed her purse and keys on the white tiled counter. "Oh my God. My heart just about jumped out of my chest."

"So, what is it?"

"What?" Her breathing attempted to steady. She noticed a lead crystal vase with a bouquet of a dozen dark red roses on her oak dining room table. She stepped closer. "These are beautiful. Oh, baby, thanks."

Mangus stood, tall and muscular with butter pecan skin, looking like Boris Kodjoe. His buffed arms were folded along his defined abdomen. His red golf shirt showed off his perfect biceps, and a quarter-peek at his wide, tattooed crucifix on his upper arm. He also had a scripted *MB* on the other arm. "Why else would you be marrying me?" Mangus' two-carat diamond stud shone brightly from his left ear.

Marina pulled her eyes away from him and then leaned down to sniff one of the velvety looking rosebuds. She touched it lightly with her fingertips. "Those smell beautiful. And they look so strong." She stepped up to hug him around his trim waist and then took a half-step back, looking up into his almond eyes. "That was just Leah."

He hugged her back. "What was she talking about?"

"Oh, she was just talking about until death do us part and something about making sure we are…like…you know, knowing who we're marrying, something like that."

"And?"

Marina gave him full attention. "I know who I'm marrying."

"No reservations? No complaints?" he asked.

"You are the man of my dreams, Mangus." She caught his visual attention and smiled. She loved every inch of his face, from his dark eyes to his pointy nose and square chin. She breathed in. His manly scent brought her comfort. She breathed out.

"And you are the woman of my dreams, Marina."

"No reservations? No complaints?" she asked.

He spoke as he looked down at her bronzed face, which was still glowing from her full, on-air makeup. "The woman of my dreams."

She batted her thick lashes, giggled, and stepped away, taking a second to slip off her shoes. "You make it sound like a possible nightmare."

"I did not."

Marina poked him in his stomach with her index finger and stepped along the ivory, porcelain mosaic tiles toward the stainless steel fridge. "I know. Just kidding." She gave a grin and pulled the right side open. She looked inside.

He leaned against the oversized oak island and crossed his arms. "Well, the fact is that you are my future wife and my life and I'll tell you one thing."

"What's that?" she asked, taking a bottle of water from the refrigerator and uncapping it.

"If Leah's still cracking on my last name, ask Mrs. Mitchell, Mrs. Watts, Miss Hyatt, what's in a name?"

Marina stopped herself from taking a half-sip just in time as her mouth prepared for humor. A bit of water dribbled down her chin. She giggled and dabbed it with the back of her hand. "Stop it now. You leave my Leah alone. Maybe because her two former marriages didn't work, she's just a little paranoid for me. She means well. Besides, I'm happy."

"Good. If you're happy, I'm happy."

She moved closer to him, stood on her tiptoes and raised the bottle to his lips as he took a swig. "Leah really likes you. And Marina loves her some Baskerville."

Mangus swallowed and took her into his arms again, hugging her tightly. She hugged him back with the bottle behind him, rested her head upon his chest and closed her eyes.

He stared up at the barren white ceiling tiles, wordless, and rocked her from side to side.

"I'm your wife for life," she reiterated. "You'll see."

Mangus shut his eyes as he held his fiancé, and she held him. He gave a deep sigh and his heart sped up. An odd sensation, like a weird chill, traveled through his body and he gave a slight shake of his shoulders to try to gently snap out of it. But it remained. Again he stared up at the ceiling. And again he remained silent.

Chapter Four

"Now you're about to fuck up."

By the middle of the following week, all seemed well as Mangus and Marina continued with their wedding plans. In spite of all that needed to be done, they both showed up for work, and made time for each other in the evenings, tying up loose ends as needed. And the one important thing they always tried to make a priority was church service. They loved their church home, *Faithful Word* in Austell. It was their battery charge and their strength, and it was the one thing they made a point of enjoy-ing together.

However, they were no-shows during service the Sunday that had just passed. Marina had to work, and Mangus had done a double shift so he overslept. But tonight was their time to get caught up by listening to Pastor Tanner's message together. And that would have been fine, if the devil had not been trying to do his dirty work.

"She needs to give it the fuck up." Marina's words were blunt and stern.

By nearly one in the morning in the cozy, sunken living room of Marina's home, Marina looked over at Mangus with scornful, dis-satisfied eyes. Her words and her stare battled with the calming feeling she'd felt all week. In an instant, the look on her face as the soft light of the side table lamp shined upon her skin was that of complete reversal.

"What are you talking about?" Mangus took steps from the glass sofa table where he'd just disconnected from his iPhone and stepped back to the olive micro-fiber couch where he and Marina had been sitting.

"I just heard you tell Melanie you were studying a lesson." Marina turned off the CD player with the remote.

"And?"

"And, you should have said *we* were studying a lesson."

"The bottom line is I let her know I was busy." Reservedly, Mangus again took his seat next to her, but did not lean all the way back as he had before.

"Busy alone? Dang, Mangus, it's bad enough I have to see her every Sunday in church. Especially since I know that when you intro-duced me after service the other day she told you there's something about me she doesn't like. What kinda crap is that?"

He grabbed his can of beer and took two gulps in one. "Marina, believe me, Melanie is just a friend. I do not want her and she does not want me." He sat toward the sofa's edge with his legs apart.

"Oh please, Mangus. Do you really think she suggested you take your time with me and slow down, just because she cares? That woman was hoping you'd be available long enough to snag you for herself."

"Please, I've been single for years and she never tried to snag me. Besides, Leah told you the same thing about her doubts about me."

"Leah knows me, and she did not say to slow down. She is one hundred percent in support of this wedding. Besides, she's my best friend."

"Okay, well like I told you before, we were neighbors years ago and that's it. She and her husband and her two boys lived down the street."

"Yes, but when they broke up, she came running to you talking about how she wished she could find a man just like you. You forgot you shared that with me I guess." Marina crossed her bare, trim legs as she repositioned herself upon the sofa in her short lace robe. She scooted back and to the right to better face him.

He took the last big sip, swallowed loudly and placed the empty can back on the table. "We have never been attracted to each other."

"Speak for yourself." Marina folded her arms.

"Plus, she's too short," Mangus said as he rubbed his own fore-head.

Marina's face spoke of amazement. She widened her eyes. "Too short? What the hell does that have to do with it? So you mean to tell me that if she were taller, you guys would have fucked each other's brains out by now?"

Mangus leaned in closer. "The bottom line is, I love you and I'm marrying you and I want you, period. I do not want Melanie."

"Then why does she feel she has the right to call you after midnight then? And by saying *you're* studying, you denied that you're even sitting here with your future wife. That might have been fine if we'd just started dating. But she knows were engaged. You should have told her you're here with your fiancé and that she's calling too late. Mangus, you're so transparent." She took a deep breath.

He touched her forearm and squeezed. "Marina."

She pulled away and leaned forward to close the bible that rested face down on the glass coffee table. "Marina, my ass. We're getting married soon and I'm still dealing with women from your single life who are still calling on your cell phone. Some of these women I don't even know. If they're your true friends, I should know them, just as you know my male friends. Just in case you didn't notice, men don't call me."

He nodded his head. "I hear you."

"I can't believe I'm sitting here going over the bible with you from last Sunday when we missed church, listening to the pastor on the CD, and you mumble into the phone like that while your back is turned to me like we're at some damn nightclub."

"I guess I didn't want to hurt her feelings."

Marina's forehead scrunched. "Oh, see now. Now you're about to fuck up. What kind of feelings would she have if she's only a friend? And why would those feelings matter more than mine?"

"You know what, here?" He sprang to his feet and trekked over to get his phone and dialed. He came back over to sit down next to Marina. "Hey Melanie. I just wanted to call you back to see if anything was wrong. Nothing? Well, you called so late I thought something was wrong. Cool. I'm just sitting here with my fiancé Marina. We're going over last Sunday's sermon and we were surprised that you called so late. Well, just make a point to not call after nine. I just wanted to tell you that. Okay. Good. Have a goodnight. Bye." He disconnected his phone and set it upon the table. He looked at Marina. "There. You happy now?"

She looked away. "Now she thinks I made you do that shit."

He sat all the way back. "I did it because I wanted to. And I don't care what she thinks."

"Oh, but you cared enough to not hurt her feelings before I got upset."

"Baby, at this point, whatever bothers you, bothers me. You come first. I told you I just want you to be happy."

Her shoulders and her voice slumped. She focused on her hands, which now fidgeted in her lap. She took a moment to breathe, just to see if surrender would cooperate and take over. "Mangus, you didn't have to do that."

He rested his hand upon her right thigh. "I did it so that we won't have anything in the way. I don't want to lose you, Marina."

"I don't want to lose you either."

"And tomorrow I'm calling to change my phone numbers, both the cell and at home."

She rested her head upon his upper arm. "I've never had a man who simply did what needed to be done without making me feel wrong or insecure."

He took her hand and squeezed. "You honor me by not having men call you. I can make sure I do the same and honor you."

"Thanks," she simply said. And then she gave a long exhale.

Chapter Five

"...treat her like a queen."

The affluent neighborhood, twenty miles from Atlanta, was lined with an abundance of tall, full evergreen trees that punched up at the summer sun, while the humid air delivered the heat with a soggy edge. The manicured lawns were rich and dark and plush from the heavy spring rain. The brick and stone, white columned homes in the gated community looked like mansions. They reeked of wealth and success.

The Baskerville's three-story home, which was planted amongst residents like Bow Wow and several Falcons players, was nestled in a cul-de-sac. It sat at an angle, with a long winding driveway and three-car garage.

As always, the spectacular insides of the Duluth home smelled of clean linen.

They all sat barefoot as they'd left their shoes at the speckled marble entryway where they belonged. Shoes worn in the house, along the expensive beige Berber carpet and pricey treated floors, was unheard of.

"So it looks like you have everything covered, Marina. I'm proud of you."

"Thanks, Mrs. Baskerville."

Her posture, like Marina's, was grand. Mangus' mother spoke as she sat upon her contemporary eggshell white sofa. Her slender back rested upon a large chocolate and white flowered throw pillow. Her cropped, jet-black hair was neat, and her long, fire engine red nails were fresh. She wore a dark reddish shade of lipstick and layers of black mascara on her fake eyelashes. Her deep earth tone make-up was flawless. Her dark chestnut skin definitely had not yet cracked.

"I'll tell you one thing, Miss Future Daughter-In-Law, it's about time you started calling me by my first name." She leaned toward the octagon coffee table and lifted her fluted Mikasa wine glass, raising her pinky in the air. "I know we haven't had a lot of time to really get to know each other, and plus I have that demanding job. But I think we need to change that." She took a lady-like sip as the room temperature Merlot subtly made its way down her throat. She lightly smacked her lips. "I say after you both get this wedding past you and come back from your honeymoon, the four of us need to get away and go on a little trip. We plan on traveling a lot more anyway. It'll be sort of a wedding gift from us."

Marina's face showed pleasure, yet a bit of timidity. "Oh, Mrs. …I mean Camille, you two have done more than enough already." She looked to Mangus' father and then eyed his mother. "I wouldn't think of you taking on an expense like that."

Mangus' father spoke from his chocolate leather Lazy Boy across from the ladies. "Oh, now you know there's no talking her out of this trip. We've been discussing it and it's something we really want to do. So just go ahead and give in, if you know what's good for you." He gave his son the eye. Mr. Baskerville wore his regular tan Dockers and a crisp white dress shirt, reclining back, flexing his bare, pale white feet that were propped up in front of him.

"Mom, that is very kind of you to offer," Mangus said, sitting in a chair that exacted his father's.

Marina acquiesced. "Yes, it is. Very kind. I'll just say thank you."

Mrs. Baskerville replaced her glass onto the black, wrought iron coaster and sat back, crossing her long, curvy legs, sounding thrilled. "You two can think about where you want to go later on. We've been blessed to travel to so many places in our lives. Any place you chose is fine with us. You know, Hawaii is beautiful. We could even go to St. Lucia, or even that Sandals getaway, they have a great package. There are so many places we could go. Hey, there's even a European cruise for twelve days. But you might be cruised out after your honeymoon, right?"

Marina said, "You can never over cruise. We're going to the Caribbean for seven days. We can hardly wait."

"I'm excited for you. And so it's a deal. We'll get away together very soon."

Marina reached over to take her last sip from her wine glass. "I still say that you taking care of the chapel, the flowers, and the reception is way more than enough." She brought the gold-tipped glass to her lips and finished it off.

"You're our new daughter. We're glad to do it. We always wanted a daughter, right dear?"

Mr. Baskerville nodded as he spoke, "Right."

His wife noticed Marina replacing her empty glass to the table. "Dear, can you go and get Marina some more dry white wine please?"

"Sure," Mr. Baskerville said, pressing down the footrest and rising from his chair and heading to the mirrored wet bar. He stepped along the cherry stained hardwood floor.

"Oh, no. I'm fine, thanks." Marina shook her head toward her future father-in-law and smiled.

Mrs. Baskerville inquired, uncrossing her legs and scooting to face Marina who sat beside her. "So how's your mom doing? Have you talked to her lately?"

"Yes, I talked to her the other day. She's doing okay."

"Are you two very close?"

Marina rubbed her own left upper arm. "No, Camille. We're not." She glanced over at Mangus and then batted her eyes back toward Mrs. Baskerville.

"Oh, I'm sorry about that. Maybe this wedding will be a way to break the ice."

"Maybe."

Mangus sat forward with his elbows to his thighs and said, "So, Mom. How have you been feeling?"

"Great, son. Are you referring to that dreaded cancer word that I refuse to claim?"

Mangus told Marina, "She's gone through chemo, and even has the doctors amazed. She's missed little to no work at the United Way, and keeps on going at full speed."

"You are amazing," said Mr. Baskerville as he approached with a full bottle of Merlot and filled his wife's glass.

"Thanks, dear." She asked Marina, "Would you like more?"

"No thanks."

"How about you, son?"

"No thanks, Mom. I'm fine. I'm the designated driver anyway."

"Good for you. Always so protective. Well, Marina, I'll tell you. Life is all about the way you think. You attract what you believe. I refuse to buy into that six-letter word, I just refuse to. I have survived so much in my life, especially in North Carolina where I was born, and where we,

Bill and I, met, and then coming here to Atlanta, where interracial couples are still frowned upon even today. You know, I broke the mold in my career, and worked to erase color lines just because I had no tolerance for people who were negative thinkers, like the people who judged my husband and me way back when we first started dating. They called me a honky lover and called my husband a darkie lover. I won't even repeat some of the dreadful words they used. But, we endured it all and stayed together. I'm proud to say I'm a strong woman of color and I'm not about to let some doctor's diagnosis define who I am. I've been through too much for that."

Mangus' face showed satisfaction. "That's my mom for you. She is a survivor."

"She is that," Mr. Baskerville said as he retook his seat.

Mrs. Baskerville smoothed the sides of her hair and then fiddled with her bangs. "I'm not trying to get on my soapbox, but I'm just saying, as far as I'm concerned, I am healthy in every way. The main focus with this family right now is Bill's retirement party later in the year, and first and foremost, your wedding."

Mangus asked, "Dad, since when are you retiring? Isn't it a little early for you to retire?"

"Son, now you know I'm about to turn sixty-four. I've been a city council member for a long time now, and I've been in public office since I left the field of medicine. I've had opportunities come my way that I've passed on just so I could be here for my family."

Mrs. Baskerville spoke with pride as she reached over to place her hand atop Marina's. "I've got a good man, Marina. And so do you. I have been blessed with two men in my life who spoil me and love me no matter what. And you are about to become a Baskerville. The Baskervilles migrated to North America from England to escape oppression and starvation and have a long heritage or being survivors. That's the blood my son and husband have running though their veins. And that, along with Mangus' African heritage, is strength magnified. I'm telling you, treat your future husband with respect and he'll do anything for you. Right, dear?" She looked at her man who was pointing to her while he grinned at his son.

"There she goes. Whatever you say, honey."

Mangus said to Marina. "As you can see, these two lovebirds are each other's biggest supporters. A real life match made in heaven."

Mr. Baskerville said, "Talk about surviving, I've survived this woman who…" and then he pointed toward his wife and gave a humorous grin.

His wife interjected, "Woman who what? Funny. You wanted a woman tough enough to stand by your side, and God gave you one. And you're stuck with me. Marina, I could have left many times. But, I didn't. You've gotta stick it out and see it through. The grass might always look greener but nurture your own dead grass. It'll grow back. And learn to forgive, you two. Above all else, learn to forgive."

"And I could have left too, now," Mr. Baskerville interjected with a smirk.

"Oh please. You know you never had one moment of doubt, right dear?"

He nodded twice. "Right dear."

"See, I always say that a woman needs a man who loves her so much that if she lies, he'll even swear by it."

Marina laughed out loud.

Mrs. Baskerville squeezed and then released Marina's delicate hand and then stood up and headed to the long, rectangular, formal dining room table. She adjusted the arrangement of a tall, cylindrical vase full of bright yellow sunflowers. "So, is there anything else you need me to do? I know you already took care of the responses. How many are confirmed?"

"We're a little bit over. We're at one-hundred twenty four," Marina said.

"Wow. That's a lot of people."

Marina told her, "I know. We can handle the reception food costs for any people over the original one-hundred."

"Oh please, Marina. We wouldn't think of it. We told the chapel to add it on to our bill no matter what." Mrs. Baskerville stepped away from the table to examine the dozen high back chairs, and then scooted a couple of them forward to make sure they all lined up just right.

Mangus replied, "Thanks, mom. Marina, just learn to say thank you."

"Thank you."

"So what else?" Mrs. Baskerville asked Marina.

"Nothing. That's about it."

"You're sure."

"Yes. It's all handled."

"I must say you make planning a wedding look pretty easy."

Mr. Baskerville said, "She reminds me of you, honey."

"Yes, she does. Kinda stubborn. But, you'll be good for my son."

He said again, "Like I said, she reminds me of you."

Mr. and Mrs. Baskerville exchanged looks.

"Marina, how about if you come on upstairs with me. I want to show you my dress. I picked it up yesterday. It is simply beautiful."

"Yes, I'd love to see it," Marina said as she stood and followed Mangus' mother down the long hallway and then up the winding staircase. They talked as they walked hand in hand.

Mr. Baskerville grinned. "She's a pretty girl, Mangus. We watch her on TV all the time. You did a good job. She seems really sweet."

"She is."

He sat back and placed his elbow along the armrest. "Well, my son is about to become a husband."

"Yes, sir. I'm ready."

"How long has it been since you met Marina at your mom's charity event?"

"Almost a year and a half."

"Really? I'll never forget when Marina walked up to that table, you dang near jumped out of your skin. That's how it was when I first saw your mother that first day of college at Duke." His face beamed in recollection.

"Yeah, when it's right you just know it."

His dad gave a firm stare. "You think a year is a long enough time to get to know someone?"

"Yes, Dad, I do." Mangus crossed his legs just as his dad did.

"Your mom and I only knew each other a few months before we became a couple, but we waited for years before we got married.

"Really? Well, you hadn't finished school yet. Marina and I are older than the two of you were."

"True, and besides, we had so many obstacles to overcome. The odds were stacked against us. My parents eventually came around to accepting the fact that I fell in love with a girl who just happened to be black, or Negro as we used to say, and her mother accepted me as well. But your grandfather, your mom's dad, never accepted me. He wanted his oldest daughter to marry someone of her own race. But in spite of all that, we've stood strong. And you, of all people, know how tough it was when you grew up."

"Yeah, I remember we had our car spray painted with bad words when I was in elementary school. And I guess I just got used to the kids calling me half-breed and white-washed."

"You would tell your mom and me that you wanted to be a police officer when you grew up. You just wanted to right the wrongs of the world." He laughed.

"I guess I do remember that."

"We're so proud of you, son."

"Thanks."

"I'm also proud of you for the fact that you put up with so many things that sometimes went on in this very house. Your mom and I sure had our moments. But I wanted you to know by example that the key to making a marriage work, is first of all…to find woman who can cook." Mr. Baskerville again laughed and placed his hand over his beer belly.

Mangus laughed. "Oh she can cook now."

"No, I'm just teasing you. The key is to make her happy. They say that when you're a little boy, you get your happiness from being given to, when people make you happy first. But you become a real man when you find your happiness through making sure she's happy first. You become the giver. Mangus, do what it takes to treat her like a queen, and you'll feel like a king. You're happy only after she's happy. And know that unless she's balanced and content, the home is not a happy home. Cherish her feelings, son. And then you'll feel respected in return. I know it's hard, but put her feelings before yours. That is, if you really love her until death do you part."

"I do," Mangus assured him.

"Then good. You'll be golden."

Suddenly, Mrs. Baskerville and Marina headed back toward them, and then stepped right into the huge country kitchen as if the men weren't even there. The ladies giggled and chatted with excitement.

"Yep, you'll be golden all right."

Chapter Six

"...don't let it happen again."

Marina had been nonstop, tending to last minute errands and following up to ensure completion of each item on her checklist. One day blended into another as though evening and daytime were the same.

The tangerine summer sun was at full blast and the clouds were on vacation. It was a bright and perfect day for a wedding.

Marina's friend from high school, named Lynn, stood in the brides' dressing room of the elegant Pristine Lakeside Chapel in Jonesboro. The furniture was off-white and provincial. The room was fancy and elegant. The crystal chandeliers shone extra bright light upon the small group's last minute activities.

Lynn admired Marina as she zipped up her friend's traditional wedding gown. Marina stood before a wall-to-wall, full-length beveled mirror. "Beautiful," Lynn said, beaming from ear to ear.

Marina blinked her long, dark eyelashes. "I feel beautiful. And I feel loved," she replied especially perky while twirling around in a slow, graceful circle as though she were a princess in a fairytale.

Marina's ivory colored lace and chiffon, beaded Madeline Gardner bridal gown had long, sheer sleeves and a formal taffeta train. It was a form fitting, A-line designer gown, low cut, and elegant, and it framed Marina's coke bottle figure to a tee. Her exuberant cleavage winked just a tad bit, her waist was cinched with the help of her snug fitting demi-corset, which helped to show off her womanly hips even more. Her blazing burgundy hair was brushed back into a bun with wispy curls coming down around her cinnamon-colored face.

"Life is good," she said to her friend as she clutched her single strand of classic pearls and happiness rushed to her cheeks.

Lynn wore a long, cream, silk dress, and Leah, who was outside of the room seeing to the final preparations, wore jet-black. Their bouquets were Marina's favorite, fresh brilliant red roses.

Lynn slid the jeweled crown along Marina's head and adjusted it perfectly, just as a woman walked in side-by-side with Leah, looking down at some papers. The woman spoke quickly. Leah immediately stood next to Marina with a look of sheer confusion.

"Ladies, I know that our wedding consultant escorted you into this room to get ready." She looked up at Marina and Leah. "But Marina, your friend here, your maid of honor, just told us your wedding is at noon."

"It is," Leah replied.

The woman again looked down at her papers. "We have it on our books for two o'clock."

Leah spoke again. "No way. As I said, it's at noon."

Marina spoke as well. "Leah, you called right, to change it to noon?" Marina's perfectly waxed eyebrows raised as though attempting to encourage a speedy reply.

"Yes, I called a while ago."

The woman checked her log again. "We do have that you called about five weeks ago, but we got another call a while after that, stating that the time had been changed to two-o'clock."

Marina's eyes were ample. They told on the pace of her heart. "No way. It has been scheduled for noon ever since Leah called, and all of the invites went out telling people to be here for a wedding at twelve-noon."

The woman paused just before she spoke again and looked Marina straight into her concerned eyes. She scanned Marina's face and beamed, as though she had just seen Princess Diana. "By the way, it's nice to meet you Ms. Maxwell. I've seen you do the news many times."

"Thanks." Marina's face was blank. Her mind was preoccupied. *Dammit*, she thought to herself. She focused to steady her breathing.

The lady dropped half of her grin. "Some of the people from your wedding are starting to show up. But, we had a last minute booking for a one-hour, chapel only ceremony at noon today. We can do yours after that, once we clean things up and set up again. She glanced at the wall clock. "But not at twelve. I'm so sorry."

"You're sorry? Why didn't you call one of the numbers on the ceremony form to confirm?" Marina asked with tension over her eyes.

The woman flipped up one paper and spoke as her forefinger browsed the handwriting. "We did. We called 404-384-0031, but it was disconnected."

Marina replied immediately, "That's Mangus' old cell number. You should have called me."

"The lady who called to change it said she was, Marina Maxwell."

"And you didn't call back to verify?" Leah asked.

"We called a number and verified. Looks like it was 678-771-4500."

Marina's chin lowered and she focused directly into the woman's eyes. She took a step toward the door. "We'll see about this. This can't be happening on my wedding day." She began to pull her dress away from her French satin pumps, and grabbed each side of her gown, high-stepping in the direction of the groom's room. She yelled as she exited. "Mangus. Where is Mangus? Mangus."

Leah spoke toward her best friend's fleeing back. "He's across the hall."

Marina marched straight into the groom's parlor, waving her pearl-white, manicured fingers in the air. The wedding manager stood beside her giving Mangus a sympathetic smile as Marina spoke. "Mangus, what's going on? The chapel manager said they have another group coming in for a ceremony in one-half hour. Someone called to change the time of the ceremony to two instead of noon."

Mangus stood in front of a floor to ceiling mirror adjusting his silver-gray bow-tie. His fellow coworker and groomsman, who was also a police officer, Ronnie, and his best friend Bruce sat down, one tying his shoes and the other simply staring at Marina. "How would I know?" Mangus turned and faced his heated bride. "How did this happen?" he asked calmly.

Marina replied, pointing toward the woman, "She said whoever called had a 678 number. Do you know who that might be?"

"What's the number?" Mangus asked calmly.

The woman again read from her sheet, "678-771-4500."

He tilted his head and then rubbed the back of his neck. He looked at Marina. "That's…that's Melanie's number."

Mangus' groomsmen looked down toward the floor and then looked away.

The pitch of Marina's voice grew higher. She spoke to the woman first, but kept her sight on Mangus. "Ma'am, will you excuse us please? Bruce and Ronnie, will you please give us a moment alone?" The men stood and quickly exited the room, while the wedding manager was right behind them as she closed the door securely.

Marina simply stepped within two feet of Mangus. Her eyelashes fluttered. Her quickened breathing pattern was now visually detectable. And then, in one instantaneous movement, she abruptly raised her right hand and walloped Mangus straight across his broad face with a flat, open hand.

The sting was evident as he squinted and then blinked his eyes rapidly, and brought his hand to his tingling left cheek. His light-skinned face blushed beet red. He patted his skin while eyeing her with a darted stare through a sheer wetness that built up from the slap.

He tried to speak slowly but his words were coated with shock and panic. "What is your problem?" He took two steps backward.

Marina gritted her teeth. Her eyes spelled that of a woman who was about to lose it for real, and her bottom lip quivered as she spoke. Her jaw was tight. Her words were loud. Her frown line between her eyes was deep. "My problem is that I asked you what was up with that bitch and you said nothing. How is nothing going on with a woman who would be so damn hurt by the fact that you changed your cell number, that she would react with enough vengeance to try and get back at you by ruining your wedding day? That is straight post-sexual madness. Did you ever fuck her, Mangus?" Her eyes dared him to lie.

He looked toward the door and then back. "No. And calm down."

"Calm down? This is my wedding day and we're gonna have over one-hundred people standing in the lobby waiting for another ceremony to end before they can get into the chapel to see us say our vows. And you never straightened out your woman problems."

"It is not my fault that she called and pulled that. If she did."

"Oh, if she did, huh? The woman just gave you her phone number. And while you're standing here being righteous enough to make your priority the fact that you and she didn't do anything wrong, maybe you can come up with a solution so we can try to make this screwy situation right as we stand here in our wedding dress and tux and tails, with no chapel to get married in. That is if we still should. Because if you don't make a decision, I will make it for you and we can send everyone home, announcing that my not-so-ready-husband is still too stuck in his bachelorhood to come on into the matrimony stage of his life. Perhaps you need more time."

Mangus took a major breath and a long blink. "Okay, that's enough. You can be mad at me all you want." He cut his eyes at Marina and headed toward the lobby door and yanked it open, walking right up to the woman who was standing just outside.

"Excuse me but, what's your name?"

"Diane Lacey." She gave him a look of slight pity, even though she tried to play it off.

"Ms. Lacey, is there a place where our guests can maybe have cocktails for an hour or so once they get here?"

Marina stood behind him, breathing down his neck.

The woman replied, "They can go to the reception hall. We can throw something together, like maybe a pre-gathering. At no charge of course." She looked back and forth between both Mangus and Marina. And then she focused upon only Marina, this time giving her a look of amazement. "I really do apologize for the confusion. The wedding party at noon is only about fifteen people or so and it should be fairly quick. I'll let you know as soon as they're out of there." She nodded as though she was seeking nods in reply.

Marina spoke up as she took a step next to Mangus. "You should ask them to wait, not us."

Mangus shook his head as he spoke to the woman. "No, that's not necessary."

Marina had one hand on her hip. "Not necessary? Mangus, you need to put your foot down and demand what you want. Your parents are spending thousands of dollars for over one-hundred people and a full reception at this facility." Marina looked at the woman. "The other party is a small group of people who only have the chapel, am I correct? Are they eating here?"

"No." Ms. Lacey tapped her pen to her clipboard.

"Then you need to make this right and ask them to wait. Not us." Marina raised her chin as though she was waiting for the woman to simply give in.

The woman looked at Mangus and then back at her list, and then at Marina. "You know what? I'll see what I can do." The woman speedily stepped away, whisking past Lynn and Leah who looked on.

Marina crossed her arms as she spoke more softly to Mangus, now aiming her words toward him only, trying to soften her jaw. "I can't believe this."

"Marina. Is everything okay," asked Marina's mother, who suddenly stood before them wearing a champagne colored, floor length dress with a high lace collar and long sleeves. She had on long teardrop, pearl earrings and held a satin bag under her arm. "I just got dropped off and saw the two of you talking to that lady. You look really beautiful." She leaned in and hugged Mangus. "Hello."

He smiled warmly. "Hello there. You look pretty. Thanks for coming."

Marina said, "Yes, thanks, Mabel. Everything's fine." Marina still had her arms crossed, but she leaned in and kissed her mother on the cheek.

Mabel made a smooch sound into the air at the same time. A moment went by as she looked at both Marina and Mangus. "Okay. Well, I'll be right out here."

"Yes. Thanks," Marina said while looking beyond her mother who walked away very slowly.

Mangus said to Marina, "It'll all work out."

She resumed the tightening of her jaw after looking around to see who else may have been watching and stepped back inside the groom's room as Mangus followed and shut the door. "Mangus, I can't make every decision for us. Every time something happens that causes a problem, I end up finding a solution. You should have demanded they make this work."

"Marina, this happened because someone intervened who shouldn't have. I can understand how Ms. Lacey would feel they're not responsible for that."

"Well, I can't. They need to have better precautions in place, like speaking to the bride or groom through reaching them at the numbers provided on the original contract, not simply returning the call of the person who phoned in. And you need to permanently handle Melanie's butt. She impersonated me."

Mangus actually gave a quarter chuckle as he looked down at his shiny dress shoes. "Let's deal with that later. Right now, let's get everyone situated."

Marina's eyes were pale red. "Lynn and Leah can handle that along with Ronnie and Bruce. I'm not going out of that lobby door where everyone will see me in my gown. It's bad enough you saw me."

"I'll be right back."

Mangus gave a quick prideful glance into the mirror at his face just as he stepped back through the door and closed it firmly.

Marina heard voices and laughter beyond the door. She turned to take in a view of herself in her elegant wedding gown and adjusted the sides of her dress, looking down at her right hand, which was a deep red. She looked at her flushed face, noticing that she needed to redo her make-up. She patted her skin with her middle finger, and wiped away a small spot of mascara. She'd hoped no one heard the sound of the stinging slap she'd just laid on her groom. The first slap from her to him, and it happened on their wedding day.

Dammit. That's gotta be the last time, she thought. "Oh Lord, why me?" she said aloud as she sat down on a tiny stool, alone in the room. She fought back what felt like a rush of tears, and blew her face with her left hand.

She heard the door open slowly and then looked over. Her sad eyes met the face of her best friend, Leah, who simply stood behind her and gently rubbed Marina's tense shoulders, bending forward kissing the top of her best friend's sparkly crown.

Marina raised her hand to her own shoulder to cover Leah's hand, and she stood.

"I can't go out there." Her eyes begged Leah.

"Yes, you can." Leah's eyes begged her.

And without another word, the two walked out of the groom's dressing room, and into the bride's room together, hugging, in silence.

* * *

Later that night, in the honeymoon suite of the fancy and elegant Ritz-Carlton Buckhead, Marina lay across the ebony and mocha bed sheets of the king-sized bed, still wearing her wedding gown. Mangus had already pulled back the snow-white down comforter and crawled onto the bed to lie upon her. She looked up at her tuxedo-clad husband while he placed his lips upon hers and seductively sucked her tongue.

As he broke away from the close-up of his wife, he spoke. "I love you Mrs. Baskerville."

"I love you Mr. Baskerville."

"And I'm glad your mother was able to come."

"Me too."

He kissed her delicate chin, and then moved his body downward, slowly and purposefully, and spread her legs apart. Mangus arranged her fancy gown just so, and placed himself between her never-ending legs. He kissed her lower thigh just above her powder blue garter belt, and then moved up toward her awaiting middle.

Marina sighed and tensed up. She couldn't see him, but she could definitely feel him. She placed her arms outward and femininely surrendered to her new husband.

Mangus positioned his mouth along her white lace panties, and moved the fabric to the left side, sticking his unyielding tongue inside of his wife, tasting her vagina on her wedding day, and pleasing her with his expertise as she moaned and called his name.

"Oh Mangus, oh, yes," she said softly to the sound of the stiff fabric of her petticoat rubbing against the sheets and the sound of the increasing liquidity between her legs.

He licked and sucked her sugar into a frenzy, and she grinded in response, adjusting her high heels as the undeniable sensation hit her toes, tensing and flexing her thighs just as he sped up his pace. Her ass muscles tightened. She put her hand over her sweaty forehead to gain composure and caught a glimpse of her triple marquis diamond wedding ring.

Her pulse raced and her heartbeat thumped and her orgasm throbbed and her man took on her full, strong release into his mouth until she…little by little…came down from her intense marital high. Her emotions overwhelmed her.

He rose up all the way, inch-by-inch to kiss her on her light brown forehead, and she kissed him on the left cheek. She remembered that cheek. She gave him full teary eyes and he took them. She said, "I'm sorry."

He gently kissed her smoky eyelid and said, "I'm sorry anything upset you on our wedding day. But, don't let it happen again."

"It won't," she promised as though her reply were a question.

"Good," he said, while she reached down to unzip his black tuxedo pants.

It was time to consummate their union, and the start of what was to be their blissful lives together as a happy couple…now the loving husband and wife.

Chapter Seven

"She called it tonsil bruising..."

The brand new, massive, one hundred-thirteen thousand-ton cruise ship swayed with a sensual subtlety, almost as though it was floating on air, as though gravity was nonexistent. The soft movement was just enough to remind folks they were being whisked away from the humdrum, everyday life of Fort Lauderdale along the grand Atlantic, headed to the spectacular mystique of the Eastern Caribbean. It was a chance to escape life's rigors and realities.

Marina and Mangus' maroon king suite had an extra spacious balcony, and the newlyweds didn't waste any time making the most of it.

Being that is was the first official day of their honeymoon, they had not yet left the comfort of their cozy room, even though the sun prepared to fade behind the distant horizon. But instead of the two of them watching the last bit of the blushed orange, majestic sunset that slowly dissipated, only Mangus was in the position to take in the spectacular view of the ship's slender bursts of shimmering lights, reflecting like sparking diamonds upon the dark ocean waters. That is, if he could indeed concentrate, what with all the titillating, sexy distractions.

He laid back and Marina, the dutiful wife, knelt at his side, with her plump, gingerbread ass exposed to the night air. He had a side view of her dark blue, butterfly and hearts tramp-stamp drawn on her lower back.

She worked her usual erotic magic. She called it tonsil bruising because her man was always able to extend his lengthy dick deep, all the way down her accepting throat, without interference from anything but her tongue and the insides of her receiving mouth. Yes, she, unlike most he'd been with in the past, was able to handle it with ease, every inch of it. And it was definitely way more than a mouthful. At times she used her hand to guide him far back, to the very depths of her oral cavity to meet her tonsils, coming down to allow her exploring bottom lip to slurp the topside of his swollen balls at the same time. She did not know the meaning of gagging. She gave new meaning to the term super head. He'd even taught her how to talk while taking pipe.

"Are you gonna give me my stuff?" she asked, giving him her naughty eyes while she folded her hands around his dick.

Mangus looked down as though showing approval. "Yes, baby." His upper head was spinning and his eyelids lowered, blocking out all visual of the paradise at sea. That view could wait. All he could focus upon was the motion of the ocean, mixed with his fast approaching sensation that was rising from between his thighs, where his lower head was being treated like an all night sucker. He tightened his ass muscles and stretched his long legs out as far as they could go.

"I feel you," she said, encouraging his gradual journey.

His moans, growing shorter and faster by the second, spoke volumes.

With her mouth, she marinated his hard, light-brown flesh with just enough saliva to ease her sliding palm, and she concentrated on repeating the exact motion, with the same intensity, with the same movement, now using both hands, over and over and over again, as she knew she was seconds away from accomplishing her giving mission.

Her new husband's hips grinded back at her. He fucked her face with his dick. She moaned an affirmative, repetitive sound, giving him loving permission to expel all that he had deep down her throat.

Her mouth was full of his meaty girth, which throbbed with pulsations that told her it was coming. And so, she groaned again, louder, finding that her own pussy was dripping and throbbing in response to the thrill of his obvious excitement. She got off on playing wide receiver.

"Oh fuck," Mangus blurted out with a deep-muzzled tone, as if he was fighting for dear life to not let everyone within earshot know that he was about to cum in his talented wife's mouth. He let out a long, slow grunt.

She then felt his juices spurting, warm and sweet, again and again, filling her mouth and tickling her taste buds. She stayed on point, exacting her same movements until he froze in place. Marina quickly housed a mouthful of his baby-making fluid, and she gave one big swallow. Her face seemed to say that it would be rude not to. She loved the taste of Mangus' seed.

"Ummmm," she said, releasing him from her oral grip, and licking her sperm glazed thick lips. At the same time, she kept one hand on his shaft, shellacking upward and downward to drain each and every secreting, white pearl drop, placing her wide tawny tongue on his tip to lick him clean, more than a few times. "Tastes great, less filling," she joked, but looked serious as a heart attack.

He sensed her humor but he was still in awe, breathing rapidly. "Woman, that was the best damn head you've ever given me. Shit."

"Nothing but the best for my new husband," she said calmly and surely with his remnant juices still permeating her tongue. She traced a circle counterclockwise with the tip of her tongue along her lips and moaned in porno fashion.

He took a deep breath and surrendered to the glow of his post-orgasmic state, melting into the luxury of the blue and white lounge chair. He eyed Marina's golden nakedness as she arose to her feet.

Her perky brown nipples were erect, pointing his way, and her smile was broad and big.

He said, "I'm fuckin hooked."

She took a few steps as her backside bounced from side to side, and she grabbed the handle to the sliding glass door, flashing a girlie grin. "I'll be right back. Do you want anything to drink?"

"No. I want you to come back here so I can return the favor." With his eyes, he grabbed her hairy vagina and shook his head. "You, Mrs. Baskerville, are so damn fine." He unglued her momentarily and glanced over at the perfectly full moon. "There's something about being out here in the night air that is so exciting."

"There's plenty of time for that, baby. We've got seven whole days to be freak mongers. How about we get dressed and go check out what this floating hotel has to offer? I can't wait."

"That's right. There is a whole world outside of this room, right?"

"You know it. I'm gonna hop in the shower. Come on in when you're ready." She stepped inside the room and slid the door shut.

"Will do." He let out a long breath and then lifted his dick as he looked down. "You all right little man? Your ass is spoiled as hell. Look at you damn near smiling. Ya greedy bastard." Mangus leaned his head back, relaxed nearly every muscle in his body and closed his eyes. "This is gonna be pretty cool. Married life is the way to go."

His dick, with a mind of its own, again grew stiff in response, as though it was checking to see where the gifted super freak had gone. It pointed in the sultry direction of her departure and smiled.

872
8112

Chapter Eight

"...glimpse of the woman's gigantic vanilla rumpshaker..."

All you can eat grand buffets, comedy packed shows, some-times generous slot machines, glamorous picture taking, duty-free shopping, all-night clubbing, and hot sex, sex, sex, filled one, two and then three days straight. They'd taken a group tour exploring the first port-of-call, which was the magical locale of Nassau, Bahamas.

Later that evening, Mangus and Marina made time for their scheduled formal seated dinners in the fancy Fontaine restaurant just to enjoy the luxury and privilege of being served, which usually included all of the lobster and filet mignon they desired.

On one of those evenings, they met two tablemates in particular, a conservative looking couple named Jeff and Kristina. He was a pastor back in Ohio, and she lived the life of a pastor's wife. The two couples laughed and talked like old friends, and agreed to meet for breakfast one morning up on the Lido deck.

And so on the fourth morning, after their regular early morning marathon lovemaking session, Mangus and Marina forced themselves to head on over and spend time with other people, as opposed to each other's private parts.

As the ship prepared to dock in St. Thomas, the foursome sat at a window table near the buffet area after piling their trays with waffles, fruit, grits, scrambled eggs, every type of breakfast meat, and home fried potatoes, and they drank fresh squeezed orange juice and sipped hot coffee.

Jeff and Kristina Willis were the epitome of class and goodness, at least from the outside.

Jeff leaned forward with his burly forearms along the tabletop. "Baby, Mangus here tells me he's a cop in Atlanta."

Kristina's hazel eyes showed she was impressed. She was a lighter shade of brown and so was her hair. "Oh really? A cop huh? That's got to be a real rewarding job." Both of Kristina's manicured hands were wrapped tightly around a pale blue coffee mug.

"It is," Mangus replied as he sat back in the lap of luxury, adjusting the brim of his deep blue fitted cap.

Jeff inquired, "And you, Marina. I hear it takes a lot of patience and understanding considering the rigors of being with a man who is fighting crime."

"Mangus makes it look easy." Beaming with pride in her pale green sundress and straw hat, Marina placed her left hand on Mangus' muscular thigh under the table. "He rarely complains, if ever. I don't pressure him, but, when he's in the mood to talk about his day, I'm all ears."

Mangus patted her just above her knee. "She's good about supporting my career choice."

Bald-headed, brown skinned and athletic looking, Jeff eyed his spouse. "Yes, my wife is too. I'm telling you, in the beginning, when we decided to jump out on this leap of faith, the devil was in full effect. There were many reasons to give it up." He spoke in Mangus' direction. "We had people in our lives who were not supportive, we had money issues, and there were times when we only had a dozen or so parishioners in church."

Kristina said, "Our congregation has grown so much, it's amazing. We stuck to it and listened to the word of God. He told us they would come. And they did."

Marina took a swallow of juice and spoke. "That's amazing to hear. I'm so inspired by you both."

Jeff beamed with pride. "Thanks. Kristina's been right by my side from the moment I verbalized my dream to her. She is heaven sent. That's the name of our church, you know, Heaven Sent Ministry."

Marina smiled. "How sweet. So how often do you get a chance to get away like this?"

"Oh we try to do this every six months or so. We have an associate pastor who handles things while we're gone," Jeff said.

Marina nodded. "This must be a real battery charging experience, just to get away."

Jeff continued as he rubbed his chin with his thumb and forefinger. "It's a time for us to let our hair down, that's what it is. We rarely even tell people about what we do for a living. They seem to freeze up and shift into their best behavior. I want people to be themselves."

"I can imagine," Mangus said as he reached for his last bite of toast and devoured it.

"Was that your first impression?" Jeff asked Mangus.

Mangus sat forward a bit and half grinned, in between trying to swallow. "Well, I'll tell you now, we're no saints."

Kristina glanced at both Marina and Mangus. "I won't ask you if you've committed yourself to Christ. I'll just say, God forgives those who sin. And we all sin."

The pastor's eyes spoke with volume as he shifted his sights over to a nearby table. "Actually, we sinned last night."

"Oh?" Mangus said.

Jeff pointed with his eyes and his head. "See that couple over there?"

Mangus turned back and replied, "Yes."

Kristina leaned forward, pressing her chest to the table. "Well, she slipped her business card in Jeff's jacket pocket while we were on the dance floor and she wrote her room number on the back."

"And?" Marina asked.

Jeff said with a devilish smirk, "We called her at like two in the morning. We had a foursome with them. He wanted to watch his woman be with a black man. And, he wanted to go down on a black woman. We had to accommodate his wishes."

Marina sat back and readjusted her white cloth napkin along her lap. "Oh my goodness. Oh Lord."

"Watch it now," Jeff said jokingly.

Marina shook her head and glanced at Mangus. "That is really, as they say, too much information."

Mangus said nothing.

Jeff flashed a major smile and leaned back, reaching over to put his empty plate on top of his wife's plate. "You two need to lighten up."

Marina explained, "We're on our honeymoon. I'd say sleeping with other people is not for us, but, you know, to each his own."

Kristina half agreed, reaching back to readjust her long ponytail that rested along her back, which was tied with a leopard print scarf. "Surely not right now."

"Now or later. I'm not saying I have a problem with what you did. I'm just saying it cheapens the meaning of our commitment and our vows if we share ourselves with someone else," Marina said as she shifted her sights out of the window and onto the view of the shore that resided behind the clear blue ocean.

"I tell my husband if it's done behind my back, that's not cool. But if I'm right there, I don't have a problem with it. We're only human."

Marina still looked away. "As long as you both agree."

"And, who are we hurting? What happens on this ship stays on this ship. "Right?" Jeff asked.

Marina looked at him and then looked at Mangus who raised his eyebrows.

Suddenly, the white couple nearby stood, pushed in their seats, and got up to walk away. Jeff and Kristina gave them a big smile. The man bowed his head. The woman gave a wink to Kristina. They kept walking.

Marina sipped her juice again and then asked, "So, Kristina, how many kids do you have?"

"Between the two of us, we have four."

Just as Kristina was explaining the breakdown of their offspring from previous marriages, Marina caught a side glimpse of the woman's gigantic vanilla rumpshaker as the couple passed. Marina split her vision while listening to Kristina talk, keeping one eye on Mangus, who not only noticed the woman, but leaned to his left, moving his body toward the isleway to cop a clear, unobstructed, unadulterated view of all the wagon she was so gloriously draggin.

Marina instantly elbowed Mangus without even an ounce of modesty. "Don't do that," she said from one side of her mouth as Kristina kept talking, and then Jeff joined in.

"Yeah, we have a good old time together. We've been married for ten years and it seems like two years. We were made for each other, that's for sure."

Marina and Mangus sat up straight and listened as the couple talked, but Marina's mind was stuck on what the nudge was all about.

Mangus tried to play it off. His forehead was wet. He lifted his cap slightly and then re-secured it. Within a few minutes, the conversation was so one sided that the four found themselves pulling out their chairs to depart at the same time.

Kristina said, "Well, it was nice meeting you. If you two want to get together again, we're in P4241. Hey, maybe we can go dancing together one night."

Marina reached forward and gave Kristina a hug. "Maybe so."

Jeff shook Mangus' hand. "And don't worry newlyweds, we won't try to get in your pants."

Mangus then shook Kristina's hand and said, "Very funny. It was nice talking to you. See you later."

As the couples walked away in opposite directions, the silence was thick. Thick like somebody had stolen something.

Chapter Nine

"...that shit pisses me off..."

Mangus spoke lightheartedly on purpose. "I never would have guessed, with them being Christians and him being a pastor, that they would have straight out freaked like that. And then to admit it, wow. Maybe they thought we'd be down for it, I don't know."

"So you think they were actually propositioning us?" Marina asked while slipping on her blue-block shades. She crossed her arms under her chest as they stepped into the heated sunlight.

Wearing baggy jean shorts, Mangus' bare heels flopped in his Nike sandals as he walked along the wooden deck. "It just seems that's not something you'd want to share with strangers unless you wanted to see if someone was into it."

"If they'd wanted us to join them, they wouldn't have told us what they do for a living. Don't you think?" Marina kept her focus forward, and pulled the brim of her straw hat down further.

"It just seemed odd for them to be so out there with it. You'd think they'd want to keep that to themselves. And God."

They passed the busy, massive pool area and then through the sliding doors near the gift shop.

Marina spoke lowly. "Maybe so. But it's not as out there as you were, poking your damn head out to get an eyeful of some white woman's ass, Mangus."

"What?" Mangus brought his eyebrows to meet his forehead, trying to catch a glimpse of Marina's expression through her massive, dark shades.

Marina then removed her sunglasses with a subtle snatch. Her eyes were pissed off. Her forehead was too. Her face was flushed. And her voice was now full grown. "Don't what me. What do you think you got nudged for? For not drinking all of your fuckin water?"

Mangus looked around. "I don't know why you nudged me. Why did you?"

Marina turned her head toward him face on. "Mangus, when you try to play things off, that shit pisses me off more than the fact that your sneaky ass can't keep from checking out every damn thing that moves. You always have to get an eyeful." She dismissed her evil eyes away from him.

Mangus focused on the decorated ceiling, and then looked ahead. "You know what? Don't start this shit now. We're on our honeymoon."

"All the more reason for you to behave."

They stopped at the elevator door and waited, as Marina tapped her foot.

Mangus sighed. He pressed the down button, twice. "Behave? Marina, I am not a child."

She adjusted her small straw purse over her shoulder and then her hands found her waist. "Then stop acting like one. Be man enough to say you were looking at her ass, that you wanted a better glance, and that you got caught."

"Whatever." The elevator doors parted. They both proceeded inside and Mangus selected the Empress deck level. They faced forward. They were alone.

The doors shut before them as Marina spoke louder. "Whatever what? Just admit it Mangus. You were checking her out."

He focused on her face and moved in closer with a stern glare. "I was not."

Marina leaned in toward him with a jerking motion. The heated flame from her mental tension traveled from her brain, down her neck, to her shoulder, and flowed down her arm and ended up pulsating in the palm of her hand. She balled up her fist and bridled it at her side. Her bag slipped down from her shoulder. "Mangus. How can you deny it? Why are you such a liar?" Her nose flared.

His eyes grew. "I am not."

She locked in on his stare. "Fuck. That's just like the time you spoke to that woman who was checking you out while we were walking to my car, and you said hello while your were right beside me and then told me you didn't say anything, like something was wrong with my damn hearing. It always ends up being my fault. Like I'm the one who's tripping. Shit, just fuckin say you did it."

He stood firm. "I told you I didn't."

"Oh, so my eyes were deceiving me, right? I may not know what people tell me, but I sure as hell know what I see."

"You can't tell me what I was looking at, Marina. Only I know."

Her heart thumped. Her fist was still tight. "Oh please. What I do know is that Jeff and Kristina were focused on me while we talked. We were engrossed in what should have been a four-way conversation. But your ass drifted off because your mind told your dick that something was available to be scoped out and you didn't want to miss it. Everyone at that table was showing respect but you."

"Oh so, the pastor and his wife sleeping with other people is respect. I was not the one fuckin her."

"You fucked with your eyes. You are married now. Stop lusting, Mangus." She gave him a daring stare.

"You are my wife now. Stop being so insecure."

"What?" Her voice cracked.

"That man has a wife who deals with him sleeping with other woman right in front of her, and I have a wife who can't even stop trying to police who I look at. And he's a dang preacher."

"Oh, so you were looking at her then, huh?"

The elevator door opened and Mangus took his first step. "You know what? I'm gonna enjoy myself on this ship. You can stand right there and argue with yourself."

Her eyes dared him. "Don't you walk away from me?"

"Watch me."

"Mangus," Marina blurted with a tense jaw.

Through steam-filled eyes, she saw nothing but his wide back stepping away from her as she extended her right arm and grabbed at his shirt, yanking it back toward her. The fabric along the seam ripped.

Mangus jerked his body and snatched his shirt from her grip as he took two steps away. "What are you doing? You're trippin."

He turned his back to her again just as she grabbed his upper arm from behind and then she began swinging on his back as the elevator door closed behind her. And then in a snap, she lifted her right foot and propelled her foot with a bursting jolt like she was punting a football, landing her pointed toe deep against his butt.

He instantaneously did an about-face and propelled around when another elevator across from them beeped and then opened slowly. An older woman stepped out. She was looking down as she rummaged through her lime green bag, and then she caught a glimpse of them just as Marina quickly stormed away toward their stateroom.

Mangus played things off and stepped behind her, within an inch of her fast moving body, readjusting his sleeve and his pride.

He asked as she speedily slid the keycard through the slot. "Marina. What the hell are you doing?" He walked in after her and shut the door with force as she tossed her purse on the bed. He threw his baseball cap onto the floor.

She turned toward him with her index finger in his face. "Don't you ever walk away from me again, do you hear me? Be a man and see to it that your wife is okay." She rolled her neck as an exclamation point.

He shook his head and walked toward the closet. His thoughts raced. He sighed and slid the door open. "Be a man, huh? Okay. I'll do that. I'm gonna get changed since you destroyed my clothes. And I'm going back out there to enjoy myself. Hell, be a lady and keep your hands, and your feet, to yourself."

She stepped right up to him. "You're gonna stay right here and make sure your woman is understood."

He didn't even look back at her. "You'll never be understood on this one until I say what you want me to hear. And I'm not gonna lie." He bent backwards to soothe his backside and then turned from right to left.

"So you would just go back out there and fuckin leave me standing here, versus admitting that your eyes were on that woman's ass?"

Mangus cleared his throat.

"Well?"

He slipped off his shirt, and hurled it onto the desk, and then snatched another from the hanger.

She stomped her right foot. "Don't you leave me. Don't you leave me, Mangus." Her voice spoke of panic.

With a jerking motion, he slid the shirt over his back and pushed his arms into the blue plaid cotton sleeves, adjusted it over his shoulders, and buttoned it. "I'll be back." His eyes perused the small desk for his sign-and-sail card.

"Mangus," she screamed in a high-pitched tone. There was an echo in her eyes of sheer desperation.

He stood still. Frozen. Looking to the side to take in her reflection through the dresser mirror. He stepped to her. "Do you see yourself? Look in that mirror, Marina." He pointed firmly.

Inch-by-inch, she raised her eyes toward her own angry, all too familiar vision. The vision she prayed would die, stared right back at her. It was alive.

"We're on our honeymoon. You're my wife. You've gotta trust me because we're supposed to be living a lifetime together." He stood behind her and placed his hands squarely on her shoulders. "We took vows for this shit, woman. We can't fight against each other like this. You can't fight me. I am a grown ass man, Marina."

"I know that."

He gazed toward the door and then snuck a look back at her face. Her wide, teary eyes were begging out loud. Her face was covered with a look of misunderstanding, but mainly with a heavy dose of deep-rooted hurt, for him and for herself.

He blinked a long blink. He stepped a big step toward the door.

Her voice was above a whisper, and it shook. "Mangus, please don't leave this room. Please." It was as if she then held her breath.

He turned back toward her frame and she came close, resting her head on his chest.

She could hear his heartbeat. It was quick and strong.

At that moment, his arms found a way to hug her.

And the next moment, she managed to find a way to just…chill.

Chapter Ten

"...please don't touch me like that."

It was the last night of their honeymoon after a full day at sea.

Mangus and Marina had gotten off of the ship a couple more times in San Juan and Grand Turks to do some sightseeing and shopping and jet-skiing and lounging in the sun. They'd even gambled a bit and won a few hundred dollars in the casino. They hit the pizza bar and ate enough ice cream to notice that their waistlines had thickened. They also made a point of hitting the gym.

They'd had enough make-up sex to last a year. Marina actually did more making up than Mangus did. They couldn't seem to keep their hands off each other.

Marina wore the dress that drove Mangus wild. It was a tight, backless, strawberry red number with a gold collar, and it was shorter than short. It gave Marina a chance to show off her golden tan, and her shapely, muscular legs. She wore gold strappy-sandals and huge hoop earrings. Tonight, she went without a purse since it would be their night to get their groove on in the nightclub called the Cabin Fever Lounge. It had rows of tables and a separate upper level for the voyeurs, and a grand, black dance floor with illuminated lights that flickered. The room was dark and the vibe was old school disco. All that was missing was the disco ball.

Mangus wore Evisu jeans and a black Lacoste shirt. He was shaking himself toward Marina as she backed it up on him with her Beyonce-like moves. The floor was packed and Mangus looked proud. More than a few eyes were on his woman.

"Damn, you look good, baby. You could be in a video yourself."

Marina snapped her fingers with every rhythmic step. "Just working it with my man, that's all."

The song "*What'cha Gonna Do*" by Jayo Felony blended into the mix.

"What are you gonna do?" Mangus asked while eyeing her hips. He began to mouth the words as though he was performing.

Marina giggled. "I don't ever wanna go home baby." She danced her way right up to him and draped her arms around his neck, clasping her hands. Her hips grinded against him. "Oh, I see, you're at full attention again."

"Can you blame me?"

"I love you, Mangus."

"I love my baby, too. You make me happy." He kissed her lightly.

"I hope so."

"Come on now, what's with all this talking? Shake your shit."

She backed away. "How's that, huh?" she asked, doing a move that looked like an x-rated belly dance.

"You got it."

"Go ahead on, you two," Kristina said, dancing up beside Mangus as her husband Jeff joined her.

"Hey, how are you two doing?" asked Mangus.

"We're good. We don't mean to interrupt," said Jeff as he looked at Marina only.

"Hello," Marina said, slightly downsizing her gyrations.

Jeff and Kristina both wore black pants and white shirts. She had on silver flats and her saucy beige hair was curled into ringlets down her back.

The four danced side by side to a barrage of songs, raising their hands in the air, and grinning from ear to ear.

Marina said, coming to a complete pause, moving in closer to whisper in Mangus' ear, "I'm about done, baby,"

He ceased his dance moves. "Okay cool. No problem. I need a cold one anyway." He grabbed her hand as she wiped her forehead with her wrist.

"Are you two giving up already?" asked Kristina. "I was gonna ask if I could cut in."

Mangus said as Marina looked on, "Oh, we've been out here for quite a while, so we're done. You two go right ahead."

"Okay, but save a little more energy for us later," said Jeff.

Mangus smiled, leading the way through the crowd.

Marina spoke behind him, placing her hand on his back. "Honey, they're sweet and all but, I don't know."

"Know what?"

"I'm telling you, they're swingers and I don't think they've ruled us out."

"Oh, so now you agree they might be trying to make a move, huh?"

"Okay, so you were right."

"Oh I was, huh? I like the sound of that."

"I'll bet you do."

They approached a corner bar table and Mangus adjusted a stool for Marina to sit.

"Thanks," she said, scooting back and re-adjusting the halter part of her dress.

Mangus stood next to her. "So, do you want to find the other club on the main deck? Or we can do something else. I just want you to feel comfortable."

"No, I'm having fun."

"What would you like to drink?"

"One of those Bahama-Mamma drinks we had out by the pool earlier. That was so good."

"Coming up," Mangus said as he stepped over to the end of the long, bustling bar.

Jeff and Kristina walked over and sat on the two remaining chairs at the table next to Marina. Marina smiled and kept her focus on the people on the dance floor, tapping her fingertips along the blacktop table.

Kristina said, while dabbing her forehead with a napkin, talking loudly, "It's like Soul Train out there. That D.J. is something else. It seems like he played one good song after another."

"Yeah, that was a workout all right."

"You look like you stay in shape."

Marina laughed. "Oh please, I'm sweating like a pig over here."

"We haven't seen you young lovebirds around much." Katrina gave a half-wink.

Jeff told his wife, "Baby, that's what honeymoons are for."

Mangus returned and set their drinks on the table, "Here you go." Marina's drink was in a light green glass with a frilly pink and yellow umbrella. He spoke to the couple. "Can I get the two of you anything?"

Jeff stood. "Oh no, I'll just get us both some water. Don't worry about it. Besides, we don't drink. I'll be right back. You go ahead and take that seat and enjoy your lovely wife. Nice dress by the way," he said to Marina. His gaze was of nothing but Marina's bare legs.

"Thanks," Marina replied, almost making it sound like a question. She took her drink in hand.

"That looks good," Kristina said as Marina stirred the long, hot pink straw.

Marina replied, "It is. It's some kind of blended rum punch with pineapple."

"Pretty drink. I hope you two have been staying out of trouble?"

"Most definitely," Marina replied, taking a sip.

"Good. You'll have to look us up if you're ever in Chicago."

Mangus said, "Okay."

"We'll be in Atlanta soon actually."

Mangus held his chilled glass of beer and titled it toward his lips. "Oh really?" He drank the cold, golden liquid in obvious gulps.

"Here you go sweetie."

"Thanks, Jeff." Kristina grabbed the tall glass of ice water and immediately took two long swallows in one. "Ahhhhhh," she said slowly, lifting her long, sweaty, naturally curly hair from her bare shoulders. She combed the back of it with her fingers. The scent of her Burberry body oil was blatant. "I'm parched." Her eyes were on Mangus. "Mangus, right?"

"Yes."

She looked him up and down. "How tall are you?"

"A little over six-two."

She set her glass down and twirled the ice cubes around with her index finger. "And are you mixed? You look like you might be Creole or something." She stuck her finger into her mouth and lightly sucked on it.

Mangus looked away toward the bar. "My father is white."

"I see. You are a very handsome man. Very handsome."

"Thanks."

Marina was all ears.

"Do the two of you work out together, Marina?" Kristina leaned over and placed her left hand along Mangus' forearm, rubbing it back and forth, and then rested her right hand on his upper thigh, coming close to his zipper.

Mangus' eyes widened.

Marina's eyes lit up. "Yes Kristina, we do. But please don't…"

"Kristina, with all due respect, please don't touch me like that." Mangus took both of her hands and removed them from himself.

Kristina sat up straight and crossed her legs, again grabbing her glass of water, and taking a quick sip. “Oh, I’m sorry. I didn’t mean anything by it.” Her eyes were still on his thigh.

Marina took a deep breath. It was as though she was struggling to count to three.

Mangus said, “I understand. But, I’m a married man, and I’m sitting here with my wife, not to mention that your husband is right here. Not only are you starting to make me feel uncomfortable, but I know you’re making my wife feel disrespected. So please don’t do that again.”

Her husband spoke as he stood next to her. “Mangus, she didn’t mean anything. My wife is just a very touchy feely person.”

Mangus took his wife’s hand as he stood, “Marina, how about if we call it a night?” He looked at the couple as Marina came to a stance. “It’s been nice. You two enjoy the rest of your night.”

Jeff said, “You too. And we’re sorry if we offended you. I hope what we told you earlier didn’t give you the wrong impression. We’re just friendly.”

Mangus grabbed both of their drinks. “Have a good evening.”

“God bless.” Both Jeff and Kristina said together.

Marina mumbled as she took quick steps, “Oh no they didn’t say God bless.”

They heard a voice behind them and both turned.

A woman spoke to Jeff and Kristina. “Hey there you two, how’s it going?”

“Hello,” said Kristina, springing to her feet to greet the white couple from the foursome’s freakfest.

Marina said as they headed toward the club’s exit, “Oh no. Just in the nick of time.”

Mangus turned forward as fast as he could and shook his head. “Baby, those two are something else.” He handed Marina her drink.

“No doubt. Thanks, because I was about to…”

“I know. We can’t say we’re surprised, can we?”

“I guess not. Hey, what do you say we try our luck again on the dollar slot machine that was showing us so much love yesterday.”

“Let’s go.”

Marina took Mangus’ hand and began a small girlie skip by his side. “I can touch your hand, right?”

“You own it.”

"I told you your ass was fine," Marina said with a giggle.

"Yeah well the way Jeff was undressing you with his eyes on that dance floor, he was about to get checked next." Mangus took another sip of his brew.

Marina raised one eyebrow as they headed in the direction of the casino. "Did that turn you on?" She gave a suggestive look.

"I guess no man wants a woman no other man wouldn't want."

"I guess you're right. And don't think you don't deserve a prize later on for your manhood."

"God bless you," he said as they laughed out loud, mainly for the fact that they were getting along.

Chapter Eleven

"...jack off in her name..."

Newlyweds Mangus and Marina Baskerville arrived home on a bright Sunday afternoon. They returned to their less than one year old, two-story house made of four-sides blonde brick. Mangus had purchased it after selling his smaller ranch home in Snellville.

He'd bought the Sugar Hill home in Gwinnett County not long after he met Marina. He had a vision of settling down and raising a family there one day, just like the large house he grew up in. He made sure there was a large yard for his kids to play, a private office, a room for a son and a baby's room for a daughter, or vice versa. He wanted a formal dining room for entertaining, and a spacious breakfast area. It was important that he had certain specific amenities and that's just what he got, including a three-car garage.

Mangus had a good eye for décor, and like his mother, most of his colors were earthy, either tan or brown or rust, and most of the textures were suede or leather. The walls throughout were warm buff and the crown molding was ivory.

Marina had sold some of her furniture before she moved in, though what she didn't sell, she donated to Goodwill, and she and Mangus planned to decorate each room, one by one over the next year or two, starting with the master suite. Mangus had done a good job, but the sitting area was empty, and Marina had designs to turn it into a private retreat for the two of them to simply kick back and relax, stress free. They'd kept all of Marina's expensive and rare artwork, as she had an intense love of art.

Mangus had done well for himself on a cop's salary, but it was the savings bonds his parent's purchased for him when he was young that added up pretty well a few years ago. And now with Marina's six-figure income, the two of them could live comfortably, and slowly add to the value of their home, as well as possibly buying other property.

This afternoon, the only thing the newlyweds planned on doing was shaking off the rigors of planes, ships and automobiles by taking a long, cozy nap, together.

They spooned each other, his hairy leg lassoed around the smooth caramel skin of her calf, as they surrendered to their cushy Cloud Nine bed in the downstairs guest bedroom. Barely tossing and barely turning, she wore only white panties. He was in the buff.

Marina opened her eyes before Mangus. She was totally unaware and uninterested as to even what time of day it was. For a moment, her intense slumber had her feeling punch drunk.

She slowly removed Mangus' arm from along her waist, and slipped out from the bed, gently resting his hand upon a copper-colored bed pillow. She raised her arms in the air and stretched them so high that it felt as though she could reach the tray ceiling. She took a second to take in the sight of Mangus, dozing with his sexy mouth open just a bit. His peaceful face made her feel good inside.

With only the dim hallway light ahead of her, she stepped along the butterscotch carpet until her feet met with cold roman tile squares of the kitchen, and proceeded toward the refrigerator for some juice and something to snack on when she noticed a plastic shopping bag on the kitchen table.

What is this? she said to herself while rubbing her makeup-less eyelids. She flicked on the kitchen light and reached inside of the bag. Inside, she found some of Mangus' old photos.

She perused each one, shuffling them like playing cards. Three or four were from when he was a young child, smiling with his father while on a fishing trip. She flashed a smile and even gave a quick chuckle when she saw how long Mangus' curly brown hair was. She noticed his resemblance to his dad even way back then.

But most of the photos, possibly a couple dozen or so, were vacation shots from Mangus and his ex girlfriend, Porsche, in the Bahamas. Some were the two of them jet skiing, even riding horses, and lounging by the pool. But two in particular were of them on a small boat with a group of people, and Mangus and Porsche were kissing. In that shot, Mangus had his hand all the way up Porsche's short skirt. Her thick legs were parted wide to accommodate his hand's desire. The tongue-tangle looked intense and his mouth was open way more than hers.

Their eyes were closed shut. She was receiving his tongue well. And she had her hand on his ass.

Marina's chin dropped instantaneously and her teeth clenched her tongue as she stood still. She closed her eyes for a minute and then reopened them, glancing down at the pictures. The more she looked at them, the more she could feel the beat of her heart accelerate. She took a deep breath. And still, she stood in place.

She shuffled through the last few pics and ended up with the last one in her right hand. She took two steps closer to the overhead light for clarity. It was a snapshot of a sight she knew all too well, which was Mangus' midsection, obviously taken in the dark and at close range, and in the photo there was a woman, who had long brown, highlighted, flat-ironed hair, that had a rich sheen to it. And she had her porcelain face positioned between his legs.

The hair on her head in that photo was the same hair as his ex-girlfriend Porsche in the other photos. All Marina could see was his curly pubic hair and succulent lips, busy lips. With one more blink all that formerly seemed to be a barrage of quick-paced heartbeats was nothing compared to the enemy attack her eyes had just delivered to her brain.

Marina held tight to her mind as best she could, and held on to three photos in particular. Before she knew it, her bare feet carried her back toward the bedroom faster than she'd walked only a moment before. "Mangus," she yelled. "Get up."

"What?"

"Get up," she said, standing over the bed. Her nipples were tiny erect pebbles.

"What?" he asked again. His skin was flushed and his eyes were half open.

"What are these photos doing on the table in the breakfast area?"

"Photos?"

She stood at his side of the bed and reached over to turn on his lamp. "The plastic bag of photos. They're on the kitchen table."

He turned his face away from the bright wattage. "What are they?"

"You tell me."

"I don't know. I know they're old."

"Not so old. Some are from what, two years ago. You and Porsche, Mangus."

He laid flat on his back. "Oh, I don't know."

"You don't know what?"

"How they got in there?"

She crossed her arms and bounced her foot. She spoke rapidly. "You put the photos in the bag, and you put the bag on the table. On our kitchen table."

He sat up and pulled the covers up to his waist. "I mean I know there was a bag that I found on the closet shelf when I was making room for your things before we left for the cruise."

Marina just gazed at him with sharp, unbelieving eyes.

"I don't know. Maybe it was the bag in my suitcase I found when I was packing. I didn't check to see what was in it."

"Obviously."

He extended his hand, half squinting. "Here, give them to me."

Marina held two of the three, without handing them over, holding them up like a slideshow. "These are the ones I'm talking about."

He took a forced look and frowned. "Oh, you can toss those. Those are hard to look at anyway." He massaged his eyes.

She dropped her hands. "Hard to look at? Mangus, what the fuck does that mean?"

"It doesn't mean anything. I don't want them anyway."

"But what do you mean by hard to look at?"

"I meant that was the vacation I planned for her, that she agreed to go on knowing she was gonna break up with me anyway. I mean I spent a lot of money for nothing."

"And today it still hurts that you got dumped? Hell, you're married now and you're still not over it?"

"I am over it." Mangus gave pressure to his temples and took a long, deep breath.

"Then you wouldn't have said they're hard to look at, Mangus."

He came to a slow stance and leaned over to grab his pajama bottoms off of the pine bedpost, stepping into them while he spoke. "You read so much into everything I say. Please cut it out. They are history."

Her tone grew louder. "Oh, there are more where those came from. More, hard to look at photos of you and the woman who left you? How about this glamour shot, Mr. Porno Star?"

"What is that?"

"I wonder. The head was so good you had to snap a picture of it so you could, what, jack off in her name when she was gone? Or did you need it to show your friends her generous head-giving skills?"

"Now that one, I can't tell you why I took that."

"Oh, I bet you could if you wanted to."

Mangus blew his exhale through pursed lips and squirmed his mouth around, standing perfectly still.

"You know, they always say, don't get with a man who was dumped because he wasn't the one who made the decision to be done. You didn't come out of that relationship on your own terms, did you?"

"Yes, I did. And if I wanted her back I could have had her. She sent those pictures to me after we broke up to remind me of what a good time we had. To me, that was not a good time. I didn't want her. I don't want her."

"Not a good time? Looked like a good ass time to me. Even finger-fuckin in front of people on a damn boat." She tossed the photos at his feet. "Mangus, when you finally get over looking at them, when they're not so hard to look at, you let me know. Let's just keep them around. Fuck getting rid of them. Look at them every now and then and get over your ex-girlfriend who dumped you after your grand vacation, after she sucked your dick all week long. Try that while your wife tries to make a life with you. Hell, it looks like you were having more fun with Porsche than we had on our honeymoon. You didn't even take one picture of us."

He gave her a slicing stare.

"What was that look for? Oh, so this is my fault?"

He stepped back and bent down to pick up the photos, and then walked around the bed and toward the bedroom door to enter the hallway. He gave a slight shaking of his head. "At least she wasn't policing my eyes every damn minute," he said under his breath.

Slam, was all he heard behind him.

The thirty-two inch tube television came crashing from the end of the dresser and slid over near Mangus' heels as his shoulders raised and he jumped, leaping at least three feet ahead of himself.

Marina stood with a scowl. "That's just plain old fucked up."

His voice belted. "What in the hell is wrong with you? You could've hurt me with that."

Her eyes welled. She shook her head and screamed, "Fuck you, Mangus, just fuck you. You need to watch what you say."

"Watch what I say? Dammit. Whatever I say, the fact is that a TV can be a deadly weapon, Marina. You're going way too far. Next thing you'll be in the kitchen grabbing a steak knife or picking up my weapon."

She was now out and out yelling. "Oh please, I didn't throw it at you."

And now he was yelling. "You can't minimize that, Marina." He pointed down at the busted television.

"See, you just don't understand me. You can't walk away and make a comment like that after what I saw. Do you still love her?"

"No."

"Mangus," she said at extra full-volume, and then she slowly lowered her shaky body down to the floor and began to cry. He hands met her face as she used them to cover her pained expression.

He stood still, shifting his stare down toward the television, and then he headed down the hallway, into the kitchen to grab the bag from the table, and stormed into the garage to throw away the pictures. But not before he tore each and every one of them into a million little pieces, whether they were of him and Porsche or not.

He slammed the kitchen door and took dreaded steps back into the room, hearing Marina weeping, but not looking at her. He bent down to pick up the older, heavy television. The picture tube had cracked and two pieces broke off, along with a few small glass fragments and one of the knobs. He took crouching steps and placed the TV on the floor next to the corner of dresser, and then came to a slow stance, walking back into the kitchen to get a broom and dustpan.

By this time Marina was sitting on the end of the bed, wiping her eyes and sniffling. With the tip of the broom, he swept up the tiny pieces from the carpet, felt around for slivers he may have missed, and took the broom and dustpan back into the kitchen.

He sat on the black leather living room sofa with his legs apart, in silence. He leaned back, crossing his right ankle to his left knee and only then realized it had been night time all along. He went back into the bedroom and Marina was in the same spot. Anger was flowing through his veins. He stepped to her, bent on one knee and asked, "What in the hell are we doing?"

She stared down at her hands. "I don't know."

He stared and frowned.

She said, "It's almost like we're being tested. Or should I say, like I'm being tested. But, I will say, that I'm sorry for exploding."

"Marina, it might be true that I should have destroyed those pictures, especially that one in particular. I know it must have been hard to look at."

"Mangus, I'm afraid."

"What you need to do is relax. You can't go off like this every time something happens that hurts you. It's not like you don't have a right to be upset, but it's the way you show your anger. Is this your way of pushing me away? Because what you're doing is losing yourself to your jealousy and rage. And the result could be that we lose each other, or one of us loses our lives."

"I can't help myself."

"You have to."

"I just love you so much."

"This is not the way to show it."

"Maybe it's just meant to be that I lose you."

"Not if you don't want to."

"I don't want to."

"Then stop. Now."

"I will."

Mangus had heard that before. It seemed unbelievable. As much as he wanted to believe her, his new wife was hot headed and hot blooded and passionate to a fault. The fire in her belly made her a spitfire in bed, and out of bed.

His nerves were a wreck but his husbandly mission was to make sure his wife had nothing whatsoever to go off about. He wondered if maybe he just stopped lying, she would be fine.

But then he told one more lie. "I believe you, honey." His pants were on fire.

Chapter Twelve

"...their sexy new neighbor..."

Sleep deprived after a long night of drama and talking, Mangus was running late for work. He prepared to back out of the middle garage, wondering what would be the best route to take to make up for lost time.

Marina had left an hour earlier after cooking up his favorite turkey bacon and cheese eggs, but Mangus was moving slow. He noticed the large, dark blue city refuse container in the third garage and remembered it was Monday. Trash day.

He went around to the other side of his car and prepared to roll the container along when he spied the tiny pieces of torn photographs inside, scattered about. He flipped the lid closed and tried to refocus his thoughts toward moving on from the incident, and he rolled the large can on wheels along, down the slight hill of the winding driveway and onto the curb near the mailbox.

The amber glow of the sun greeted him. He looked up and breathed in the fresh morning air, and then remembered he was behind schedule.

As he turned to rush back toward his ebony Escalade, a high-pitched voice greeted him.

"Hello," she said.

He turned in the direction of the voice and immediately stopped. "Hello. How are you?"

She walked closer to him. "I'm good." She simply approached and looked at him. Her full, cocoa lips parted to expose her perfect white teeth. She wore a precision haircut with spiky bangs, and she was the color of whiskey. She had on an orange tube-top and tight, pencil-leg jeans. She was both busty and hippy. "Trash day snuck up on us, huh?"

He said, "Yeah, I guess so. It would be nice if I could remember to put the can out the night before. Usually I remember when I hear the sound of the truck making it's way down the street."

"I know what you mean." She stood before him, big boned, with glossy lips that shimmered in the sun. She wore black framed, designer eyeglasses.

"I wouldn't think you've had too many weeks of missing Mondays. Did you just move in?"

She licked her lips after every sentence or so and then continued to smile. "I've been here five weeks already. I moved here from Los Angeles. I don't know why we haven't run into each other before now."

"Oh, well welcome. We were out of town for a while. My wife and I."

She simply stared and simply smiled.

He snuck a peek at his gold wristwatch. "Listen, I'm running late to work but it was nice meeting you."

"Oh no problem. I'm sorry. By the way, my name is Maxine. Maxine Butler." Her sexy voice was as curvy as she was. She extended her hand.

"Hello Maxine. My name is Mangus." He shook her soft hand and released quickly, placing his hand in his pants pocket.

"And your wife's name is Marina, right?"

"Yes."

"Oh okay, I thought so."

Mangus looked curious. "Oh, so you've seen her on TV?"

"TV? No."

He pulled his keys out of his pants pocket and looked down to position the car key. "Well, she's a newscaster. Some people tend to recognize her."

"No. I haven't watched much news in Atlanta. I'd probably notice a newsperson from Los Angeles quicker than one out here. Soon enough, I'm sure I'll see her." She blinked slowly. Her lashes waved his way.

"How did you know her name?"

"I know her name. And I know your name."

"Okay." He nodded as though waiting for more.

"I've heard her yelling your name more than a few times. And I've heard your voice, too."

He paused and then jingled his keys. "Oh, we were talking loud, I'm sorry about that." He then gave a quick look to the sidewalk and prepared to take one step back.

"I don't mean to intrude, but, if you ever need or want to talk to someone, I'm here."

"Why would I need to do that?"

Her pleasant face and her understanding eyes accentuated her words. "I don't mean to embarrass you, really I don't, and I can tell you need to get going, but, Mangus, it sounds like she gets pretty angry."

"You know, with all due respect, I don't know what you're talking about."

"Let's just say, I'm not talking about your name being called out in the heat of passion." She kind of snickered but seemed to check for his reply.

"Okay." He looked toward the garage. "Look, I really do have to head to work. I don't mean to be rude. But I need to get to the station in about ten minutes, and I've got a twenty minute ride ahead of me."

"No problem. You're a policeman?"

"Yes. So, again, it was nice meeting you, Maxine." He again extended his hand.

This time, she grabbed it, and held on as she spoke. "You too. I'm an accountant and most of the time I'm working from home, so if you ever need me, just knock. I'll see you around." She released her grip slowly and then pivoted gradually as she sashayed away, briefly looking back with a lasting girlie wave, topped by a parting wink.

He turned toward his ride just as he remembered he was running late. His mind remembered but his eyes didn't seem to care. They just had to. Just for a second. So, he carefully and momentarily looked back to see…to see if she had it. And she did. She was gifted with a backside. "Yeah, later. Take care," he said far too quietly for her to hear him, but he said it nonetheless.

By the time he hopped in his truck, backed out and pulled off, Maxine, their sexy new neighbor, was gone.

Chapter Thirteen

"...making up was her specialty."

"Baby, listen. About last night."

"Marina, no problem," Mangus said, taking surface streets and making every effort to avoid long traffic lights.

She simply spoke sweetly. "Baby, please try to understand what I'm saying. It's so hard for me to see those pictures, intimate pictures of you and your ex, especially when the photos were sitting on the dining room table that we share. And for you to say that..."

"Let's move on."

"Okay." She paused. "I just wanted you to know I appreciate the fact that you tossed them and I want to make it up to you." Each word was flavored with demure.

"No need."

"See, I know you. I know you're still bothered. What can I do?"

Mangus came to a four-way stop and proceeded when he saw that the guy who had the right of way was playing slowpoke. "Just let it go. Give me a minute."

"Okay. I've only got one afternoon newscast today and then a meeting with a youth club president at five. So I'll probably be leaving at around six. Will you be home by seven or so?"

"I should be."

"Good. And let's make sure we go to church on Sunday, okay? I think we both could use a little spiritual food right about now."

"Uh-huh."

"See you later. And be safe out there."

"I will."

Mangus ended the call. He realized he had no choice but to get on the highway since surface streets were moving so slowly. He took the onramp and then decided he'd take a minute to call his best man. He touched the cellular screen with his index finger and selected his boy's office number.

"Bruce Houston please. Thanks."

A few seconds went by.

"This is Bruce."

"Hey man, how's it going?"

"Hey Mangus, what up? When did you guys get back?"

Mangus made his way to the fast lane. "Yesterday afternoon."

"Where are you? Sounds like you're rollin."

"I'm headed to work. Running late actually."

"Not even one day back in-between, man. That is true love of work there. You are devoted to protecting and serving I see."

"Just back to real life. So what's been up man?" Mangus asked.

The sound of a door closing could be heard in the background. "Nothing much. Actually, I hung out with Carolyn last weekend."

"Carolyn? You going back there?"

"I don't know. I've been out here in bachelor-land a while and everyone I meet I seem to compare to her. It's tough to find the one nowadays. I ran into her at Trader Joe's on Roswell buying that Two Buck Chuck Chardonnay we used to drink, and she looked good as hell, dude. I just had to cut out the cool ass routine and break down and ask if I could call her. We talked that night and hung out at Stone Mountain Park the next day and next thing I knew she was at my house all damn weekend. It was like we never missed a beat."

"That's good to hear. Carolyn's cool people. You sound good."

"Well, what about you, Mr. Married Man. How's the life of the wedded and snatched up?"

Mangus pressed the button to turn on the radio and selected a local old school station. "It's cool."

"Bro, I know Marina wasn't too happy at the wedding. And I can't believe Melanie pulled that stupid ass cock-block move. But, Marina sure turned it around by the time you two said your vows. There wasn't a dry eye in the house, as they say. Even the brothas got a little weepy."

Mangus managed a smile. "That toast you gave was straight up. I really appreciate it."

"Hey, you made a decision to step up and be a devoted, one-woman man. I've got nothing but respect for you. You and me, we've been side-by-side ever since we were rockin the crew socks and the Velcro kicks."

And then Mangus managed what was probably what he needed most, a moment of laughter. "Thanks, man."

Bruce laughed too and then asked, "Hey, how about if the four of us get together one day soon? Carolyn and Marina have never met, but I'll bet they'd really hit it off."

Mangus hurried along to the next exit. His voice quickly shifted back. "I'll bet they would."

"You all right, dude? You sound tired as hell, for real."

"I'm about as sleep deprived as they get."

"Oh, see, I forgot. You're still on your honeymoon and shit. Boy is tapping it on the regular now that you got the papers, huh." Bruce sounded as if he had clapped his hands together.

"Yeah, I've got the papers." Mangus found himself a block away from the station.

Bruce asked, "You're in this for life so make it right."

"No doubt. Listen, I'm about to pull up now. I'm about to get this workday going. Hey, let's get in nine-holes later next week. Let's talk and figure out a day we can get an early start before work."

"Sounds cool. I'll get at you, man. And catch up on your sleep. "

"No doubt."

"Holla at ya boy."

Mangus sat back, even though he was more than five minutes late. He listened to the song on the radio. *You and I* by Stevie Wonder, the song he and Marina played at their wedding. It was just about to end. He turned it up.

In my mind we can conquer the world. In love you and I, you and I, you and I.

The melody took him back to Marina walking down the isle in her angelic white dress.

Him standing there at the altar waiting for her.

The moment he slipped the diamond ring on her finger.

The vows they made to each other.

He felt a rush of emotion.

It had been a little more than one week since he'd married Marina, and already, second thoughts had started to creep into his head like an unexpected, unwanted visitor. It wasn't like the euphoria he'd imagined of being a new spouse. The feeling he'd so looked forward to. The feeling of having a life of love and bliss. The love was there, but the prospect of bliss looked bleak.

His phone sounded to announce a text message. He selected the view icon.

Meet you at 7:30 tonight in the living room in front of the fireplace with your birthday suit on. Marina the stripper will be putting on her one-woman show. Don't be late, Dolamite. From, Your Wife. ☺

He managed a semi-smile.

As usual, making up was her specialty.

*   *   *

At 7:29 p.m., the framed eleven-by-fourteen cruise portrait from the formal night of their honeymoon stood proudly, smack dab in the middle of the taupe granite mantle. The smiling newlyweds were adorned in their black evening attire, facing each other and interlocking hands like it was a prom photo.

The romantic words of Robin Thicke filled the darkened air. The only illumination was the flickering flames of the wood-burning fireplace. The popping sounds of the wood on fire made subtle crackling noises in the background. The scent of the smoky wood ablaze made a perfect dancing flame that added to the allure. Lavender incense smoldered near the fireplace hearth.

Marina strutted into the living room as Mangus lay upon the crème down-comforter on the floor. He wore his light brown skin and a twinkle in his eye.

Marina was naked, and she took long, slow, sultry steps toward him, dragging her toes along the plush carpet as she stepped. All she needed was a pole. Her belly moved in and out and back and forth like Shakira. She shifted her hips from side to side, and had a long red scarf in her right hand. She twirled the silk fabric in the air, and around her back, and down along her belly, and along the roundness of her behind until she reached him.

She stood over him and tickled his chest with the soft silk, and then brought it to his face, lightly tracing his chiseled nose and generous lips. His eyes met the exact spot of her hairy vagina. He'd always liked it unshaven and wild. And from the moment they met, she had always kept it just the way he liked it.

"Hey there, bad boy, whatcha got?" she asked, tracing his crotch with her sheer accessory.

"Your best friend."

"Why don't you show me?"

He looked down at himself and adjusted his partner. He was at full-attention. "See what you made me do?"

"I see. That's pretty impressive. Hey, I hear you can eat a mean pussy," she said, still working her hips.

"I can."

"I hear you're the best."

"I am."

"I hear you can make a woman cum in one minute."

"I can." His confidence was obvious. He spoke as though it were a promise.

"Show me," she demanded with a whisper, circling the scarf around his closely shaven head and allowing it to drape along his manly neck. She held on to both ends of it and pulled his head closer.

"No problem," he said. He knelt while she stood over him.

She immediately secured her legs to straddle his mouth, and he leaned his head upward to meet her awaiting split. She braced herself.

"It smells good. That's that sugary shit you wear. Can I stick my tongue inside?"

"Yes," she said with a sexy moan.

And stick his tongue inside he did.

Marina jerked and squeezed her butt cheeks tight, bending slightly to secure her pussy against his face at just the right level. He grabbed the depths of her ass from behind. Major spillage escaped between his fingers.

Then he traced the outline of her lusciousness with his tongue, kissing her satiny skin and licking her pinkish meat. He made his way up toward her hardened clit, and precisely secured it between his lips with his tongue, almost in a "U" shape to exact its design.

She jerked. "That's it. That's what you do so well."

He moved his head slightly from left to right to get his pressure and grip correct, and then he sucked. He sucked and flicked and sucked and licked and sucked and tweaked her tip, and pressed his head in and out as her clit seemed to grow a full two inches long, like it was a snake and he was the charmer. He gave head to her clitoris. That was his trick. And it was working, as usual.

She grinded against his face, looking down to see him work his magic. She could barely see the tip of his nose along her hairline, but she could feel it. She clenched her teeth and looked up, dropping the scarf along his backside and grabbing the back of his head, holding on for dear life.

Her leg muscles tightened and she could feel the blood rising from somewhere, and it was coming fast. She was about to blow.

She screamed at full force, as loud as she could. "Ahhh, Mangus. Mangus, fuck you Mangus. Damn you."

And she burst her orgasm right into his waiting mouth with a force that propelled her throb three long times until she had no choice but to back away as she could no longer take the enormous, x-rated sensation.

He watched her as she stood back with her head spinning. She grabbed her own clit and cupped her pussy with her hands. "Get away from me," she said, ending with a giggly laugh. Her face was as red as her hair.

He laughed too. "Can't handle it, huh?"

"I don't know what the fuck you do down there, but you need to teach some damn classes."

"Oh please. It's all about pleasing you. You make me want to do it right."

"Shit, any woman would have a hard time sustaining that one."

He sat back with his dick protruding like it begged to not be forgotten and he licked his lips like L.L. "Now bring that sloppy wet pussy here so I can fuck what I started."

"Yes, sir," she said, giving him a stiff handed salute. She stepped toward him. "Where do you want me?"

"Right here, on top of me." He laid back, securing a throw pillow under his head.

"Yes, sir," she said again as she slowly bent down to lay upon him and spread her legs to each side, securing herself as she grabbed all of him with her hand and guided him to meet her buttery opening. "See what you did?" she asked after she fingered her juices for a second.

"That's my pussy," he said with a deep, growling voice.

She lowered herself fully onto his width and length and took all of him in.

Inch-by-inch he took over her entrance, grinding to the left and to the right while he lay on his back, being treated to most men's favorite position. She then rode his dick with a bounce and a bucking motion that mirrored a porno flick. Her ass jiggled so violently that it seemed to have a mind of its own. But before she could give him what he deserved in return for her climax, she let one go again and shocked even herself. The direct hit of his wall-to-wall dick always did the trick in finding her sweet spot.

She shook her head and threw her hair from front to back, shaking her moneymaker wildly. "Fuck, Mangus. Damn. Uggghhhh." Her passion filled shouts signaled the strength of her orgasm.

Marina had it bad.

The audible was almost barbaric.

The lust was so strong it was visible.

Mangus squeezed his wife's rolling gluteus maximus with extra strength and slapped one side. As the sound it made hit his ears, he straightened his legs and said, "Yes, yes, that's it. That's..." He flexed his thighs and stretched his pronounced calves and pointed his toes and shut his eyes. "Dammit," he said, erupting all up in her, first with one long, powerful squirt, and then with shorter bursts that seemed to go on forever.

He waited until the full expulsion subsided before finally opening his eyes.

Marina leaned over him, collapsing her sweaty breasts upon his chest and said, "That's my boy. You came good for Mamma, didn't you?"

"Uh-huh," was all he could say. And then he stuck his thumb in his mouth.

Marina laughed and felt his warm juices start to escape. "Ahhhh, don't make me laugh. Shit. Wait," she yelled, carefully rolling over onto her back and closing her legs tight. "Keep this up and I'm gonna get pregnant for sure."

"Uh-huh," was still all he could say. The pussy afterglow had him by the balls.

Chapter Fourteen

"Trying to bridle my tongue..."

After forty-five minutes of praise and worship performances ending with *Miracle Worker* by the exuberant and talented Sunday Morning choir, the pastor stepped to the pulpit.

Tall and authoritative looking, and dressed in a tailored, maple colored three-piece suit with a patterned sage green tie, and cinnamon Alligator shoes, Pastor Todd Tanner was sharp as usual as he ran it down the way it should be told.

He always seemed to be preaching to each and every person individually, as though sharing a personalized lesson written especially for him or her. He had a way of bringing everything home in a down to earth, easy to understand way in which his congregation could relate to. He had a knack of making everyone feel as though they could survive the peaks, and the trying valleys of life, knowing that the light was just around the bend, just at the dawning. And today was no different.

Every seat in the new, *Faithful Word* super mega-plex cathedral in Austell was full. With marble columns and diamond archways and two, extra wide-screen overhead projection monitors, the three level, octagon auditorium was serving its purpose. The building fund collections had obviously been fruitful, and had multiplied greatly.

Marina and Mangus always sat toward the front in the middle section and were secured into the comfort of the emerald green theater style seats with their respective leather bound bibles in hand. All ears.

"Today's message is the difference between being given to and being made. Given to and being made. When you become broken, you ask God to make you. When you are made, it indicates there is a process involved. How many people have been broken or are broken today?"

Almost all of the churchgoers raised their hands, along with Mangus and Marina. More than a few shouts of hallelujah floated through the place.

He stepped from behind the oak podium. "I know there are times when I'm feeling broken, and believe me, in the past, I was broke-down broken. That's why I'm standing here today. I thank God for my setbacks because every setback is a setup for a comeback. Can I get an amen?"

"Amen," Mangus and Marina said in unison, looking directly at each other. Mangus grabbed her hand and rested their joined hands upon her black skirt.

"Life is what you make it, not about what you've been given. It's about what you make out of what you've got. God makes us into who and what we need to be. You get back up when you fall. But falling is meant to happen. It's a part of life. However, failure is the result of people quitting. There are things you may not want to do, but you still need to do them. You have to change something in the realm of your spirit in order to see results. But be faith-filled and patient. You know why? Because, something that is made, takes effort and time.

"You know, the devil uses heavy artillery to delay our progress, and to deceive us into thinking that things are worse than they really are. And the devil will distract you and break your focus. Not to mention that he will make you disappointed in yourself to the point where you focus so hard on your every failure that you get discouraged and give up."

His tone grew louder and his voice rougher. "Anything that is to be successful will be fought by the devil. God will let us lose things and hit rock bottom, but promises of God are inherited through faith and patience. Faith and patience, Faith and patience. Say that with me."

Everyone said. "Faith and patience." Mangus squeezed Marina's hand. She squeezed back.

Pastor Tanner continued to speak for close to an hour, and read from John 16:20 on the threshold of pain, and Matthew 14:6 on the healing while hurting, and 2nd Samuel 18:18 on the absence of pain.

As the choir began to hum and sounds of the keyboard began to linger softly in the background, Marina and Mangus closed their bibles and zipped their cases, sitting quietly, shoulder to shoulder.

The Pastor's deep voice was mixed with hope and excitement. "And so, I want you to not be a victim to your situation. You know what? God will touch you when you bridle your tongue, when you cool your anger, when you say I'm sorry, I was wrong. There is a high cost for low living. Hope deferred makes the heart sick. So rise up and raise your level of consciousness. Ask God to make you a servant. When you can't help yourself, you should throw yourself on the horns of the altar and ask God to make you. Tell God you can't do it by yourself. Ask him to suck all of the sickness and negativity out of you. Ask him to heal you and make you well.

"I want to ask those who need to be made, who want to be made, to come forth and fall to your knees upon the altar. If you grew up without a parent, or you lived on the streets in poverty, or you were exposed to drugs, or got mixed up in a gang, were pregnant as a teenager, or someone abused you, hurt you, left you, disappointed you, come forth now and ask God to make you. Come out of the other side of the darkness and into the light, so that you can be a servant to others. You have been tested so that you have a testimony."

Slowly, more and more people arose from their seats and headed toward the altar. Single men, couples, families, elders, and teenagers, all stepped up for the altar call.

Mangus was an official member of the church he'd joined years ago. Marina had not yet joined. She sat up straight, with her head bowed and her eyes closed, and did not move a muscle.

"May we bow our heads and hear these words. Father God..."

Moments later, Pastor Tanner finished his final prayer and excused the parishioners as the choir and musicians serenaded the closing.

All of the charged up, smiling churchgoers slowly headed to the back of the sanctuary to exit. As they approached the south exit door, Mangus was greeted.

"Hi, Mangus. Haven't seen you here in a while." The feminine statement came from a tall, light skinned vision in baby pink. Her monochromatic, streamlined suit had a defined waist that showed off her figure-eight shape. Even her leather clutch and Jimmy Choo platform pumps were pink.

Mangus looked to his side to eye her as he and Marina stopped. Marina took his hand and stood to his right. "Hi. Porsche, this is my wife Marina."

Marina nodded once.

Porsche said, "Hello. I know who you are. I've seen you on the news." She immediately locked eyes with Mangus. "Wife huh? Well, congratulations."

Mangus said after a barrage of blinking, "Thanks. I thought you moved away."

"I did. I mean just down to Columbus." Porsche batted her eyes while looking Mangus up and down in his blue-gray suit.

Mangus asked, looking puzzled, "But you drive here every Sunday for church?"

"Oh yes, Pastor Tanner is one of a kind." If Paula Patton had a twin, it would have been Porsche.

"Yes, he is," Marina said, giving a tiny smile. She held on tight to Mangus, gripping his upper arm.

Porsche gave full focus to Marina. "Did Mangus tell you we'd come here every Sunday without fail? He's the one who introduced me to this church. Without him, I wouldn't even have known about the good Pastor."

"Oh really? No, he didn't tell me that," Marina said, keeping her visual upon Porsche's shiny, tinted brown hair, and on her unforgettable lips.

"Mangus, no kids yet? I know how much he loves kids." Porsche femininely waved her hand toward Mangus.

Marina said, "We just got married not long ago."

"Oh, so newlyweds, huh?"

"Yes," Marina replied, and then bit her lip, finding herself looking left to right, eyeing no one in particular as people walked by.

"Well, you've got time."

Mangus looked as though he'd had enough. "You know what…it was nice seeing you."

"You too. Talk to you later, Mangus."

The couple proceeded on. "Goodbye, Porsche," Mangus said without looking back.

Oh, but Marina did look back.

A few women greeted Porsche.

Porsche looked back at her.

Neither smiled.

Marina looked forward. "Forgive me Lord," she said softly to the hot afternoon air as they stepped outside.

"For what?" Mangus led the way quickly.

"I'm trying to think of something nice to say. Trying to bridle my tongue, as the Pastor put it. She's very pretty. Even prettier than her pictures, huh?"

"Okay. I hear you."

"And she must make a good living, with her designer shoes and all. Funny. What was that, one week ago she was an issue in our lives and here she is today on this lovely Sunday morning, in the flesh, in our faces?"

Mangus could feel the sarcasm radiating from her hand. "That's in the past."

"It won't be a part of our past if we have to see her every week. I think that's crazy to drive so far for service."

"I can't control who comes to church." Mangus spotted his car and proceeded down the last row.

Marina dropped his hand and shifted her shoulder bag to her other arm. "Yeah, but that's like the third ex that's been under my nose since we started coming here together. Did you introduce all of your women to *Faithful Word*?"

"What women?"

"There's Melanie and Lizette."

Mangus looked back at her. "Melanie and Lizette come to the early service." They arrived at his truck.

She looked away and gave him the silent treatment. But not for long. "Dear God, I am trying," she said as he opened the passenger door for her and she stepped inside.

He stepped around the back and looked up at the sky, and then opened his door, taking a moment to remove his suit jacket as he spoke. "Look, Marina. See, I know you. You wanted to check Porsche and you didn't. I think that's great. But hey, we can't schedule our church services around certain women who we might run into. Our marriage has got to be stronger than that." He hung his jacket on the back seat hook.

Marina put her purse on the floorboard between her feet. "But when you think about it, it always seems to be your women who are an issue. How come it's never my exes who show up in our lives, at our church, in our photo albums."

"I can't tell you," he said as he got in the car, put on his dark shades, and turned on the ignition. The normally long lines to exit were short and he was pleased.

Marina turned the air conditioning to full blast and aimed the vents her way. "Well tonight, why don't we bring up the name of my old boyfriend while we're in bed and you let me see how you like it. Or better yet, let's go to a restaurant right now and I'll lean over to check out a man and then I'll fantasize about him while you're down there with your tongue stuck inside of me. How would you like that?" She placed her bible in the back seat.

"That's ridiculous. I've never put you through that," he said as he pulled off.

"Well it sure feels like it. If it's good for the goose, it's good for the gander. But, I would never do that." She crossed her legs.

He patted her on her leg and grinned. "I know. You're an angel."

"Now see, you are not funny." She eyed his hand and then the profile of his face.

"You aren't either," he said.

She looked away.

He asked, "Anyway, where do you want to eat?"

"Let's just drive through McDonalds."

"Okay." He waited until the cars began to exit and then said, "By the way, isn't little Naomi, that foster child, staying over tonight? The agency called this morning while we were in the shower and left a message."

"Yes," was all Marina said.

"And she's going to work with you tomorrow, right?"

"Yeah." Marina placed her elbow along the window frame and stared out of the window into space.

"That's nice of you to do that."

"Well, I love kids. They don't know how to hurt folk's feelings. Not until we teach them how, that is."

Mangus nodded.

"I guess Porsche and I have one thing in common. We know how much you want to be a father."

"Soon enough. Soon enough. Faith and patience," Mangus said as a deep reminder of where the two of them had just spent the past nearly two hours.

Marina cut her eyes away and gave a blank stare to the bustling world outside of her passenger seat window.

She quelled her tongue with all her might.

She had a fight on her hands to restrain her own oral anatomy.

It was as though she was fighting back a lioness.

She grunted audibly.

Mangus focused straight ahead and said, "No worries."

Chapter Fifteen

“This bitch needs to back the fuck off.”

The next morning, Naomi, a ten-year-old girl from the *Melon Heart Agency*, sat downstairs in the den with Marina, while Mangus was upstairs getting ready for work.

Marina was already wearing her on-camera, teal pantsuit, as she stroked the keys of her laptop, finishing up sending a few emails before she and Naomi headed out for the day.

Naomi was sitting on the floor near Marina, drinking apple juice from a drink-box straw, and watching the new, large plasma television. Marina bought it when she also bought a smaller version to replace the one in the downstairs bedroom.

“Can I get you anything else for breakfast, Naomi?” Marina asked, sitting back in her stocking feet.

“No, ma’am, I’m full. Thank you.”

“Are you sure? I can make you some more bacon and eggs and fruit if you’d like.”

“No thank you. I’m fine. Why didn’t you eat what Mr. Baskerville and I had?”

“Oh, I just eat oatmeal. I’m not a big breakfast person.”

“Yuk. Oatmeal is nasty,” Naomi said, making a matching face.

Marina smiled and kept her eyes on the computer screen. “What do you normally eat?”

Naomi fidgeted a bit as she talked. “Just cereal. Or toast. We don’t eat a lot of fruit.”

“I see.”

Marina prepared to copy a file to her flash drive as she found herself looking at Naomi. Naomi was a medium brown complexion and she had long, bushy eyelashes. Her eyes looked like ebony buttons. She almost looked Indian. Her curly hair draped down her back, and her face was wide. She had pierced ears with little gold hearts, and long fingers that went on forever. She’d chosen to wear her dark blue jeans and a yellow short sleeve top with a tiny pocket over her heart. Marina smiled at the sight of her. Naomi kept her sights on the animal show on TV.

Marina asked, "Did you have fun last night?"

"Yes. I'd never had slumber party with popcorn and Kool-Aid before. I've slept on the floor before though."

"Oh really?"

"Yeah."

Naomi again focused on her show and giggled at the sight of a dog walking slowly up a flight of stairs with a tiny shot glass filled with water atop his head. He didn't spill a drop. She then looked up at Marina with a wide eyes and a soft, excited voice. "So my real mommy and daddy died."

Marina instantly looked down at Naomi with her entire focus. "Oh they did, huh? I'm sorry to hear that. I'll bet that was tough."

"I don't remember though. I was only six months old."

"Oh I see. Do you have any brothers or sisters?"

"No. It's just me. Well, I do have an older foster family sister. Her name is Jessica. She's white." Naomi sipped the last bit from her juice box and it made a slurping sound. "Sorry."

"No problem." Marina's face showed understanding. "Is your foster sister nice?"

"Sort of. She just doesn't have time for me. She's sixteen."

"Oh, so she's in high school. I'll bet she has a lot going on."

"Yeah. But her mom is nice. But Jessica doesn't have a father either."

Marina smiled. "So the two of you have something in common."

"Yeah, but her dad didn't die. He just didn't want to her." Naomi's eyes skimmed the room.

"He didn't want to her?"

"No. He's never even met her. But she said she tried to call him. He just doesn't call her back."

"I hope that one day he does. Dad's are very special."

Naomi glanced back at the television. "Not my dad. Do you have a dad?"

"Yes. Well I did. But he died when I was young." Marina kept her hands on the sides of the laptop.

"Oh. Did you get to say goodbye?"

"No. But we were very close."

Naomi looked upward and examined Marina's face. "So do you look like him?"

"I think I look just like him."

"I'll bet you have a mom."

"Yes, I do. Why do you say that?"

Naomi explained with vibrant energy as though she had things all figured out already. "Because you're not adopted. Most kids who are adopted don't have moms. But some of my friends end up having a mom who adopts them. And sometimes they have a dad who adopts them, too. Sometimes both. I wish I had both. Do you look like your mom?"

"I think so. A little bit."

"Do you have any pictures of her?"

"I think I do. Somewhere." Marina scooted forward.

"Can I see? Please."

Marina placed her laptop on the coffee table and stood up. "Wow, I'll have to look in one of my old photo albums." She walked to the walnut entertainment unit and opened a cabinet down below. She bent down and pulled out a white album. "Let me see. Wait, actually, I have some recent photos of her from our wedding album." She flipped through and then headed back to sit down. "Here it is."

Naomi sat up on her knees and peeked over at a photo of Mangus and Marina standing next to her mother at their wedding. "She's pretty. Wow, she's taller than you."

"Yes she is."

"I don't know if my mother was tall. I don't have any pictures. I heard the social worker say that my dad killed my mom. And then he killed himself. I was there."

Marina took a slow, deep swallow. She forced herself to speak without appearing stunned and without there being too long of a pregnant pause. "Oh, my goodness. I'm sorry you had to over-hear that."

"I'm strong. I can handle anything."

Marina nodded. "It seems like you are very strong. I'm very proud of you." She put her hand on Naomi's shoulder and lightly massaged her upper back.

Naomi lowered herself back down and then placed her empty box of juice on the table.

Marina put the photo album back on the table and then shut down her laptop. "Listen, how about if we get our shoes on and get ready to go to my job?" Marina came to a stance.

Naomi showed her amazement. "Your job on the TV?"

"Yes."

She stood in an instant. "I saw you one night when my foster mother told me about you. You looked pretty. And you look pretty now."

"Oh, thanks. You look very pretty too."

Naomi stood close to Marina and offered a hug at Marina's hip. "I'm glad you let me spend the night."

Marina leaned down and hugged her back. "I'm glad you came to spend the night."

Naomi looked at Marina with a wide-eyed stare. "Can I come back again after we see you on TV?"

"I think you're going home later on today when we're done at the station."

"Station?"

"The news station, where I work," Marina said.

Naomi released a breath. "Oh. I thought you meant where the police live. I've been there before. When my last foster brother kissed me I was there. He got into a really bad fight with his father when his dad saw us, and they got arrested. They made me wait for the lady to come and get me. But I got taken to another foster family really quick."

"Wow, Naomi, you've been through a lot, haven't you? I'm so sorry."

"Can I please have some more juice, ma'am?"

"Yes, you may."

"Thank you, Mrs. Baskerville. I like your name."

"You do? I know it's not an easy name." Marina walked over to Naomi's over night bag. "Listen, here are your shoes. You be a big girl and put them on and I'm going upstairs to say goodbye to Mr. Baskerville. And go ahead and get yourself more juice from the fridge."

"Yes, ma'am."

Marina headed up to the master bedroom.

Mangus stepped away from the desk chair and then sat on the edge of the bed, leaning over to tie his work shoes.

Marina said at a low pitch, "Honey. My heart is just breaking. I can't believe what this little girl has been through. It makes me feel so bad that kids come from situations like hers."

"As much as we'd probably all like to trade in our parents, I suppose it can always be worse."

"Shoot, Mangus, it seems your childhood was like Ozzie and Harriet."

"Please. My mother and father? Not quite."

Marina stood at her dresser and made a selection from her many fragrances. She sprayed a bit of Lovely by Sarah Jessica Parker onto her wrist and on the side of her neck. "Well, we know mine wasn't. Baby, she actually asked told me her dad committed suicide after killing her mom."

"Wow. That's some serious talk for a ten-year-old."

"She's led a serious life already," Marina said, preparing to lean down and give her husband a kiss.

Mangus looked up at her and puckered his lips. She put her hand on his back and met her lips to his. The sound of their smack was loud.

But also, at that very moment, a quick chime sounded on the desktop computer.

"What was that?" Marina asked, looking toward their corner desk.

Mangus said, "I don't know. Probably my AOL buddy signing in or out."

Marina then stepped to the walk-in closet and grabbed her black high heels. The sound chimed again.

Marina exited the closet and said, "See, that's it again. Is that an IM?"

"I don't think so," Mangus said, taking his wallet and keys from the nightstand and placing them in his pocket.

"Well check it," she said, slipping on each shoe as she balanced herself.

"How?"

Marina pointed toward the flat screen monitor. "Minimize the screen you're in. Mangus. Now don't act like you don't know how to check an instant message."

He walked toward the desk and sat back down in the brown leather chair, maneuvering the mouse to reveal the AOL screen and the tiny IM box.

It read, *Good morning, Mangus. How are you?*

And the second one read, *Been to the Lace Lounge lately?*

“Who’s that?” Marina asked as she stood behind Mangus.

“Looks like it’s Melanie.

“Melanie?” Marina’s voice grew.

“Yes.”

Marina poked her head forward to get a better view. “What? She’s got some nerve after what she pulled. What does she want?”

“I guess to say hi.”

“And to ask you about a strip club? She seems mighty cozy with her message, Mangus. How long have you been hearing from her?”

“This is the first time.” He closed out the two boxes and closed down his email in-box as well.

Marina had one hand on the back of the chair and one hand on her hip. “Oh, the first time that I just happen to be standing here, huh? Usually, I’m out of the house by now.”

“I’m telling you I haven’t heard from her.”

“Mangus, answer her back.” Marina’s tone was no-nonsense.

“I will.” Mangus then placed the cursor over the icon to shut down the program.

Marina’s voice jumped. She popped him on his shoulder with her right-hand fingers. “Wait. Do it now.”

His eyebrows dipped. “Keep your voice down. Naomi’s down there.”

Marina stepped to his side. “Mangus, if you don’t, I will. I’m sick of Melanie’s ass.”

“I’ve got it.” He shooed her away with his eyes.

Marina was now talking with her hands. “You need to remind her…no, tell her that you’re married now. See, that’s what I mean. I don’t have men sending me any damn messages. The men I dated all know the deal. But see, I straightened them out even before we became engaged. Hell, she must feel it’s okay to do this. Doesn’t she know this is my computer, too?”

He scooted the desk chair forward a bit. “Yes, I’m sure that’s obvious.”

“It’s not too obvious, I guess. Tell her.” She accentuated the last two words with urgency.

“Wait.” He gave a half-glance back at her.

"Tell her now. I have to go. I'm not playing." Just as he reopened the program and logged in to his email, Marina stepped closer to the screen and yanked Mangus' hands away from the mouse. "Let me do it. You're gonna say something nice and pleasant. This bitch needs to back the fuck off."

Another IM chimed in. He spoke fast and put his hand on hers. "Marina, get away from the keyboard. I said I've got it."

Marina was one level below yelling. "I am not playing, Mangus. What does it say?" Their hands battled.

"Mrs. Baskerville, are you mad?" Naomi asked from the door-way. Her forehead was scrunched up and her mouth was turned downward.

Marina immediately switched gears. "Oh, no, honey, I'm not mad. Did you put your shoes on?" She stepped in Naomi's direction.

"Your voice hurt my ears." Naomi rubbed the side of her neck and raised one shoulder upward.

Marina stood in front of her and offered a hand to the top of her head. "Oh, honey, I'm fine. I was just talking like, you know, happy loud. You didn't do anything wrong. Let's get ready to go. See, I've got my shoes on too." Marina pointed down at her feet.

Naomi nodded and went back down the first few steps and Marina spoke to Mangus just before she exited the bedroom door. Her jaw was flexed. "Mangus, handle your business. Or else I promise you I will."

"Marina, have a nice day. And you too, Naomi. It was so nice meeting you," he said loud enough for her to hear.

"Yes, sir," she said as she stepped.

He said, looking back toward the door, "We'll see you again soon."

"Maybe tomorrow?" she asked with a bigger voice.

"We'll see. Enjoy yourself," said Mangus as he turned back to the computer. "Bye Marina."

"You just handle your business." Marina shot him a look from behind as he began typing away.

She took the steps back downstairs and again conversed with Naomi.

"I like it here. You're so nice," Naomi said as they exited the door from the kitchen to the garage.

Naomi hopped in the backseat and Marina strapped on her seatbelt.

As they drove off with the morning sun watching over them, Marina noticed the new, and very womanly next-door neighbor, who was watering the lawn while wearing short-shorts.

Marina looked mystified as she wondered who the big-busted woman was. Their stares met.

Marina smiled and waved.

Maxine waved but did not smile, and then turned her back and continued aiming the hose.

Marina's thoughts raced. *Who in the heck was she?*

"Do you work far away? I can't wait to get there," said Naomi from the back seat.

Marina half focused. "No. Not too far away, honey. We'll be there in a minute."

"My foster mother told me life is what you make it." Naomi spoke while flipping through a tiny children's book about ballerinas.

Marina looked back at her new neighbor's curvy image in the rear view.

Maxine turned back around and watched Marina drive away.

Marina shook her head and concentrated on her ten-year-old mentoree.

"Yes, your foster mother is a smart lady. Life is what you make it indeed."

Chapter Sixteen

"...men who suffer in silence."

As the garage door gradually lumbered up, Mangus, who was dressed in his work pants and a tan golf shirt, stepped to his SUV and reached in to hang his fresh-from-the-cleaners police uniform on the backseat hook.

"Mangus," he heard a voice say.

"Yes."

"I wanted to give you this. I'm sorry. Good morning."

He turned around and saw Maxine standing at the entrance of his garage door, looking summery and cheery, holding something in her hand. He said, "Good morning."

She stood before him with her ample lips and hips, looking as though she'd been sweating from pole dancing. Her hair was a bit wet, and her white cotton top was drenched to her skin. "I know you're on your way to work, but, I have something for you."

He took steps toward her, eyeing only her face on purpose. "What is this?"

"It's a pamphlet. It just has some information you might need."

He looked down at her hand. "What kind of information?"

"Information on domestic violence?"

He reached his hand out and took it, perusing the cover. "What makes you think I need this? When you approached me before, you probably just heard an argument. One argument."

"Mangus, like I told you before, I've been there. And I've heard more than one."

Mangus looked at her and then back down at it. He extended his hand to give it back to her. "I'm sorry you took the time to bring this over here, but I don't need this."

She kept her hands at her side. "I understand your reservation. That's normal. Especially for a man."

"Maxine, right?"

"Yes."

"Man or woman, that doesn't have a thing to do with my life."

"Like I told you, I can hear the yelling."

"The yelling?"

"Please don't be offended by the fact that I'm bringing this up to you. You seem like a nice man, and I really have the best of intentions. I'm not giving you this to embarrass you. I want you to be informed. You're not alone. There are a lot of men who suffer in silence. And there are resources. I know I might sound like a commercial to you, but there's no other way to say it. Your wife is abusive to you. And you are a victim."

"Oh, okay. And you know all of that from what you might have heard on the other side of a wall? I think what you're hearing might be…well, it just isn't like that." He again stared only at her face. "Maxine, please understand that I really think this is very kind of you. But I am not in need. I can take care of myself. This is a normal marriage and we are fine."

"I don't think either one of you are."

"I'm being honest with you. I'm telling you I'm fine."

"Just be honest with yourself. That's what matters."

"What, are you some psychologist or something?"

"I had a husband who was a trip. We got into it nearly every day and it took me years to get out of that relationship. He was abusive and he was cruel. I know the signs. I know the sight of it. I know the smell of it. And I surely know the sound of it."

Mangus dropped his hand and folded the pamphlet in half, sliding it into his pants pocket. He leaned against the back hatch of his SUV.

"Mangus, you can leave it at work but just look through it. Please."

"I will."

"Good. There's a number on the back. I don't know him personally, since I had a female counselor, but I know this gentleman deals with men specifically."

"Mangus backed away from his truck and said, "I'm gonna head out now."

"Okay," she said as she nodded, pulling the damp fabric away from her chest area.

"You have a good day." Mangus spoke his words toward her neckline, and then a few inches below, right at the top of her cleavage.

"I will." She caught the location of his eyes. She looked down. "Oh, I was trying to fix the water spigot and…I got water all over me…well,

I got a little wet." He looked away and she crossed her arms along her stomach. "But, anyway, I did want you to have it."

"And now I do."

"Yes, you do. Well."

He said, "You'd better get inside and dry off."

"I'll do that." She took one large step back.

"I'm gonna get going. Have a great day."

She spoke as she walked away in the direction of her house. "You too. I'll check on you later."

"No need."

"I'm right next door," she yelled.

"See you later, Maxine," he said while stepping up and into his car.

"Be safe," he heard her say.

Mangus took a little extra time before he put his ride in reverse, just a second or two, and then backed out and headed to work. He found himself in the mood to simply talk.

"Hey Mom, what's up?" he said with his earpiece to his ear.

"Not much. It's good to hear from you. How are things with you?" she asked from her cell phone.

"Good. I'm on my way to work."

"I see. How's married life treating you?"

"It's fine."

"I know we haven't talked but a quick second when you guys called to let us know you made it back, but you've been on my mind. So, you've been getting used to married life, huh?"

"Yeah."

"And how's work going? What kind of calls have you been going out on?"

"Oh, some little kid who ran away from home yesterday, and then there was a fight at a bar. One of the guys ended up getting shot when he left but he survived."

"Oh my goodness. And I heard about some guy who shot and killed a cab driver due to road rage. Was that your county?"

"Yes."

"I'm telling you. It must be a full moon."

"Maybe so. "

"I must admit I worry about you, but you know that. Some people are just so angry in this world. Things happen so fast, at the drop of a hat. It's like everyone's on edge and then they simply snap. Things can turn out to be tragic in the blink of an eye. You just be careful out there in those streets, Mangus. Every time you walk in that house safely you need to thank God."

"I do. How's dad?"

"He's good. I'm in the grocery store since I'm off today."

"Oh, I thought you were on your way to work. You mean you have a day off?"

"Yeah. Amazing, huh? I scaled down my hours so that I work three days a week right now. I need to show them they can get along without me. Even though they call me about fifty times a day."

"I'll bet they do. Well good for you. You deserve that."

"Thanks, honey. So, I just have to ask. Last night your dad and I talked about how soon you two might decide to have children. You know we need some grandkids to spoil at this stage in our lives."

"Marina and I have talked about it. But, it's a little soon right now."

"I can imagine. The first thing you need to do is get used to having someone around morning, noon, and night. It takes time. Are you happy, son?"

He said right away though his tone was low. "Yes, Mom. I am."

"Okay now. Marina seems like a sweet girl and I know you two didn't really have time to go to marriage counseling, but I'll tell you one thing that worries me. I just didn't feel comfortable saying it before but I think I need to tell you. Because you know I don't hold my tongue."

"What's that?"

"Marina doesn't have a good relationship with her mother and that bothers me, especially when a female is to not close to her mom. Sometimes you'll see girls who are distanced from their fathers, and I guess that tends to make more sense. But a girl who grows into womanhood needs her mother. Moms bring a strong sense of self to a female."

"I never thought about that."

"Have you two talked about it? I mean, I hope I'm not being too nosey, but why are they so distant from each other? It was like at the wedding, they barely said two words."

"Mom, Marina's father was murdered. He was killed when Marina was fourteen years old."

"I knew he died but I didn't know he was killed. How?"

"He was shot."

"Wow."

"Marina was really close to him. And not as close to her mother, so things probably just grew more distant after that."

"My goodness. Fourteen is a critical age for a young girl. And so did her mother raise her on her own after that?"

"I guess she tried. But Mom, Marina's mother was on drugs. She was an addict. So, Marina kind of raised herself. She had good grades in high school and put herself through college on scholarships and grants. And she's made a good life for herself, in spite of it all."

"Oh my God."

"From what I know, her mother stopped using when her husband died, but she went through what Marina thinks was some kind of depression, and I'm pretty sure it was like Marina was on her own. I think they've just have some bad memories between the two of them."

"That is sad. Very sad. Maybe Marina doesn't ever want to be a mother. If not, I guess I could understand."

"Oh, she wants that more than anything. We had a young girl over here last night who she's mentoring."

"Good. So have Marina and her mom talked about what happened?"

"I don't think so. I think they talk maybe twice a month. But from what I know it's never about the past. And it's usually pretty brief."

"My goodness. Thanks for sharing. I know things are sacred between a husband and a wife, and I know you are very private, so I appreciate you for opening up. But when I saw her mother at the wedding, there was just something about her, like there was like a wall between them. She was very cold. Almost like she was ashamed of herself."

"True. They were distant."

"And for Marina to be so outgoing and warm, I just don't get it. They're like day and night."

"Maybe."

"Mangus, I say that as her husband now, you've got to encourage her to talk it out with her mother. Marina needs to talk to her one-on-one and clear the air. Life is too short. And that could very well be something that affects her in other ways. I'd just love to see those two break the ice and forgive. Whatever it is."

"I would too. It'll get better."

"Son, I'm sorry. I know you surely didn't call me to talk about something so deep. I've been standing here in the Publix supermarket smack dab in the middle of the produce department, squeezing pears for ten minutes."

Mangus smiled out loud.

"But, really, I just feel so bad for her. And for you."

"I'm fine, Mom."

"Are you sure?"

Mangus took a second but gave his reply. "I'm fine."

"Okay, well, we want to make dinner for you two soon if you can get away."

"I'll talk to Marina."

"Please do. And don't forget to encourage her to spend some time with her mother now."

"Thanks," he said as he continued his drive to work.

"I love you, Mangus."

"I love you. You and Dad."

He hung up feeling a little bit more, patient. For the time being.

As soon as he began to settle into deep thought for what was left of his commute, he received a call.

"Hello. How are you?"

"Good, Marina."

"Are you at work yet?"

"Almost. How's Naomi feeling about being there?" he asked.

"Oh she's loving it. Everyone's giving her a lot of attention. She's a sweet girl."

"Yes, she is."

"Mangus, I forgot to tell you that I've got this banquet tomorrow that the organization called *No Child Left Behind* is putting on to honor a few people, and I'm one of them," she said sounding low-key.

"What's that about?'

"Mainly education for children. You know the specials during sweeps period I did to promote their events? That's what it is. I just wanted to see if you can go with me since it's a Friday night. It's at the Ritz in Buckhead at 7 p.m."

"I should be home way before then. Sure."

"Good."

"And congratulations."

"Thanks."

Chapter Seventeen

"You're the sneakiest mothafucka..."

"And so tonight, we introduce to you to our final recipient, a woman who has given back to the community since the inception of her career," said Sherry White, the gray-haired president of the *No Child Left Behind* organization. "She has won numerous awards, not only for her skills as a journalist, but also for her tireless efforts in supporting causes for the betterment of women and of children, as well as AID's and cancer charities. Her commitment to our cause in educating our youth has been frequent and valued. And so, tonight we present the Troy Duncan Volunteerism Award to Marina Maxwell Baskerville." The woman waved her hand toward the podium as Marina stepped up, and offered a warm hug.

As the applause sounded, Marina took the heavy award into her hands and placed it to the side of the microphone. She adjusted the bottom of her tailored, silver pantsuit jacket, and ran her fingers through the sides of her curly hair and looked out amongst the many well-dressed, smiling guests.

She fiddled with her short strand of pearls, spoke from memory, and from the heart. "Thank you, Ms. White. Wow, I am so honored to be here tonight. I always feel a little bit as though I don't deserve to actually receive recognition for what I do with my time. I do it because it is truly in my heart, and in my head, as I am very aware of what's going on in the world today." She shifted her weight from her right leg to left, and readjusted the microphone closer to her chin.

"To sit back and watch and not participate in life, to me, seems like a waste of my time. And so I try to make the most of my days on this earth, not only through my efforts, but also through my position in the world of journalism. If I can help to spread the word or if people come out because they are suddenly aware of these organizations because of my announcements or appearances, whereas they were not previously, then that is my reward." She placed her hands along the side of her eighteen-inch crystal obelisk.

"I have always felt strongly about empowering women and striving for an equal share for women in society. We are not second-class citizens, and especially as a black woman, I have felt so much pride in who I am, that to enter the outside world and find that the opinion of some is that we are not valued is troublesome to me. But my main focus has been and will continue to be on children…our future.

"Sadly, our children have been victimized in incomprehensible ways and they're born into situations without their permission. They love unconditionally and we tend to teach them to be conditional and to behave in unjust ways. Their impairments are usually based upon something that they have learned from us.

"I've been given to in so many ways. I have a great career and a wonderful, loving husband, Mangus Baskerville, who is sitting right there." She pointed to him and he pointed back, as both smiled. The people in the room made a point to find him, offering a brief applause. "I am blessed with health and a beautiful home. And so the notion of giving back only seems fair.

"I came from a place of poverty and survived situations that some would swear had to be fictional. But they weren't fictional. They were very real. And in spite of it all, I survived. I was a straight 'A' student in high school and by the age of sixteen, graduated with a full scholarship to attend a college in Los Angeles. All it took was one person to tell me I looked like a newscaster, and I changed my major and had big dreams of sitting at an anchor desk delivering the news. Once I transferred to a university here in Atlanta, my role model quickly became Monica Kaufman and I pretended I was her, every night while sitting in my dorm room, I'd play news anchor. And now, I'm living my dream.

"I am a survivor and I'm thankful and proud to stand here today, in front of you, accepting this award. Recently, me and my husband's Pastor said that people can be given to, but that the true reward is when we are made. I feel as though I have been made into a woman who flipped the script so to speak on my circumstances, though yet and still, I have more making ahead of me and I look forward to that.

"I look forward to what *No Child Left Behind* continues to stand for and accomplishes, and I, Marina Baskerville, vow to be there along the way to support you with my time and energies so that we can continue to educate, empower, and help guide our children to be happy and productive members of our society through raising their levels of self-esteem, and raising them to value their worth. I thank you very much. Goodnight."

Marina lifted her award and backed away. She turned and looked down as she took the two steps from the stage, making her way back to the table of eight people.

Mangus was standing along with everyone else, applauding and watching her. She stood before him. He hugged her tightly. They kissed lightly upon the lips.

She nodded to those at her table and then took her seat, carefully setting the award near her place setting. Mangus picked it up with both hands up and read the inscription and gave her an approving glance as everyone else sat back down.

Later, Mangus and Marina mingled in the spacious, garden-like courtyard of the hotel just as the sun began to set. As was the usual in the ATL, it was almost 9 p.m. and the darkness of nighttime had not fully shown its face.

Marina stood beside Mangus near a table with a few other people as Mangus, looking dapper in a charcoal suit, talked to the program's director. One couple sampled the crab cakes and spring rolls and Marina followed suit.

With her appetizer plate in hand, Marina's station manager came up and introduced her to a gentleman. "Marina I'd like you to meet Ryan Logan who runs the organization called *ONE*. It's an organization for non-violence education."

Marina nodded and said, "Hello Mr. Logan."

"Hello Mrs. Maxwell, I'm sorry, Mrs. Baskerville. It is indeed a pleasure meeting you. We've heard so much about your efforts through the years and we appreciate someone with your visibility having such a strong commitment to children and education. It is inspiring," said the short, stout man with coffee bean skin.

"Thank you, Mr. Logan. I don't do that much really. Just a few causes when I can."

"Your modesty is admirable. I know your schedule is busy, but we have an event coming up and we were wondering if you'd be able to appear as our Mistress of Ceremonies. It's a local event so there wouldn't be travel involved, but I'm sure we could arrange some sort of appearance fee for your time. We'd be honored."

"Oh, I'm sure we could work something out. Perhaps we can talk about specifics at some point. You can call or email me at the station." Marina pulled her business card from the side pocket of her small clutch. "And I don't take fees for my time, Mr. Logan. But thank you."

"Well, thank you for even considering it. I'll be in touch with you."

"Sounds good."

"Oh, and one more question," he said just after he'd prepared to depart.

"Yes."

Just as Mr. Logan was about to pose his question, Marina looked to her side to see Mangus standing alone right next to her, looking down at his drink as he took a sip.

Slowly approaching on the other side of the table were two glamourous looking, sophisticated women, with pretty faces, talking to each other as they stepped. They walked on by to an area behind Mangus and Marina. Mangus still glanced downward.

"Mrs. Baskerville, if you would consider writing a small commentary for our website that focuses upon your position regarding non-violence, not only domestically, but globally as well, we'd really appreciated it. We have a major email campaign next weekend that we're launching, and to perhaps have your image on our homepage would serve our cause well." He spoke excitedly.

"I'm sure I can do that," Marina said as she looked at Mr. Logan, and then noticed a large, paned window behind him. And in that window, she saw a reflection of her husband, Mangus, turning his torso around as he looked back and tipped his head and turned forward again.

"I will let them know," said Mr. Logan.

Marina looked behind and saw the two women sitting on a brick bench…just the two of them. No one else stood near them. Their legs were crossed. Their skirts were short. Their heels were high. Their full tops were low cut.

"Please do. It's nice to meet you. Oh by the way, this is my husband Mangus Baskerville," she said as she grabbed on to Mangus' left arm. Tightly.

"Hello sir. My name is Larry Logan. I'm with ONE, an organization which your wife has so graciously consented to providing a personal statement for, and perhaps an appearance as well."

"Nice to meet you Mr. Logan."

"The pleasure is mine. Well, the lovely couple that you are, you two make sure to enjoy the rest of your evening."

Marina said, "You too. Talk to you later."

Mr. Logan stepped away.

Marina said from the right corner of her mouth, "Let's go." She set her plate on the table and balled up her napkin, tossing it into a nearby trashcan.

"You haven't finished your appetizer."

Marina took two steps and then looked back at Mangus and then back at the ladies, who were looking smack dab at Mangus as he set his drink down.

Marina continued threading her way through the crowd and then out of the hotel to the valet area.

Mangus followed. "What's up with you?"

She said nothing.

"Then why…"

"You're the sneakiest mothafucka I have ever met in my entire life."

His eyebrows jumped. "Oh Lord, here we go." The valet stepped up and Mangus handed him a yellow ticket, giving a painted on smile. He placed his dark gray Oakley shades over his eyes.

Marina stood still, tapping her foot with her arms folded, looking forward. "Stop acting like everything happens to poor little you. As if I only get upset when I just feel like picking on Mangus. I saw you."

"Saw me what? What did I do now?"

"Yeah, that's always the question." She turned to face him, fighting to keep it down. "You're just plain old sneaky. There I was standing right next to you. How many times do we have to go through this?"

"What?" Mangus' face did not give away the fact that he knew they were about to get into some deep, dark, drama.

The valet pulled Mangus' car around and another opened the door for Marina as she stepped up and into the passenger seat with a pleasurable face that defied her angry head.

"Thank you," she said while looking down.

"Yes, ma'am. You have a good evening," the man said at the same time that Mangus got in the driver side and closed the door. He pulled off.

She went off. She rolled down the window and her reserved tone exploded into full-fledged screaming. "I saw your ass turning around to check out those two women who were behind us, and you had the fuckin nerve to nod to them to let them know you saw them."

"I did not," Mangus said loudly, with a look of amazement and exhaustion.

She continued to shout, turning her body toward him. "I am so through with this. Why do you lie at the first sight of getting caught? I could see it if you had a woman who didn't care that you check out women. But, you know it's a problem. You vowed to stop this shit. And you still sneak and do it anyway. It's like you just decide in your mind that the chance of getting caught is not as important as sneaking a peek. I don't fuckin get it."

"Neither do I. You didn't see me looking at anybody." He turned up the radio volume.

Marina switched it off with force and then flailed her hands around, close enough to his face for him to feel the wind. "I saw your reflection in the fuckin window, and I wasn't even trying to see it. You turned around when my back was turned. See, you know what you did, but you still deny it until I break it down for you first, just so you can see how much I know. Your game is sour." He could feel the heat of her breath and sprays of her saliva as she talked.

"Marina…"

With raw aggravation in her eyes Marina suddenly pressed her hand toward his face and smacked Mangus on his forehead, and then she snatched his sunglasses from his face while she pulled on his arm.

"Dammit, stop it, he yelled." Mangus wrestled his arm free as he fought to focus on the road, blinking and twitching his eyes. "What the hell are you doing?"

She broke the glasses completely in half, tossing them out of the window. She shouted, "Did you look back at them or not?"

He looked straight ahead and yelled, "Fuck. I guess I did, dammit."

She shrieked in amazement. "You guess? What are you guessing about? You made a conscious, bastard-move, effort."

He rolled up her window from his side of the car and locked the doors. "Marina. You are losing your damn mind. So fuckin what, I heard something and when I turned, one of them smiled so I smiled back. I didn't turn with the intention of who was back there first."

"Oh please. You saw them walk by just like I did. You made a of point of seeing where they ended up and your ass got busted. I wasn't even trying to police you."

"I told you I heard something." Still with shocked eyes, he continued to concentrate on his driving.

Her voice stayed loud. "Mangus, just stop lying. Dammit."

"You stop yelling."

"Hell no." She hollered at the top of her lungs and squirmed through her mental discomfort, scooting away from him. "I will fuckin jump out of this car if you don't for once admit what you did."

He kept one eye on her. "Calm the fuck down."

"No." She reached to her right and grabbed the door handle.

Mangus immediately pressed the accelerator and sped up as quickly as he could.

She ranted and kicked her feet. "Stop this car."

"I am not stopping until we pull up in the garage."

She again leaned within a few inches of his face. "Why can't you admit it?" She repeatedly poked his right bicep with her index finger.

He tore across the road and was choking the steering wheel, trying his best not to look at her. "I didn't."

"Mangus," she howled.

He turned a final corner fast and furious. "Calm down, Marina."

"Pull this fuckin car over." She banged her fist upon the padded leather compartment that separated them.

"No."

She turned toward the windshield and saw that their home was a little bit away. "Let me out of here." She grabbed her clutch bag and leaned down to take off her shoes.

He came to a slow crawl at the stop sign less than a half-block away.

Marina braced herself to hop out and he took hold of her upper arm, squeezing it and pulling her back toward him as he sped up again, yanking her to him.

"Let go," she yelled.

He removed his hand and reached up to the visor to press the remote, glancing over to see his new neighbor who was just pulling her new cherry red Z into her garage. He kept his hand on Marina as she writhed about, and quickly pulled into the garage.

Chapter Eighteen

"...his dick went limp."

"I hate you," Marina said, stepping out of the car barefoot with her shoes and purse in her hands, slamming the car door.

Mangus got out and slammed his as well, even harder. "I hate this shit we go through. This crap is stupid and unnecessary." He gave a hard press to the button on the wall to close the garage.

Marina burst through the door into the kitchen and threw her things on the counter. Still, her voice was deafening. "What is stupid is that you're man enough to try to be slick, but not man enough to say, hell yeah I did it."

He stood right beside her in the kitchen. "What's all of this anger and jealousy with you, Marina? I told you to keep your fuckin hands to yourself. I am so tired of this shit."

"Then keep your eyes to yourself," she said with a shrill.

His words did not budge. "I will continue to look where I want to look. And I was not checking them out."

"I saw you."

"You can't tell me what I was thinking. What is wrong with you?" His scowl was deep.

"First of all, this was my special night. I was fine until I noticed you noticing them. Hell, I knew you'd check them out. I know your damn type." She walked away, past the dining room and into the den, plopping down on the loveseat, crossing her arms and legs.

He followed her yet continued to stand. "My type? According to you, any woman is my type and every woman wants me. Now cut this shit out. I can't have this."

She looked up at him, still speaking with piercing words. "You cut out what you're doing and I won't be like this."

He leaned downward to speak closer as though it would make a difference. "Oh, you won't, huh? So how do I cut it out? Do I wear a damn blindfold and hold your hand for you to lead me around every fuckin place we go?"

"Don't be sarcastic, Mangus. That's ridiculous. I'm saying I need you to be aware of what you're doing. You're still doing this shit. Why? Why can't you do it during all the other hours of the day that you're not with me? Especially after all that we've been going though already. Why?" she asked as she unfolded her arms and banged her hands onto her own thighs.

"For the last time, I was not."

"You were not what?" Her words were ear splitting.

"Marina, you need to stop." He stood up, tall and firm.

Marina stood up and leaned in toward Mangus, continuing to belt out her words. "This is about your dick, not me."

"It's always all about you. You're crazy." He cut his eyes and prepared to step away.

"What? You fuckin jerk," she screamed and propelled her fist straight into his rib cage. He tripped when his foot bumped the leg of the sofa and he fell onto his back.

She kicked his torso and hurriedly threw her body on top of him, swinging at his head with jabs and punches. Her fingers bit into his neck and cheeks, and she slapped the side of his face repeatedly as he shielded himself with his hands.

He turned to look up at her and she socked him, catching to corner of his mouth.

He felt the pain pound through his bottom lip and grabbed her wrists, squeezing with all his might. In one fail swoop, flipped her onto her back, slammed her onto the carpet and sat on her, along her waist, squeezing her wrists.

"Get up." She squirmed and huffed and puffed, kicking her legs, trying to twist her hands free and tossing her head from left to right, over and over.

"No."

"Get up, Mangus. I can't fuckin breathe." Her eyes looked manic.

"That's because you're so damn excited. Calm the fuck down." His eyes were pissed.

"Get up, I'm gonna pass out." Her shorts breaths were obvious.

Mangus still sat upon her. "You breathe right and you'll be fine. Take a deep breath and relax." He let go of her arms and she immediately tried to swing at his face again.

"Dammit," he yelled. He grabbed her wrists again.

"You bastard." Her pained face was balled up as tight as her fist.

"Marina stop."

She tried to raise her hips and squirm away. "Get up."

"No."

"Dammit. Why can't you just stop when you know it bothers me?"

"Look, I wasn't checking anyone out. Now stop. This can't go on anymore. I'm telling you right now."

"Mangus," she yelled, squirming as he held tighter.

"This is getting worse. You didn't act like this when we were dating and now it seems ever since we got married, you are so damn possessive. I am not a possession. You have to know that." His words were strident.

She turned her head away and screamed, "Let go of me."

"No. Now look at me," he demanded.

She jerked her face toward him, wearing grimacing frustration. "What?"

"No matter where I look, or who you think I'm checking out, it doesn't fuckin replace you, Marina."

She turned away and scooted her hips from left to right.

"Look at me. I said look at me."

She again glared at his face.

"You were all I ever wanted. Someone fine as hell, successful, and into God, or so I thought. That's why I married you. I didn't wait all these years of being single to marry you and then run off with some woman who's standing behind me who you think I want to be with. I'm not leaving you for another woman. You need to be more secure than that, Marina."

"Dammit. I see you do that shit, and then you always turn around and deny it."

"I'm not interested in those women." He started to downshift his grip a bit but not his voice.

"Of course you are. That's why you fuckin turned around. You stand right next to me and at the same time, you fantasize about other women."

"I don't."

"You do. And how do I know you don't think about them when you're fuckin me." She looked down at his grip. "And please let go of my arms."

He slowly released her and stood up.

With a deep frown, she rubbed her wrists and then rolled to her side. She knelt and then stood, and then frustratingly plopped down upon the edge of the sofa.

"Marina, that is not something I do. I'm so damn turned on by you that I can't think past the way you make me feel. Hell, my dick gets hard when you walk by, or when I say your name, woman. I love you."

She couldn't help but notice the obvious bulge in his pants.

He continued, "This side of you is the complete opposite of who you are when you're not jealous. You just got an award tonight. You're honored all the time. People love you and see you as this angel. But who are you, really?"

She shook her head. "I don't even know."

"Marina."

Her voice seemed a few levels lower. "I get so jealous. It's just that I love you so damn much. I want you to want only me. Is that so wrong? Why can't you just stop?"

"What I know is that we're all gonna look at people. And we might even see someone we think is good looking. You might see a guy who's handsome, but that doesn't mean we abandon our mates because there are good-looking people in the world. And damn, Marina, don't you know that I see men looking at you all the time? Did I trip when you were talking to that man tonight? I trust you."

"But that was business and you know it. Plus, I would never speak to or acknowledge a man who was checking me out. Especially not with you standing right there." She massaged her hairline.

"But don't you notice them looking at you?"

"Yes."

"Then don't you think that means you're looking at them to even notice?"

"But if you saw me looking at someone, I'd admit it. You never admit it."

"I would."

She looked up at his face. "Were you looking at her?"

He thought about the promise he made to himself to be honest. "I told you already. I looked back. Now, can we please cut this shit out? This is crazy. Please?"

Her face seemed to show she'd lost the argument.

He stepped toward the fireplace and put his hand along the mantle.

She said, "Please come here." Marina scooted back.

"What?"

"Come here." Her index finger scooped the air from his direction to hers.

He turned and stepped in front of her. She slowly unzipped him, little by little. His pants traveled to the floor and he stepped out, one foot and then the other. She guided him back a bit so she could kneel down to meet him, took his manhood out of his boxers, and kissed him as his hardness stared her in the face.

"This is not the answer to our problems," he said, looking down at her.

She gave him bedroom eyes.

She slid his underwear down and off, and opened her mouth wide and sucked him and licked his long shaft up and down. She took him in and bobbed her head up and down, but within seconds, he reached his hands under her arms, backed away from her mouth, and brought her to her feet.

Her eyes waited for him to say something.

But he didn't.

He leaned her back along the couch, abruptly removed her silver, silk pants, and spread her legs from west to east, moving her purple V-string to the side. He lay on top of her and raised her legs back with his forearms, found her greasy entryway and gradually pushed himself inside, penetrating her walls.

"Damn. You feel so hot."

"You got me hot." She squeezed his dick tighter with each grind.

"Turn over. You wanna fuckin know what I've been looking at? I've been looking at your ass all night. That's what I've been looking at. Shit," he said as he exited her throbbing pussy. Her pleasure cream covered his dick.

She slid her underwear down and off. She mounted herself up on all four and perched her ass toward him while he took off his pants. It was heads down and asses up.

He fingered her. "This is where I live right here. This is the only ass I want."

He stuck himself inside and they moaned together.

"Do your bounce so I can see all that yellow ass move."

She braced herself upon her elbows just right and did her hip jerking, booty clap. Her ass moved along for the ride like it had its own zip code.

She yelled out, "Where are your Timbs, baby? Put your Timbs on like you did when we first met."

"See," he said tightening his eyes as he removed himself. "You're really ready to get punished tonight, huh?"

"I'm ready."

He raced up the stairs taking two steps at a time, jerked open the closet, grabbing his tan Timberlands and ran back downstairs, shoving his feet inside without lacing them up.

He marched over and took a firm stance behind her, bending his knees to adjust his hardness to her exact level of entry.

Her body quivered to beg him to enter.

He shoved his dick inside like he was still mad at somebody.

She jerked and yelled. "Shit."

"I'll show you what I'm about to do, fuckin with me like you do," he said while poking every inch of her depths, going all the way back inside. He looked down and saw her ass wiggling like Jello. He pumped away and grunted with each thrust. He placed his hands on each side of her wide ass, and worked her body back to meet his grind. The sight of her sexily drawn tattoo that lived on her lower back fueled his fury. The sound of her cheeks meeting his balls was loud and nasty.

Her eyes were closed. "Uhhnhh, uhhnhh."

He talked shit. "See, I've gotta keep my dick inside of you for you to act like you've got some damn sense, huh?"

"Uh huh," she said, moaning like she was stuttering.

"I see your ass is cooperating now. Talk to me."

She looked back at him with a porno glance. And then, she talked shit. "Sexy huh? Sexier than that big ass white woman on the ship you were checking out."

He said nothing. He gripped her waist.

"I know you had your eyes all up her ass, watching her phat white cheeks shift as she stepped, wondering what it would feel like to get her up on her knees so you could fuck the shit out of her like this."

He said nothing. He again grabbed her ass.

"And those women tonight at the hotel. You saw something you liked. Must have been her big ass tits you snuck a peek at before you got caught. I know my man, shit."

He said nothing. He leaned forward and placed his hands along her upper back, still digging deep.

"Reach under me and grab my tits. I've got tits too, dammit. Grab 'em."

He did just as she said.

"I want to milk every damn drop of that sperm you've been wanting to shoot from watching all these women who get all up in your fine ass face every day. You know those smiles mean more than just hello. You know when you're getting hit on. Don't you?"

He finally answered, "Yes." He spoke at a low tone.

"You were looking at both of them weren't you?"

"Yes." He spoke louder.

"You wanted to fuck that white lady from behind, didn't you?"

He again grabbed her ass tighter this time. "Yes," he said even louder.

She bucked. "And you thought that one woman who smiled at you today was fine as hell. I know you did, you wanted to tittie fuck her, right?"

"Yes. Yes. Oh fuck," Mangus said, busting a long, fast moving nut all up inside of his woman. "Fuck, Marina."

She slowed down once he froze in place. "See, I know you. You felt that shit?"

All he could do was nod.

She moved forward and motioned for him to back up. "Now get up so I can get undressed and go to bed. I have a long day tomorrow," she said, almost laughing at him.

He held on to himself as he pulled out, cupping his hand. "You are one freaky woman."

"Well, I see you're freaky right along with me. I'm gonna let you slide on that one."

"What?"

She stood up and headed to the stairway. "Mangus, I'll be in the shower," she said cheerily, as though his x-rated skills had once again tamed her beast.

"I'm right behind you," he said, popping her on her ass. It bounced up and down as she turned.

He went into the downstairs guest bathroom. His dick was still hard. He stood still over the snow-white commode to release his liquid waste that filled his bladder. He flushed and then turned around to face the sink when he caught his reflection in the mirror. His left cheek was scratched. His neck was scraped and bleeding. And his left eyelid was bruised and swollen.

Instantly, his dick went limp.

Chapter Nineteen

"Is Marina still jealous?"

"Man, what's that shit on the side of your damn neck?"

"What?" Mangus asked, talking to Bruce as they rode along in the golf cart at the Bobby Jones golf course.

The very early morning sun was already giving off its melting heat. The clouds had just evaporated under its intense fierceness.

With his long, squared, dark chocolate face, Bruce was behind the wheel. He looked to his right, puzzled. "Did you two buy a cat or something? Damn."

"A cat? Please. I scratched myself lining myself up the other day." Mangus touched the area of his neck where he'd earlier applied Neosporin. He pulled down the brim of his black golf cap with the white Nike swoosh.

"Well you must be fuckin blind 'cause what little hair you ever let grow is on your head, not the side of your neck."

"I know that." Mangus shielded himself from behind his new tinted sunglasses.

"What up, man? You can't afford to go to the barber shop anymore?"

"It's just an every now and then thing, dude. I line myself up just like you need to do." Mangus examined the top of Bruce's long curly head of hair.

"Oh please. Don't hate the Indian in me. You need to put something on that shit. It's red as hell."

Mangus lifted up the knit fabric of his shirt collar. "I did and I will. Hell, stop looking at it. You need to be getting ready to keep an eye on the so-called game you're about to be losing. It'll be a slaughter."

Traveling at a slow pace, Bruce maneuvered the steering wheel along a sharp curve. "Please. I see you're wearing all black since you'll be in mourning when it's all said and done."

"Man, no matter what color I wear, there will be no losing for me. I don't lose."

"That's what you say now."

"Man, when was the last time you beat me?" Mangus asked.

"Like, whenever the last time we played was."

"Bruce, you lie like there's no tomorrow."

"Prove me wrong?"

"I'll prove you wrong in a few hours, I know that much." Mangus looked around the rolling green hills and up at the powder blue sky. His mind traveled back to the fight with Marina. The fury in her face kept flashing before him. He recalled the look in her violent eyes and he shook his head. "Man, this is the life. Hey, how's Carolyn treating my boy?"

"Better than better. There's something about going back that makes you appreciate so much more. Makes you wanna do better."

"Yeah, but getting back can be risky too though. Then you end up having new people in between and folks you need to back away from again."

"Yeah true. But it was all worth it. We're flowing like we never have."

"That's how it should be."

"Let me tell you, Carolyn is so cool about everything all of the sudden. She doesn't trip about anything. She's down for whatever, man. We even stopped at this strip club the other day when we were driving back from Charlotte. It was broad daylight. We saw these huge billboard advertisements, over and over, mile after mile, but I didn't dare even act like I noticed. And then right before the exit she said to get off the highway so we could have a drink there. It was this bunny ranch type place, dude. It was actually called *Chic and Strip*. The chicken strips were nasty but they had some fine ass white women in there. And most of 'em were hittin on Carolyn."

"No way. Was she into that before?" Mangus asked looking impressed.

"No. I mean she never said it would be a problem. But I never would have thought her conservative ass would be cool with it. My dick was hard for two days after we stepped inside. And baby girl even asked me to pay for her to get a private dance. One of those where she lays down instead of sits down. It was behind this black curtain. I couldn't see shit. She even picked out the girl. Or should I say the girl picked her."

"Oh man, damn. And you didn't even get to watch?"

Bruce spoke with his chest poked out and with extra enthusiasm on his face. "No. But when she came out, she was hot as a fuckin tamale. She pulled out her own money and tipped the girl twenty dollars. And then she handed me money to tip the dancers on stage."

"Now that is a turn on. Every man's fantasy."

"Now don't get too jealous, dude, but you know I got me some head in the car on the way home."

"Bruce, you are lying. I can't even picture Carolyn doing all that."

"Carolyn let her hair down that day. Man, I love that girl," he said shaking his head. He turned down the final straightaway toward the first hole.

"Oh Lord. You two have totally earned your freak card."

"She's my main girl," Bruce admitted.

"Oh, so haven't totally erased the competition then. I thought you said you did."

"I did, but you know how it is when we take those calls or run into folks. We're all human."

"Well, human just means we're straight out dogs according to Marina."

"Is Marina still jealous? Even after snaggin you and getting that expensive ass wedding ring."

"She can be pretty possessive." Mangus again pulled on the brim of his cap.

Bruce reached the green and turned off the ignition, setting the parking brake. He sat back and continued to talk. "That possessive shit is stressful. I don't know how you do it."

"Sometimes I don't mind, but to be honest with you, she does tend to catch my ass. Just when I get a split second look or some shit, she just happens to be on it."

"Oh, so she's policing you. That shit is not cool."

"I guess if there's nothing to catch, you can't get caught."

"Well what are you supposed to do, stare at the damn sidewalk? That is gonna grow tiring fast."

"It already has." Mangus gave a long sigh as he reached into his pocket and pressed the touch screen to power down his phone.

"I'd say she's got Cupid's chokehold on you, boy."

Mangus replied, "Maybe so. Sounds about right."

"Yeah, but trust is major though. So what's up? Are you two trying to work through this? This is new for you. I don't think Porsche was like that, was she?"

"Not really. But Porsche was so full of herself. She wouldn't dare take the time to notice who I looked at. She probably wouldn't even believe that I could have ever thought about looking at anyone but her."

"That's just self-confidence, dude." Bruce stepped out of the cart and stretched.

Mangus got out as well, heading toward the back. "Yeah, well, even Porsche got on my nerves. This relationship and marriage stuff is all about give and take. I try to balance it out. Hell, Marina does have her positive sides."

"I guess if her jealousy is the only negative, you can work around that. What other complaints do you have?"

"Nothing worth talking about. We'll get it right." Mangus grabbed his golf bag.

"If anyone can deal with it, it's you. I say you two should talk it out. Tell her what the deal is. You know women love that talking shit. Hell, that communication crap makes my ass itch."

"I know what you mean."

"Well, you're one hell of man, I know that much. And you're not the type to fool around. She needs to know that. As many times as I've tried to throw some no-strings pussy your way." Bruce rummaged through his tweed bag for a new box of golf balls.

"I don't know what you're talking bout."

Bruce asked, eyeing the fairway ahead of them. "What about Melanie? Where's her crazy ass?"

Mangus positioned the pin into the grass. "She moved to L.A. last I heard."

"Last you heard? From who?"

"Man, she sent me an email letting me know."

"See what I mean. Sometimes, you can't get rid of 'em."

"This one I don't plan on hearing from again. I had to set her straight after what she did when she tried to screw up the wedding."

"Cool. Does Marina know you hit that?"

Mangus tried to focus. He placed his ball upon the tee and stood back, nine-iron in hand. "Come on now. I'm ready to get this started and hit this tee shot. Stop trying to delay your ass whoopin."

"You're the one who'll be in mourning, wearing all black with your lying ass."

Mangus prepared to step up and fought to clear his heavy mind.

Bruce joked as he moved back to give Mangus his space. "Make sure you at least get it on the dance floor, Tiger."

"Ha, ha, Mr. Comedian. Be quiet."

Mangus focused. He looked down and then up, and down and then up, and then down. He pulled back his club, all the way up high, twisted his right leg, kept his head down, kept his wrists adjusted, and met the club to the ball, mentally exacting all the he'd learned about his follow-through, making a careful and skillful, long in the back quarter shot.

Bruce shielded the sun by placing his hand just over his eyes and looked way off into the distance. "Damn man, you hit the hell out of that one, player. Mangus the husband just might have a new game."

Mangus managed an ear-to-ear grin as he discovered that he was dead on the green, within a few feet of the hole. He said confidently, suddenly stepping with a swagger, "This hole is a par-4, so this just might end up being an eagle."

Bruce still looked toward the green. He picked up his jaw. "You're living the life."

Just that quick, again Mangus' thoughts slipped back to the mad-woman look on his wife's face. "Your turn," he said. He then joked just to seem normal. "Get your ass kicking pads ready." But his marriage was far from normal. He again looked up at the sky.

Bruce gave him a crazy look. "Boy, next time, take your damn shades off. No, on second thought, leave 'em on. I ain't never seen nobody hit the golf ball with shades on," Bruce said as he stepped up.

Mangus gave a strained laugh. He hoped his fake smile looked authentic. He focused on relaxing, blocking out the stress of his marriage.

If golf couldn't do it, nothing could.

This time it was Marina's voice ringing in his ears. *I hate you*, he heard her say.

By now, he was starting to believe it.

Chapter Twenty

"I told you she was crazy."

Mangus was behind the wheel of the brand new, white Interceptor police cruiser as he and his partner patrolled the area near downtown Snellville later that morning. "Hey, welcome back, man. How've you been?"

Ronnie said, eyeing the outside vision from the passenger seat, "Can't complain."

Both Mangus and Ronnie were suited up in the uniform gray pants with dark jackets, adorned by their Gwinnett County badges.

"What'd you end up doing on vacation?"

"You know, just hung out at home most of the time. And then I headed out on a weekend trip to Arizona to this spa."

"Spa. You, the macho man, at a spa? With who?" Mangus asked, again wearing his dark brown sunglasses.

"With my family. You know, parents and brothers."

"Your wife didn't go?"

"No, man. She had to work."

"What'd your big ass do at a spa?"

"We stayed in this timeshare my parents had and just hung out, you know, played cards, eating, and then got massages, and swam. It was cool. I hadn't been with my entire family in years."

"I'll bet that was a trip. You got a massage?"

"Yeah."

"Alright. Anyway, I don't know how your parents got all three of you together in the same room."

"My brothers and I are cool. We've gotten over a lot of that stuff I told you about last year."

"Good. Because life is short, dude," Mangus told him just as a dispatch call came in.

"Unit 128H, see the woman, AS3 assault victim, at 340 Falcon Ridge Drive in Snellville. Code 2. Domestic."

Ronnie pressed the button on the microphone and said, "128H, 10-4." He scrolled to the end-call button and flicked the navigation switch. He entered codes into a small computer. "That's right down the street. Probably some man going upside his wife's head again. I'll never get that to save my life."

Mangus made a sharp right turn and pushed the speed limit. "You never know. Maybe she's blaming it all on him."

"She? The woman. A woman can't hurt a man."

"All it takes is one time for her to pick up something and it's all over."

"Yeah, well, some of these dumb ass men need for these women to pick up something. But, either way, it seems to me the women end up taking 'em back anyway."

Mangus pulled up into the driveway of a small, dingy, white frame house and both he and Ronnie exited the vehicle.

An older, large black man with a trimmed gray goatee walked toward them from the front door, talking loud. "You've got to take her away. See what she did to me." He pointed to his dark-red ear. "She damn near yanked my ear off and then kicked me in my thigh and trashed this house."

Mangus said, "Sir, where's your wife? It is your wife, right?"

"Yes. She's...I mean *it's* in the kitchen."

"I'm right here. And who you calling it? I'm the one who called them. Don't you come out here trying to act like some victim. You are a madman." The Hispanic woman, thin and short, had mascara stains under her eyes, and her cotton blouse was ripped along the neckline. Her short, jet-black hair looked mussed up.

"I'll talk to her," Ronnie said. He approached her. "Come with me, ma'am. They stepped into the dirty, filled to the ceiling garage while she kept looking back at her husband. "What happened?" he asked.

She cut her eyes toward him as she spoke. "He just woke up and snapped when he saw me looking around in the closet. It was like he lost his mind. He said he thought I was just getting in from a date. I told him it was twelve-noon and he just started going off about me staying out, saying he'd been waiting up for me all night. I told him he was crazy."

Ronnie noticed her baby finger was bleeding. She had a bloody paper towel in her other hand. "I see your finger is injured. Can I see your I.D. please? What is your name?"

"Cecelia Jones," she said, stepping to the side door to mine through her purse, which was on the chair by the door. She handed it to him.

"Mrs. Jones, what happened to your finger?"

"He pushed me down and then yanked me back up and started yelling in my face. I grabbed on to his shirt sleeve once I saw that my head was near the corner of the nightstand as I fell, and he twisted my hand back and my acrylic nail popped off, damn near taking my own nail with it. It hurt like hell."

"You need to run some cold water on your hand. And then apply pressure. Fingers tend to bleed heavily." Ronnie looked her over. "Did he hurt you anywhere else? I see your blouse is torn."

"He did that trying to push me away from him."

"Why?"

She talked as if she was crying yet her eyes were tearless. "Shoot, I was gonna break his finger too. I thought mine was broken."

"Mrs. Jones, your husband is pretty big for you to try to hurt him back."

"Well what am I supposed to do? Sit back and let him think I'll take that mess? My mamma didn't raise me to take mess from a man or anyone else."

"Hopefully you'll never have to again. Now my partner is gonna let me know what's going on with your husband, and then we'll probably take him in. We don't tolerate domestic abuse. Since you say he pushed you down, and as a result, you have an injury, we're within our rights to arrest him for domestic assault."

"Good."

"Have you ever had to call us before on him?"

"No."

Mangus walked over to Ronnie as the man waited by the patrol car. Mangus asked, "Ma'am, did you hit him first?"

"No," she said as though she swore on a stack of bibles.

Ronnie asked, "Why?"

Mangus spoke to Ronnie as he took a step closer. "He said she attacked him."

"This little woman?" Ronnie asked, pointing his finger back at her.

"Yes." The lady took a step closer to them and was all ears. "Ma'am, please step into the garage for a minute."

She walked over near the wall as they continued to talk.

Ronnie asked, "So he says she went off on him?"

"That's what he says."

Ronnie said, "I think they were both whoopin each other's asses. I say we take him in just so he can cool off." Ronnie looked over at the man who had a deep frown-line between his angry eyes. "He still looks pretty mad."

Mangus said, "If you ask me, she should be the one who goes in."

"But she called us."

"And"

"You fuckin mothafucka." All of the sudden, the woman flipped into livid mode and sprinted in her bare feet, straight to her husband, within a foot of his chest, just as he put his hands up to block her.

Mangus leaped toward and her, pulling her back, and twisting her arms behind her as he spun her up against the car.

She shouted, "I'm gonna kill you. You stayed out all night and went to see some bitch. I know your old ass." The look on her red face was maniacal. She cried hard like she had been cut deep.

"Is that what he said happened?" Ronnie asked.

"Yes. I tried to tell you." Mangus then spoke to the woman. "Ma'am, we have probable cause to place you under arrest for domestic assault and for terroristic threats." With one hand, he took his handcuffs from his belt, flipped them open and secured them tightly along her wrists.

"See, I told you she was crazy." The man pointed at her and nodded as though he was relieved to be believed.

Ronnie told him, "Sir, she has injuries as well. Turn around and place your hands behind your back." The man frowned and slowly turned as Ronnie cuffed him, too.

"I'll call in a request for back up. She'll go in with us," Mangus said as he opened the back door of the patrol car and placed the woman, who was now suddenly quiet, in the back seat.

"She had me fooled on that one," Ronnie said while handcuffing the man.

"Yeah, the women usually do. That's why one slip can get a man locked up."

"They'll be back together within the week."

"Maybe not," said Mangus, pulling out his report book, and then leaning into the car to use the radio.

Chapter Twenty-One

"If you keep me mellow,
I'll keep you mellow."

It was past eight in the evening by the time Mangus made it home from his long day. The lingering smell of smothered chicken filled the air, along with the sweet scent of burning vanilla bean oil.

Mangus had already been upstairs to take off his clothes, and had just come back down wearing checkered, drawstring pajama bottoms.

Marina was in the den, sitting amongst the dim light, with her feet propped up, wearing a pale yellow silk robe, watching a rerun of *Deal Or No Deal*.

She gave him a quick glance. "I just put your dinner in the refrigerator if you're hungry."

"I grabbed something earlier. Thanks."

"No problem." She spoke a few seconds later. "How'd your game go this morning?"

He took a seat on the other end of the sofa, sinking down just to the right of her. "Cool. I lost."

She turned her attention to him. She paused her eyes at his perfectly defined pectorals and then snapped out of it. "What? You never lose."

His tone was dry. "Well, I did this time."

"What's up with you?" She took in a side view of his face and saw that his eye was still red.

"Nothing."

"Something happen at work?"

"Marina, I'm fine."

She put her hands up in surrender and readjusted her position, reaching down to rub her feet and then staring back at the TV. "My mom called and asked if we could take her to the doctor tomorrow."

"What did you say?" he asked.

"I didn't talk to her. She left a message."

He scooted forward a bit and looked at her. "You know what, I've been thinking we need to make more of an effort with your mother, or should I say, you need to. I mean she did end up coming to the wedding. And I'm not sure she's as healthy as she tries to make us think."

"Why do you say that?"

He explained, "She just seems like she's moving slower, and all of these doctor's visits."

"She's just good about her monthly checkups. She's fine."

"Are you gonna call her back?"

Marina hugged her upper arms. She thought. She waited. She said, "Yes, actually. I will." She cozied deeper into the softness of the sofa cushions.

Mangus lowered his eyes, almost predicting her next reply, "Do you want me to take her?"

"It depends on what time she has to go. If it's late, I guess I can."

He nodded. "Good." He looked at the program and then back at her. "You know what Marina? We need to talk. We need to talk about a couple of things, actually."

"Sure. I need to talk to you, too. But you go first. What is it?" She shifted her legs around and turned to face him.

He looked as though he was making great effort to choose his words. "Honestly, it's about us. And about your temper."

"Okay." She did not blink.

He leaned forward to grab the remote and turned off the television, placing the remote on the end table next to him. "I know you love me. I know you've been through a lot in your life, and I've spent a lot of time taking all of that into account, trying to understand you from the inside out."

"Okay."

"But, baby, your anger, and your mood swings. I mean, they just seem to be coming more frequently from out of nowhere. Not only on the cruise, but ever since we got back."

She looked toward the plastered ceiling for a minute and then back at him. "Well, Mangus see, on the cruise there were a lot of moments when I did actually bust you. You must admit it."

"Please let me finish."

She rubbed her hands together. "Okay."

"Marina, you see things from your view, and what you see is me being a jerk, checking out women, and acting like I'm single, and I can't judge your feelings. You have every right to think that. But, I have my view too."

She eyed him. "And what is that?"

"I think you seem to go in spurts with your temper, almost like you're in a certain mood at times, maybe more so than at other times. Well, honestly, I think you tend to overreact."

Her eyebrows seemed confused. "Overreact? You know what?" Marina stopped. She took a deep breath. She spoke calmly. "I have to admit that my moods do seem to come and go, and I think that it mainly happens when it's really close to that time of the month. I think I've always had really bad PMS and sometimes I look up and find myself in the middle of a mood before I even realize my period is starting."

"But I also think it might be something else."

"Like what?"

He leaned to the right and scooted back, bringing his right ankle to his left knee. "Like, have you ever gone to the doctor to have them check you out, maybe to see if they can put you on some kind of medication?"

"Medication for what? For my PMS? Because that's really all it is."

"Or just in general, medication. Like, I know there are certain syndromes or disorders we can experience that cause us to not act like ourselves."

Marina exhaled and twisted her mouth. She looked down as she talked. "Disorders? Mangus, to be honest with you, most times it's just you. I react to you. If you keep me mellow, I'll keep you mellow."

He cut his eyes away and then back to her. "Did you read that somewhere?"

Her sights snatched him. "Did you read about the disorder thing somewhere? I think what I said is true."

"Well I think that's a huge responsibility for me to try to live up to. That puts a lot of pressure on me and makes me responsible for your moods. I can't take on that duty."

"That's a husbandly duty, to keep your wife happy."

"Well let me ask you. Who keeps me happy?"

Marina did not miss a beat. "I keep you happy be respecting you, and not checking out other men, and not lusting over your friends or some stranger, and not going to male strip bars, and not having my exes texting and sending me IM's. Melanie had the nerve to send you instant messages after she tried to ruin our wedding. I would have cussed a man out if he did that."

"I'll bet you would."

She stared at him "What does that mean?"

"Marina, you can't just go around cussing people out, confronting someone who doesn't live up to what you think is right, and basically, well…I think you're trying to change me."

Her eyes opened wider. "Change you? Don't you want your wife to trust you?"

"That the operative word. You don't trust."

She scooted away and turned to rest her arm along the top of the back cushion, placing her hand under her chin. "Well, hell, maybe you're just not trustworthy."

"It's cool if that's how you see me. But if we argue about who's right, then we get nowhere."

"It's not about who's right or wrong. It's about you understanding that I do have flaws."

"I get that. We both have flaws. I don't see you accepting mine. But I'll tell you one thing. You cannot, I repeat, cannot, put your hands and feet on me again, throw things at me again, and yell at me like I'm some evil enemy. I am your husband. I am a man. And I demand your respect."

"Maybe I don't know how to do that. Maybe, you'd be better off with someone else." She crossed her arms.

He kept his sights hammered to her face. "I don't want someone else. I want you. And I want you to learn how to stay calm. I see you with your friends, and coworkers, and with little Naomi. When it comes to the rest of the world, you are loving and beautiful and your heart is as big as the sun. You just have a hard time controlling your temper with me. Your husband. The closest person to you. And it's wearing on this brand new marriage already."

She blinked quickly and then looked down and over toward the carpet. "I don't know what to say. I've said I'm sorry."

"And for every sorry, it happens again. What we need is some type of therapy. Maybe even through church. We need God in our lives. We need intervention so we can keep this marriage going. Until death do us part, remember?"

"Mangus," she said, seeming to search for a suitable reply.

"Marina we need this."

"I thought you weren't into therapists." She paused, and then met his eyes again. "I'll look into it."

"Good. I look forward to it. In the meantime, what do you say we get on the computer and play a game of scrabble?" He worked his smile to help encourage her.

"I'm cool with that." She smiled back. And then she asked, "You did send that IM back didn't you?"

He stood up and headed to the office to get the laptop. "Yes, I sent it. I blocked her, and I handled it." His words had quickness.

"Thanks."

He spoke from the other room. "So is that what you wanted to talk about?

"Huh?"

He reappeared with the slender, chrome computer and took a seat next to her. "You said you wanted to talk to me about something."

She shook her head, flashing a pleasant face. "Oh, no, it was nothing."

Marina thought back to the new addition to their neighborhood, but decided to let it be. Suddenly, it wasn't important. Not at that moment anyway.

Chapter Twenty-Two

"What do you think my issues are?"

The next afternoon, under the low hanging clouds and muggy summer heat, Marina and her mother exited the doctor's office of the Tower Medical Center in Lithonia and walked at a snail's pace to Marina's car.

Marina noticed that her mother really had begun to walk slower and that she'd lost weight just since the wedding. But she still hadn't lost her trademark backside.

Even though both could have fired away a barrage of questions, most of the drive to the doctor's office had been fairly quiet, other than a bit of random small talk, and the ride home was no different.

"So, Mabel, that went well," Marina said after helping her tall mother in the car. She then went around to enter the driver side, wearing jeans and a navy tank top.

Mabel's words were monotone. "Yes it did."

"So, the doctor said everything is fine?" Marina glanced over at her mother's hands.

"Yes."

"Are you sure?"

"Marina, why are you asking me twice?" Mabel scooted down the fabric of her bone colored, short-sleeved dress and then wiped her forehead. She used her toes to slip off her ballerina-like shoes and leaned the seat back.

Marina backed out of the space and headed out of the parking lot. "It just seems like you've been rubbing your hands together ever since I picked you up. And you've been breathing hard."

"I've just been trying to get in and out of this cute little car and walk up those stairs. Plus, it's hot out here."

"Yes, it is."

"My joints just get a little stiff every now and then, both my hands and my knees. I feel fine." She adjusted the air-conditioning vent to make a direct hit upon her face. Her short bangs blew back slightly.

"When do you need to go back?"

"I'm not sure."

"Mabel, I saw you make a follow up appointment."

"It's sometime next month, I think. I have the appointment card in my pocket book."

"It just seems like you go to the doctor a lot."

"I'm keeping an eye on my health. If I don't, no one else will. I don't eat as well as I should. Plus, you know, all of those drugs in my system for so many years can catch up at any minute."

There was more silence as Marina drove the short distance to her mother's place. During one of Marina's long inhales, she took in a whiff of her mother's trademark scent of Tresor. It hit her brain like a memory boost. She found herself focusing on making nice. "Well, I'm glad to see that you go to the doctor."

"How are you and Mangus doing?"

"We're fine."

"Good. Do a better job than I did."

Marina gave a brief half-laugh.

Her mother said, "And your job is okay? Are your hours easing up a little?"

Marina played with her hair with her left hand and had her right hand on the wheel. "It all depends on who's on vacation. For now it's an eight hour day."

"Good."

"One thing I'm gonna do though is get into therapy."

Her mom turned to look her way. "Therapy for what?"

"I'm going to see a psychologist."

"Now I don't see why that's necessary."

"I do."

"That's so new fangled. Back in the day we'd just pray and if that didn't work, we'd pray some more."

Marina kept her eyes on the road. "Did praying work for you back in the day."

"Prayer is why I'm still here."

"I see."

"What's a psychologist gonna do for you that God can't?"

"I have a lot of issues to work through. Issues that could be the reason I have a hard time right now." Marina switched hands on the wheel and placed her right hand along the gear shifter.

"Hard time with what?"

"You tell me. What do you think my issues are?" She stopped at a traffic light and signaled.

"Not that my opinion would matter but I think your main issue is anger."

"Anger? Why would you say that?"

"You've been angry ever since you started high school."

"Really?" Marina proceeded on and made a right turn.

"Really. And you know it. If I could have done better, I would have, I just didn't know any better."

"Well, I'll give you credit on that one. I am one angry woman, that's for sure."

"You're just mad at me."

"No, I'm mad at me."

"That makes no sense. Blame it on me."

"I blame it on life. And though I might need to work through it, I need to deal with it. Understanding is the first step to moving on."

"I moved on and still never understood it. It is what it is," Mabel said while looking through the passenger-side window.

"Well, call me new school, but I've got a marriage I want to keep together."

"Yes you do. Mangus deserves to get you at your best."

"Yes he does."

"I really like him."

Marina pulled up in front of her mother's place and put on the brake. "I know you do."

Mabel looked at her daughter. "And Marina, by the way. I'm sorry. Sorry for whatever I did or said or didn't do, or chose to do. I'm sorry."

"Okay."

Mabel leaned down to pick up her purse, slipping back on her slippers. "Well, thanks for taking me."

Marina opened the door and hopped out. "Hold on, I'll walk you inside."

"No, it's okay," Mabel said just before Marina closed her own door.

Marina yelled through the window, "Mabel, you stay put. I'm coming around."

Mabel pulled on the handle to begin to open the door. Marina pulled it open further and said, "Come on."

Mabel took Marina's hand and got out. "Thanks."

"Do you have your keys?" Marina asked, closing the car door and then stepping up the short walkway with her mother.

"I do. They're in my hand already."

They reached the doorway and Marina opened the screen. Mabel turned the key and took a step inside.

Marina said, "Well, I'll see you later."

"Yes. Later. Tell Mangus I said hello." Mabel's back was to Marina.

"I will. Goodbye." Marina turned and took a step.

"Goodbye, daughter."

Marina paused, and then walked again, applying a sliver of a smile as she made it to her car.

Mabel then closed the door between them.

Chapter Twenty-Three

"...a bridge over these troubled waters."

It was already after seven that evening and Mangus was on his way home in his Cadillac truck from a day that included being called to a deadly auto accident near I-85 and a teenager who ran away from home because of an abusive father.

He usually tried to shake things off by listening to music or tuning in to a local radio sports talk show.

He gave a few cleansing breaths, shook his shoulders and maneuvered down the highway. No sooner than he turned up the radio did his cell vibrate from inside his pants pocket. He turned the radio back down.

"Hi son. Where are you?"

"Hey Dad. Just headed home from work."

"Where's Marina?"

"She should be home by now. She took her mom to the doctor."

"Good. I'm glad to hear that. How's her mom doing?"

"She said she seems a little tired."

"What's wrong with her?"

"Nothing that I know of. But then again, her pride is the size of a mountain."

"That's the women of my generation for you. Listen, can you stop by here for a minute?"

"Sure. What's up?" Mangus asked.

"Oh nothing much. It would just be good to see you. Besides, your mom wants to talk to you."

"Okay. About what?"

"I'll let her tell you."

"I understand. I'll be right over." Mangus readjusted his mental sense of direction and made a u-turn.

Mangus' mind raced. Within fifteen minutes he arrived at his parent's home, rang the doorbell, but still used his key to go inside. He removed his shoes as he closed the door, noticing the familiar aroma of one of his mom's usual home cooked meals.

His mom and dad were sitting at the kitchen table. Mangus stepped to his mother and gave her a hug.

"Hey Mom, how are you?"

"I'm okay," she said, sitting with her legs crossed in her velour sweatpants and long white blouse.

"Just okay?"

"I said okay."

"Dad?" Mangus' faced begged for more words from someone.

Mr. Baskerville sat across from her, sipping on a glass of cranberry juice. He swallowed and then said, "She'll tell you."

Mangus pulled up a chair next to his mother. "Okay, so you're okay but you have something to tell me?"

She spoke slowly and kept a smile on her face. "Today I had a physical, you know my routine check up I get. And well, I had a colonoscopy. The procedure is simply awful even though they gave me pain meds and this light sedative. It takes forever. Like an hour. It rips you of your dignity, if you'll excuse the word rip. You just lay there and they invade your body from behind with this long, lighted camera." She used her hands to demonstrate a visual of the length of the enemy object.

Mangus did not crack even a glimmer of a smile. "Mom. And?"

"Well, they needed to remove some polyps. Like five small growths."

"Polyps?"

"Well, there were some in my colon. I'm told that's my large intestines, but either way I say it's my rectum."

"Mom," he said anxiously.

She just went ahead and said it. "And they need to test them. They seem to think they've been there for a while. They said over time they can be, well, you know, pre-cancerous. But they're not."

"They told you they're not?"

"They'll give me a call once they biopsy those little boogers. I already know they're not pre anything."

"Mom, have you had any symptoms or anything? I thought you said you felt fine."

"I do feel fine, now that that camera's not probing me."

"This is not funny," he told his mom with no-nonsense eyes.

"Mangus you know I believe life is all about your attitude. Don't be so serious. The good thing is that by removing them early, they won't have a chance to grow and possibly develop into cancer of the colon. That would not be funny."

"How did they remove them?"

"While they were doing that digital thing they tightened this loop and severed them I guess. Off all the places for folks to be piddling around in...why my exit?"

Mr. Baskerville said, "Honey, you are silly. You'll be fine." He showed a comforting face.

Mangus asked, "And why didn't I know so I could've been there?"

"Son, I'm fine. You didn't need to be there worrying. We decided we'd tell you now once we found out what was going on. But my goodness, you'd better lighten up. Sad faces are not welcomed here. Bill, I knew he'd do this."

"I know you did."

"Mom, I'm happy that you told me. And you're right, you are fine."

"Thank you, son. And tell Marina not to worry. I'm not going anywhere just yet. I'm not even a grandmother yet. You tell her that."

"All in time."

"I'm sure you know what's best. Your dad said she went to see her mom. I'm glad to hear it. Really glad to hear it."

"Me too."

"Do you want some dinner? I made some pot roast and potatoes."

Mangus stood with heavy shoulders and pushed the chair in. "No thanks, Mom. I'm going to head home."

"Okay, dutiful husband. You're just like your dad."

"Yes, I am," Mangus said. He leaned down to embrace his mother.

She said, "Goodbye. Thanks for stopping by so quickly."

"Thanks for calling me, Dad. I'll call you tomorrow."

"Deal."

This time on the way home he sat still and quiet. He drove from Duluth to Sugar Hill and barely blinked. His thoughts had traveled into the deepest part of this mind and his heart fought to not race in equal measure.

He stopped one block before his home and pulled over. He prayed out loud, trying to bring to mind all that Pastor Tanner had taught him. *Dear Lord,*

Come into my heart and into my home. You are my Fortress and my Strength. Father God, as in Psalm 91, I ask that You will command the angels to guard in all ways. I call upon You and ask for long life for my mother. And lift my burdens Father. I feel the weight upon me. Please show me a bridge over these troubled waters. I ask this in Your name. And so it is. Amen.

Chapter Twenty-Four

"...a lot of things to work through first."

Within a couple of hours, Mangus and Marina lay in bed under the comfort of their Egyptian cotton sheets, both on their backs. Both staring at the ceiling. The only light in the room was from the gold lamp next to Marina's side of the bed. The fan above spun a breeze big enough for the both of them.

"Mangus, have you ever thought about adopting?"

"No. Why would we? We haven't tried to have kids of our own first."

Marina's arm rested behind her head upon a pillow. "Well, I mean there's no real set way of doing it. There are so many kids out there right now who need love…like Naomi."

Mangus turned to face her. "You're not thinking about us actually adopting Naomi are you?"

"It did cross my mind."

"Naomi is just one of the many kids you mentor. Soon, you'll want all of them."

"Naomi is special. And, I think we'd make great parents."

"So do I, but we've got a lot to work through first."

"You're talking about the therapy. That'll happen and we'll be fine."

He looked back up to the ceiling. "First things first, Marina. First things first."

She shifted gears. "Anyway, how's your mom?

"She's had a colonoscopy. They need to check out some growths they found."

Marina turned slightly to her right to view his face. "Growths?"

"They just need to check and see what's up. They'll let her know."

She'd watched his lips move. "Oh my God."

"She'll be fine."

She leaned her head up and scooted back. "Wow. Well, we just have to believe they caught them in time."

"They did."

"What a trip. Our parents are getting all of these checkups all of the sudden. What's up with that?"

"They're getting older. At least they're making an effort to see the doctor."

"Well, I know one thing. Of all people, surely your mother will be just fine."

He shifted gears. "Marina, there's a meeting at church next week. A few pastors will be there to meet with couples in the ministry for about an hour."

"Like couples counseling?" she asked.

"It's called marriage enrichment."

"How do you know about that?"

"It was on the back of the program from church last week."

"What time of day is it?"

"I think it's in the evening."

"Let's go then." She scooted down and lay flat upon her back again.

"Good," he said, leaning over to Marina's face to plant a kiss on her cheek.

She said, "I have an appointment with a therapist tomorrow on my own though."

He adjusted his pillow and turned onto his stomach. "Good for you."

"Goodnight, honey," she said, leaning over to turn off the lamp.

"Goodnight. I love you."

She secured herself comfortably, facing the other way, and scooted her butt back toward him. "I love you back."

Chapter Twenty-Five

"They should have taken me away from her."

"I'm really not a bad person. It's just that sometimes I can't seem to stop myself from my jealous behavior. I mean, when he looks me dead in the face and turns things around on me, it just pisses me off."

Marina spoke strongly as she sat upon a skirted, light aqua sofa in a large rectangular office with a tall window view of Atlanta's massive, lush green trees. The office walls were filled with awards and diplomas. The room's décor was perfection.

Sitting across from her in a provincial style, high back conversation chair, the thirty-something blonde marriage-family counselor looked like she could have been an actress on *Desperate Housewives*. Only she looked anything but desperate. She was tanned and skinny and gave an air of having the most perfect life. Like she had it all together. But Marina figured maybe she'd experienced just enough crap of her own, that perhaps she was indeed able to relate to the very folks who sought her well-balanced expertise. Or maybe she was just living vicariously through the stories she was told. Either way, the woman had found a way to make it look as though she was hanging onto your every word. She looked interested as hell.

And so, Marina spilled her guts as best she could, trying to answer questions to really tap into the core of who she had become lately. The times when she gave her husband something he no longer wanted to feel, the times when she acted like a stark raving maniac.

"How does that make you feel?" the therapist asked as she titled her head just a little.

Wow, Marina thought, *it feels good to be asked a sentence with the word feel in it.* "Very angry. And Lord knows I try to fight it. It might not seem like it to my husband, but honestly, I try to be calm. I try to be levelheaded and not react. Especially when deep in my heart, I believe this man is secretly fantasizing about these women. I've never suspected a man of doing this before."

"Tell me, what were your previous relationships like?"

Marina sat with her legs crossed. Her hands moved about. "There were three of them and they each had their own set of issues. See, when I was in high school, I had a popular boyfriend who fooled around on me, but I told him off and never saw him again. I never even suspected it. It was sort of a joke we played on him. When I was in my early twenties, I dated a guy for two years. We had no issues with trust whatsoever. And then I found out not only did he have two women, but he had two cell phones, two apartments, and basically two separate lives. And my last relationship was with a jerk I lived with. Out of the blue, when I came home early one day, I caught him in bed with another woman. And he had the nerve to call me the next day and say that he loved the other woman, and loved me too. But that he'd decided to choose me. I guess I was supposed to be thrilled by that. What an irresistible offer."

The therapist had a notepad in her lap and pen in hand, but didn't write anything down. "So you've been fooled around on a lot. You basically have trouble trusting. Trusting men in general. But I want to know where that started. It could have been your first boyfriend, or earlier. How about you tell me about your father?"

Now, Marina thought, *maybe this is the twenty million dollar question.*

"My father was murdered. I was there. My father died right before my eyes." Marina uncrossed her legs and paused. She took a long inhale, and released it while her shoulders fell hard. She interlocked her hands onto her lap, and spoke while looking at the wall, as though watching a video.

"My mother had been fooling around on him. He found out. He found us, my mother and me. We were at a bar somewhere on Campbellton Road. She always took me to the catch-action nightclub when she'd go out flirting in general, or when she'd go out to meet him. His name was Teddy. He wore long, dirty dreads. And Teddy had the means to get my mom as high as she wanted to get. My mom fell in love with him. And my daddy knew it.

"I'd sit away from the actual bar area, at fourteen-years old, sipping on soda and munching on peanuts while my mother, usually scantily dressed and tipsy, conversed somewhere nearby. To this day, I'm an expert at shooting pool and playing ping pong just from all of the games I'd play to pass the time. The men always gave me looks. Odd looks. After all, my body was shapely. It was a skinny version of hers and we both had these rear ends. I never wanted to show my legs. They'd stare at my legs. One even touched my arm and squeezed it a little too long. I hated that place.

"Mom used to tell Dad we were over her best friend Edwina's house. She'd take me with her as an alibi. She'd always include me in her night-out-on-the-town marathons. I'd learned to lie to my very own father. For her.

"See, Daddy was my heart. He always read to me and taught me things. He was funny and he was kind. But that day, he simply snapped.

"He appeared out of nowhere while I was in Mom's burgundy Thunderbird at around one in morning. As usual, she'd climb into Teddy's blue car, which would be parked next to ours, and they'd get in his back seat while I just sat in the car and waited. See, I'd hear them. I'd actually hear him. I'd actually hear her. She sounded like a porno queen. Her voice was always deep and sultry. It was loud and dirty. The sound of her voice makes my skin crawl still. She was loud and dirty, even though I was in the car right next door. I think she was too drugged out to even care.

"But this one particular night, while I sat and waited, Daddy came from out of nowhere and he walked up to the blue car they were in and began yelling like he was possessed. I'd been reclined all the way back on the cold leather seat with a blanket on my legs, trying to talk my head into taking me someplace. Sleep maybe. Anyplace. Just somewhere. And then I heard him. I knew that voice. I leaned up to peek out of the window into the dark, and it was him in the flesh. I don't think he saw me. His shouts still ring in my head. 'Mabel, get your ass out of that car. Now.' I can hear his voice. I hear his voice still. Every so often I can still hear his voice.

"My mom and Teddy sat up in the back seat. I could barely see them from the neck up since it was nighttime, but a car passed by and the headlights lit them up. I could see that Mom's hair was a mess. She looked fearful. I could see her eyes good and they told on her terror. Teddy's eyes were not fearful. His eyes showed dare. And then I heard a pop. And in as quick as the sound of that pop, he…Teddy…shot my father. He pulled the trigger, and all I saw in the stillness of the chilly night air was a burst of white light. One quick burst, and that was it.

"Daddy had fallen to the ground. I screamed like I had been shot myself. I scooted closer to the door and looked out of the window as another car passed by. My daddy, my handsome, tall, loving daddy, lay still, with the side of his head split open against the wheel of the car of the man who shot him. I leaned out of the window and saw my father's brains blown out."

Marina waited and looked down for a moment. She hadn't noticed that a tissue rested in her hand, and that layers of tears covered her cheeks and had dripped onto the neckline of her gray dress. She dabbed her eyes and patted her cheeks and sniffled loudly. She again glanced at the wall.

"Mom hopped out of the car with her clothes askew, and fell to her knees to pick him up from under his arms. 'Get up,' she cried, scooting him away from the car's front tire, hugging him to her chest. I turned away and again screamed bloody murder. Teddy kept his headlights off, pulled away, and disappeared.

"Later the next week, after Teddy had been on the run, Mom and I were driving home from the funeral when all of the sudden, from out of nowhere, something hit us. It was another car. The hood of our car was bashed in. The other car had flipped over and landed up against a tree. Teddy died in that accident. He was trying to kill my mother. He was trying to kill me. But, it didn't work. At least not physically anyway.

"Mom has never dated since. And she has not driven since. The guilt has eaten away at her. The terror has all but driven me mad."

The therapist waited for a long minute to make sure Marina's words had ceased. She noticed Marina's eyes had broken away from the wall, and so she spoke. "Marina, I surely understand that considering all you've seen with your very own eyes, and all that you were subjected to, all of the secrets, all of the grown up experiences at a time in a girl's life when she's experiencing being a pre-teen, all of the hormones and emotions, and then the anxiety of losing a father so violently right in front of you, that it is all life changing and life choking. And I'm sorry you had to go through that. Very sorry."

Marina missed the look on her therapist's face as she only took in the sight of the balled up tissue in her hands. "I think I've hated my mother more than any other person in my entire life."

"What do you think made your mother make those choices? Do you think it was the drugs?"

"All I know is, my mother was an adulterer. And she abused me by putting me in those situations, and by making me lie for her. And she exposed me to witnessing her lover kill my Daddy. How do I ever forget that?"

"You may never forget it, Marina. Never. But believe it or not, you can get over it. See, we all make certain choices at certain times. The question is, do you believe your mother meant to purposely hurt you?"

"Intentional or not, my mother put me in the position to be abused, and to die. My mother is the cause of my father's death. They should have taken me away from her. But they didn't."

"Have you ever confronted your mother?"

Marina continued looking down. "No. She simply makes me angry."

"And see, that's the word. Angry. Your anger will never be resolved unless you come to terms with your mother. You can choose to resolve the issue regarding your mother on your own, in this way, but I suggest you do it in conjunction with talking to her, too. You need to understand her story so you can change the direction of your life. You need to confront her and get your feelings out in the open while you can."

Marina shook her head and gave a sniffle. "I can't."

"You have to. You just simply have to forgive her. Otherwise, you will not survive your anger. Your anger will survive you."

Chapter Twenty-Six

"...swallowing the brunette cognac whole."

"Hi Camille."

"Hi there, dear. How are you?" Mangus' mother asked Marina.

"I'm fine. How are you?"

Camille's smiling voice was like audible sunshine. "Great. Just great. I just hung up from Mangus. I told him I'd call you myself. I wanted to thank you for sending those beautiful flowers. You know gladiolas are my favorite."

"Good. We're glad you liked them."

"Mangus tells me you saw your mom. That makes me happy."

"Yes I did. I took her to the doctor. But Camille, how'd it go with your test results? Did they call you yet?"

"Marina, you know I'm perfect in every way. One word I will use is the word they used, which was benign. I'll just say that I'm blessed. Those little suckers were found and removed in time. I wanted to tell you myself."

"Oh, that is such great news. I'm so happy. And I know Mangus is relieved." Marina spoke with cheer and relief.

"You know, my son has a way about him. He holds things in sometimes, but he does tend to worry. I want him to stay up and know that he can't hold everything inside. He has to let it out. He has a lot of pride. You'll see it on his face though he might not say it."

"I know."

"I'm sure you do."

"Oh yes."

"Well, you two be good now. I'm gonna get back to my computer and read over this presentation for tomorrow."

"Okay. Good luck. And thanks for calling."

"Goodnight, Marina."

"Goodnight."

Marina hung up and placed her pink-jeweled phone upon the sofa where she sat. She had a pleased look on her face. Things had worked out for her mother-in-law. Marina enjoyed Mangus' mother's energy. She wished she could be so upbeat. But since a long time visitor had been lurking on Marina's back, it seemed challenging. It was her own mother. The thoughts of her mother seemed heavier than ever lately.

Marina had been to see her therapist twice already. Through the church, she kept reaffirming the biblical lessons she'd been learning, particularly about cooling one's temper and coming in from the other side of darkness. And added to that, her counselor had given her suggestions for how to really forgive her mother. She said what you resist, persists, and that she had to take the first step. But Marina was having a hard time, not only dialing her mother's number, but even imagining how she would attempt to begin the long overdue conversation.

She glanced at the phone as it rested right next to her hip. The smart thing to do would have been to pick it up and just dial, though she couldn't seem to command her hand to do it. It just seemed easier to avoid the issues, just as she had done for nearly fifteen years.

Suddenly, her cell sounded again and out of all those listed in her contacts, the caller I.D. read *Mabel*. She picked up her phone and pressed the answer button, bringing it to her ear with caution as though perhaps God was reading her mind; as though He knew that she was again practicing avoidance.

Marina sat up straight. "Hello Mabel."

"Hey. How are you?"

"I'm good. How about you?"

Mabel replied in her gravelly voice. "I'm good too."

"Good."

Mabel said nothing.

For no reason, Marina examined the rounded shape of her short, dark purple fingernails and then shooed away imaginary lint from her black pants. "Mangus isn't here."

"Oh no, I called to talk to you."

"Okay." Marina's ears were focused.

"I got a call today from someone you know. They asked me to give you their number, and, well…I wanted you to know just in case he calls you at the office or something. He said he hasn't talked to you since high school. I told him you're happily married."

"Who's that?"

"It's Howard, your ex."

Marina's mind rewound. "Howard Henry? I wonder what made him try to reach me after all this time?"

"He said he's with the Atlanta team now. He got traded and moved here last month, at least I think that's what he said."

Marina rested her back upon the curved sofa back. "I heard."

"Oh, so you knew?"

"Yes. That was pretty big news."

"I thought he was still in Washington somewhere."

"No." Marina paused and rubbed her bottom lip along her upper lip. "So what did he want?"

"He said he just wanted me to give you his number. He said maybe the two of you could have lunch. I have the number if you want it."

Marina's reply was immediate. "No, I don't. But thanks."

"Okay."

"Mangus and I don't really communicate with our exes."

"I understand."

Marina took a deep breath and said, "And Mabel?"

"Yes."

"Would you mind if I come by, this weekend. Just for maybe an hour or so? There's something I need to talk to you about."

"What's wrong?"

"Nothing really."

"I don't think you've been here for an hour before."

Marina cleared her throat. "Probably not."

"But okay. Let me know when so I can make sure I'm home."

Marina gave a long blink and then she stared at one of her colorful pieces of abstract artwork on the wall before her. "Maybe on Sunday, late morning."

"I'll be here."

"Thanks Mabel."

"Now you've got me worrying about what it is."

"It's just a girl-to-girl talk."

"I see. I can only imagine."

"I'll see you then."

"Goodbye daughter."

Marina scooted her eyes to the ceiling. "Bye." She tossed the phone back onto the sofa and stood, walking straight into the kitchen.

It had been a while since she felt as though she wanted or even needed a strong drink. But she stepped right up to the liquor cabinet and perused the selections. She looked past the rum and vodka and whiskey. Her eyes stopped upon the large, unopened bottle of Hennessey. She opened it.

She opened the other cabinet, grabbed a highball glass and poured the amber liquid inside to the rim. She sniffed the fluid and sipped it and swallowed and sent the burning sensation down her throat as it traveled to her belly. It made her eyes squint and her jaws tingle and her insides heat up. She smacked her lips and closed the cabinets, heading back to the sofa with her potent drink in hand.

Marina sat still and crossed her legs and thought. She sipped again and again, until she heard the kitchen door open and close. She placed the drink on the end table as Mangus suddenly entered the den.

"Hey, what's up?" he asked, stepping to the coffee table and placing his keys and the day's mail on top.

She leaned against the cushioned arm of the sofa and rested her elbow along the edge. "Nothing. How's it going? How was your beat today?"

He bent down to kiss Marina on the lips and then placed his jacket on the love seat. "Uneventful." He could sense her liquored up breath. He glanced over at her glass and smiled.

"Oh the Yac, huh?"

She grinned slightly. "Yes, the Yac. Honey, I'm really happy about your mother. She just called."

"Yeah, that's definitely a major relief. Major relief."

"She's a great lady. Hey, Mabel just called too."

"Really?"

"She called to tell me about my ex. You remember the guy I told you about who I dated in high school. He played ball up in Washington?"

Mangus plopped down upon the other end of the sofa. "Yes."

"Well, he got her number somehow. Anyway, he asked her to call me and tell me he wants to have lunch now that he lives here again. He's playing ball with the Hawks now."

"I know."

"Oh, you heard he got traded?"

"No. I heard he was trying to reach you. Your mom called to ask me if I was okay with her telling you. She really wasn't sure if she should even let you know. I told her it was fine."

She gave him a stare. "My mom asked you first?"

"Yes."

"Oh my goodness. That woman." Marina shook her head.

"She didn't mean any harm. Besides, I'm fine with it."

"Oh, so you're fine with me going to lunch with him?"

"I didn't mean I was okay with it like that. I said I was okay with her telling you. I told her it would be your decision."

"My decision? So if I said yes, you'd be cool with your wife meeting an ex over a meal?"

"I would trust your decision."

She asked with an unhappy face, "But damn, don't you even have an opinion to share with me about it? At least some sort of emotion that would at least let me know you even give a damn. Are you okay with everything? Does anything piss you off?"

"This doesn't. Where'd all that come from? Besides, you already know I'm not the jealous type." Mangus reached down to take off his work shoes.

"And why not?"

"I wasn't raised that way. Besides, like I said, I trust you."

"Well, hell, do you trust him?"

"I don't know him."

"That's my point."

"What do you want me to do? Tell you hell no, you can't go and forbid you from seeing an old friend. It's just a meal." He splayed his legs out in front of himself and scooted back.

"See, you're acting this way because that's exactly how you'd want me to act. But you're not really okay with it. I don't believe it."

"You come home to me at night. You're my wife. And I know you wouldn't do anything to violate the trust and our vows." He quickly sat forward and balanced on the edge of the cushion for a minute and then shot to his feet.

She spoke to him as he took a couple of steps. "Don't you ever think you know a woman that well. Ever. You know what, Mangus? It's okay to show your feelings, to be vulnerable and express your concerns sometimes. Do you think God will strike you down if you're actually guilty of the word jealousy?"

Mangus grabbed his jacket and stepped toward the stairway "No. He hasn't struck you down yet."

"Fuck you, Mangus. See, it's that kind of thing that makes me want to meet him."

He stood at the base of the stairs. "Don't meet him to prove a point to me. I'm telling you I'm fine with your decision. As long as he knows you're married, I trust you to keep it platonic."

"Yeah. A wife having lunch with a man she once fucked." She cut her eyes with force.

"Well he's not fuckin you now."

She scooted over toward the middle of the sofa and made sure her body was facing his direction. "Okay. See. Here's what I'll do. No matter how you act, no matter who you are and how you handle situations, I still have to be me. And the me that I am does not and will not meet with other men when I have a husband. Like it or not, and as much as you'd like me to go ahead and do it because then it would give you that same right, I'm not doing it. I told Mom to tell him no. I am mature and committed to my husband."

He shrugged his shoulders. "That's fine. I honor your decision."

"Fuck you, Mangus."

He switched his jacket to his left hand and pointed his right index finger in the direction of her mouth. "I've had about enough of your fuck you comments, Marina. You keep it up."

"And what if I do? What then?"

"Just watch your mouth."

A heartbeat later, she found herself springing from the sofa and standing within six inches of him. "You know what?" Her hand was balled up and braced at her side.

He looked down at it. "And watch your damn fist. As a matter of fact, watch yourself."

She blinked and pivoted and took a few steps, finding her awaiting drink as she sat back down toward the end of the sofa. "Goodnight, Mangus. And don't go upstairs sneaking online to check out Big Brown Booties Gone Wild, or IM Melanie, or email Porsche to ask her why we didn't see her in church last week." She made more room in her glass by swallowing the brunette cognac whole, like it was water, placing it back down on the table.

"Grow up," he said while leading upstairs.

"I'm about to," she blurted as invisible smoke seeped from her ears.

Her head spun and invisible smoke seeped from her ears. Marina slowly picked up the highball glass, and sniffed its potent scent, and then she suddenly hurled it at the wall where Mangus had stood. The glass made a small dent in the wall and broke into tiny pieces along the floor. The little bit of potent alcohol dripped along the wall.

She dropped her head into her hands and began to cry.

She heard him from upstairs say just before he closed the bedroom door, “And clean that shit up.”

“Oh, it’s about to be cleaned up all right,” she yelled back loud enough for him to hear.

Chapter Twenty-Seven

"That sweet stuff between your legs must be gold."

The lavish and tranquil *Spa Sydell* in the upscale, bustling Perimeter area was their meeting place. Leah and Marina had not spent any real, quality girlfriend time together since before Marina's wedding.

After nearly two hours inside, the best friends stood outside on a Wednesday afternoon, talking before heading to their respective cars.

Marina stood with her sage gym bag over her shoulder. Her hair was pulled back into a short, curly ponytail. She was makeup-less, wearing a rayon, black and white *Atlanta* sweat suit and large round shades.

She said, "We have got to make a point of getting massages more often. That lady gave me one of those deep tissue, find every crevice, rub your cares away massages. Damn, I needed that." She stretched out her neck from left to right to left.

Leah held on to her leather bag while she pushed back strands of hair that had fallen into her sweaty face. "I know what you mean. Mine put my butt to sleep. Plus, I'd have paid her good money to rub my titties." Leah placed her hand over her heart, standing pretty in her white cotton shirtdress and thongs. A tiny red rose tattoo resided on her ankle.

"You are a freaky fool."

"That's why you love me. What ever happened anyway? Seems like we went to the spa once a week a while back."

"Probably because our jobs geared up. Plus, I admit it. Being married has been a lot like a full time job. But, hell, you should know that."

"Please. You can have marriage. Though I must say, I am proud of you. You do seem happier being a wife for life. And your focus is definitely on your husband."

"Maybe a little too much."

"You still have those concerns about Mangus being too nice, or is nice growing on your ass?"

"Mangus will be Mangus. He's just kind-hearted and forgiving to every damn body. I was told to take him as he is and love him through his faults. Lord knows I have enough of my own."

"You were told?"

"Girl, my ass is seeing a therapist."

"Like a psychiatrist?"

"Hell no. She's a counselor. She says it's all about how we perceive things. Anyway, like I said, I'm finding out that I have a lot to learn."

"Now, Marina, you want me to believe that you just decided after all these years to see a counselor to work on your issues, but you waited until you got married. What's really going on with you two?"

"Don't make it into more than it is, Leah. Besides, Mangus and I agreed that we might even need to go into therapy together, mainly through the church. Plus, I believe what happens between a husband and a wife should stay between a husband and a wife. We'll work it out."

"See, Marina, I know you. And one thing I know and love about you is your passion. You're loving to a fault and you'd have my back if I was getting car jacked. You'd give it all you've got before we got our asses kicked." Leah imitated a one-two punch. "And I also know, just as well as you do, that Anthony and you used to be at each other's throats on the regular."

Marina aimed her hand Leah's way. "That was back then."

"Okay, back then. This doesn't have anything to do with the fact that you slapped the shit out of Mangus on your own wedding day."

Marina's jaw dropped. She put her hand on her hip. "Excuse me."

"I'm just saying. Why all the sudden are you being so secretive about your marriage? I'm your girl. And we girls talk about everything. But now all I get is you talking this flowery, surface shit. I'm not buying it. If you and Mangus are getting counseling after you got married, and not before, it's for a reason. I am no fool. No I am not."

"Leah. It's just..."

"Just stop. You can keep trying to put on a happy face if you want, but I tell you one thing, pride does go before a fall. Don't you fall on your ass, now."

"For real, I'm telling you we'll work it out."

"Okay. You say so. But heck, that's what friends are for. You know I like Mangus so don't trip about it. I won't go hating on him. And you know I love you no matter what."

"Yes, you do."

"So, I ask again, since you do have a tendency to fly off the handle, has your temper gotten better?"

Marina stood tall. "The love of the right man, a good man, is what I need. Someone who understands me."

"Understanding you, and putting up with what Anthony put up with before you left him are two different things."

"Get it right. I left Anthony because I caught him cheating, not the other way around. Besides, Anthony was all wrong for me. Mangus is who I'm married to. And he and I will work out our issues. Together."

"Like I said, that pride will work against you. If you ask me, you got that from your mother. Don't end up alone like her."

Marina shook her finger. "That's why I'm not telling you anything ever again. You know too damn much about me already. Excuse me but, I'm working on staying married. Hell, you're the one who needs to find you somebody. What's up with all this Marina intervention? Who the hell are you sleeping with?"

"Same old same old."

"D.J.?"

"Girl, that man has me hooked. I can't get enough of his ass. And I seem to be more forgiving and more accommodating than ever. That's not even like me. I think I'm dick whipped."

"Join the club."

"Hell, you're the one who always had 'em whipped. Once you put that snappa on a brotha. That sweet stuff between your legs must be gold." Leah rolled her neck, grinning.

"Whatever. All the good pussy in the world won't keep a man around if that's all there is."

"Hell, that and a good meal will keep him just fine if you ask me. Anyway, like I told you before you got married, just don't fuck this up."

"Excuse me. How do you know it's not Mangus who could fuck it up?"

"He might not be an angel, but you're definitely not one."

"You know what Leah? I've had about enough of you. I've gotta get home. Since I got off early, I'm gonna make my man some shrimp and snow crab legs, and pick up a bottle of champagne and seduce his sexy ass all damn night long. All this sex talk is making me horny."

"That's my girl. Work that man."

"I plan to. I'm going home to my husband. How is your little Negro doing anyway?" Marina asked.

"Oh yeah, I forgot to tell you. That little Negro moved in with me."

"What? When did this happen?"

"Two weeks ago."

"And you didn't tell me?"

Leah took a step in the direction of her white convertible Bug. "Hell, you obviously don't tell me a damn thing anymore, so, hasta la vista."

"Leah."

Leah kept walking. "Goodbye."

"Call you tomorrow, girl. And tell D.J. I said hello," Marina said loudly.

"Love you."

Marina pressed her car alarm. "Love you back."

A middle-aged black lady was about to get in her Cadillac, which was parked next to Marina's ride.

Marina saw her looking and nodded.

The woman said, "You're Marina Baskerville, right?"

"Yes I am."

Her voice showed her excitement. "I almost didn't recognize you with your sunglasses on. But I'd know your face anywhere. You're in our living room almost every day. I just love you. My daughter wants to be just like you when she grows up."

"Oh really? What's her name?" Marina asked.

"Valerie. She's twelve."

Marina opened her car door. "Well, please tell Valerie I said hello. And tell her to stay in school. A degree is a must in this business."

"I will. I surely will. And Marina?"

"Yes?"

"Keep the faith," the bubbly woman said, using her fingers as quotation marks.

They both smiled and both got in their cars.

Marina was still smiling as she pulled off.

Those three words that she knew so well brought a feeling of happiness to her heart.

She held on to her smile all the way home.

Chapter Twenty-Eight

"Jealousy cramped her stomach and lived in her eyes."

Cheerful and energized, Marina hit the local Kroger and then stopped by the Package store for some chilled, very expensive champagne. She drove along the traffic-free highway and hurried into their pristine subdivision, knowing Mangus would be home within the hour.

Marina dashed inside and before long, placed the crabs and shrimp in a pot, half full of water. She turned on the burner and put the champagne and ebony stemware on ice. She then hurried upstairs to shower.

Afterwards, she sat on the fitted comforter and lotioned up her legs and arms with sugarcane body cream, thinking about which bra and panties set she should wear. *Probably the light blue*, she thought.

She rehearsed the visual in her mind. He'd be shocked that her car was in the garage, he'd step through the kitchen door while she obediently fell to her knees, servicing his dick as he wished, and then she'd step away with his hand in hers, leaning over the kitchen counter while he grinded upon her backside, and she would turn around and feed him the buttered up seafood, juicing him up with the bubbly so he'd be good and ready to butter her up in return.

Marina heard a car outside and stepped to the bedroom window, peeling away the silk drapes. As she stood nude, she saw that Mangus' SUV was pulled up in front of their house. And their new neighbor, Maxine, was standing beside his car, leaning down, talking to him. She was wearing white denim short-shorts and a tiny sleeveless tee that read *Sweeter Than Honey*. And from what Marina could see from the side, it looked as though Maxine was very braless. The white tee, against her toffee skin, appeared to be having trouble with its double-D contents, not to mention that the bugs on the headlights were showing.

Mangus leaned his buffed, tattooed arm out of the window, and Maxine leaned her blessed, abundant torso further toward him. He had a look on his face that was familiar. It was similar to the look he'd worn when he and Marina first met at his mom's United Way event. It was a look of being impressed and being hopeful. It was a look that he and Maxine seemed to share as their pleased faces danced. It was a look of discovered chemistry. Marina could see every single solitary tooth in Mangus' head.

Her mind took off like a runaway train. She rushed around to find her short bathrobe and threw it on in a millisecond, taking two stairs at a time to the bottom level, and then into the garage. She pressed the remote on the wall, and stood as the garage door lifted, inch-by-inch.

Her hands were on her hips while she positioned herself just far enough into the garage for him to see her. Jealousy cramped her stomach and lived in her eyes.

He'd already been focused on the unfolding garage door with a look of wonder. And just then his eyeballs spotted her. His previously pleasant chin hit his defined chest. His mood had morphed into nervousness in two-point-two seconds flat.

He stared at Marina as though he'd been discovered on the show *Cheaters*, shifted into drive, pressed the accelerator without even saying his goodbyes, and aimed his guilt-ridden black truck into the garage ever so slowly, as Marina backed up just as slowly. He parked his ride right where it lived, where it belonged, next to his wife's ride.

Maxine stepped away in her bare feet, walking while looking back. If looks could kill, it was Marina who would have been dead on the spot. But Marina's eyes paid Maxine no attention.

Marina's eyes were busy hurling question marks, even though Mangus had a few questions of his own.

"What are you doing home so early?" Magnus asked as he stepped out of his car, still wearing his cop clothes. He shut the car door briskly.

"I've got a better question. And I think you know what it is."

"Marina, that was not what it looked like."

"What do you think it looked like?"

"Based on the look on your face I can imagine it didn't look too good."

"Based on the look on your face before you saw me, it had to have been good. How much rhythm are you gonna give up to her?"

He walked inside the house as he spoke. "It wasn't anything like you think. I pulled up and she called my name and asked if she could talk to me for a second and I stopped to listen to what she had to say, but only for a few seconds."

Marina asked, closing the door behind them, "She called your name? How did she know your name?"

"We met the other day."

"Oh really? She came over to you to meet you, or you approached her?"

"She came over to me when I was putting the trash out."

Marina leaned back against the island. She had her hands on her hips. "Funny, she never came over to introduce herself to me. From what I remember, she shot darts my way when I smiled at her the other day. Personally, I didn't think she was a very friendly woman. But she sure looked friendly just now."

"Please. I don't even know her."

"That's why we flirt. It's the first step to crossing the line. People do it to cast out the net to see who's receptive. And she looked very receptive."

"Marina, it was innocent."

"Innocent doesn't look like that. Innocent women don't wear shorts that show the crack of their asses and bend over in a married man's car. She's acting like she's trying to get her ass kicked, that's what she's doing."

Mangus stood near the dinette. "I can't help what she does."

Marina unfolded her arms and spoke with the accompaniment of her right hand. "Yes, you can. You can pull your ass on into your garage and close it behind you, just like I would do if some half-naked stud lived next door. And shit, where's her man at anyway?"

"I don't know."

"See, this is just what I'm talking about. You get all turned on and flattered, and then you try to play it off. You know I never would have even known about this if I hadn't come home early. You never even told me you met her the other day. If she was some wrinkled up old lady you probably would've."

"I didn't tell you, because, well because I knew you'd react like this."

"I see. So, you add to it by giving that Jezebel the time of day every time I'm not home?"

Mangus' glare was one of her being silly. "No. I haven't even thought about it enough to plan some strategy."

She poured a bucketful of angst on him. "Well think about it. Think about what it takes to keep this home happy. We have a vixen living right next door, along with all the other problems we have. Do you think you might be able to at least past this test, Mangus?"

"Oh, like God put her there so we could work through your trust issues." Mangus headed out of the kitchen and into the den, rummaging around to look for the television remote.

Marina followed him. "No, not my trust issues, your issues when it comes to feeding your ego through women."

"So now it's me feeding my ego?"

"That's what my counselor said."

He shot back. "She probably said that after telling you that you're insecure."

"See. Why is it you can't be understanding and apologize for the fact that it looked like you two were about to swap spit at any moment?"

"I don't owe you any apology for talking to our next door neighbor."

She hissed a savage whisper and approached Mangus, standing right near his chin. "You are such a fuckin…"

"You raise your hand and…"

"And what?" asked Marina, returning his dare. She did not blink.

He cut his eyes and she noticed.

Her rage shifted straight into fifth gear, and with a sudden jerk of her body, she instantly laid a quick, flat hand across the left side of his face.

Mangus stood very still. His cheek remembered. His mind rewound and his ears rang. His back teeth clenched and his jaw twitched. He stepped back physically and mentally.

Her voice choked up and shook. "What? What, with your smart mouth? What the fuck did she want to ask you anyway?"

His eyes stood firm. "None of your business."

"None of my business?" Marina grabbed Mangus' upper arm and pulled at him with all her might. He took a firm grasp of her wrist and easily removed her hand with a yank.

"Don't you touch me again," he blurted. The veins of his forearms made themselves visible.

Marina's scowl spoke volumes of defiance at the same time she brought back her right arm and balled up her fist, wailing one straight-on, blunt sock after another upon Mangus' chest. He turned his back and covered his head, waiting for her to finish her frantic flogging upon him.

Marina continued to wail. "What the fuck did she want? Telling me it's none of my damn business. You dumb ass mothafucka!"

Marina's robe flew open and slipped loose from her shoulders, draping down her arms. She used one hand to pull it back up, half into place as her breasts hung free.

Mangus stood up straight and kept his eyes on her instability, even though his back was half turned. His silence was icy.

She stood strong with her feet braced one in front of the other. "What the fuck do you have to say now? You're such a damn punk!"

He edged away from her being. "Are you finished?"

"Maybe. Maybe not. Maybe I need to go next door and talk to that fuckin bitch who's seducing my husband? What do you think about that?"

"You won't."

She flung her words. "Don't act like you know me so well. And whether I'm around you or not, you could at least act like a faithful, committed husband. Pastor said a husband and wife should never do anything when the other is not around that they wouldn't do if they were. If I was sitting next to you in that car, would you have pulled up to talk to her and flirted?"

Mangus shifted his focus and took a quick sniff. His eyes darted toward the kitchen and he said, "Something's burning."

"Dammit," she said, turning to rush into the kitchen to find the seafood cooked up into a dark, burnt mess at the bottom of the pan. She turned off the burner and grabbed a potholder, swooshing the air back and forth.

Mangus followed behind her.

Marina still fussed as she tossed the pot into the sink and flipped on the water. She spoke amongst the steam. "And here I was, coming home early to surprise you and cook for you and fuck my husband. I was feeling so good about us."

"So was I," he said, grabbing his cell phone and keys from the kitchen counter.

"Where the fuck are you going?"

"Shut up." He didn't even give her a glance.

"You are such a jerk," she said while turning around as she snatched open the drawer and screamed bloody murder at his back.

When Mangus turned around, Marina had fully extended a long steak knife up in the air toward the top of his head.

He propelled toward her with his hands raised, and brought his right foot forward, making a strong sweeping motion at Marina's bare feet. Her legs wobbled, she lost her balance and propelled backwards, with the knife flying out of her hand, bouncing onto the tile floor to the left of them. It landed right next to Mangus' foot.

He scooped it up into his hand. His eyes were stretched to the limit. "Oh so now you have really lost your damn mind. Now you're gonna pick up shit and use it on me? This is out straight madness."

He stepped back and kept an eye on Marina who lay flat on her back, with all of her naked body exposed.

She made a groaning sound as she fought to adjust herself. The pressure knocked the breath out of her. She saw stars. She turned to her side, putting her hand along her backside, flinging her robe closed. Pain exploded in her hip. She squinted her eyes and flicked her aggrieved gaze away, knowing her tears would carry no weight. "Get away from me," she shrieked. And indeed her face was wet with tears.

"That's it," Mangus said, in a masculine voice. He tossed the knife onto the counter. His chest raised and lowered with obvious intensity. "I told you this would happen. This shit is over." His heart rate was like a barrage of popcorn in a kettle. He did a one-eighty and marched out the door, slamming it behind him.

All Marina heard was his engine starting up and the sound of his wide tires backing out. She sat up, but did not get up. Her brain screamed.

What had started as an afternoon of pleasure and surprise had turned into an evening of jealousy and violence.

Frustrated and tired, Mangus aimed his car anywhere it wanted to take him. He sat behind the wheel in his police uniform, after having just been assaulted. And not assaulted by a stranger, but by his very own wife. Someone he loved.

He thought back to when they first met, and back to that first slap on their wedding day, and he thought back to the cruise, and back to all of his wife's other emotional reactions to the many situations that plagued their young marriage.

He knew it was way past time for counseling. Perhaps it was like closing the barn door after the horse had been stolen. Had it been stolen? What would his buddy Bruce have done? Probably given his woman a firm beat down and packed his things, and then he would have left for good. What would Ronnie have done? Probably called one of his own buddies on the force before his woman could have even began to call 911, just to make sure he didn't end up another statistic of a big, strong man who had the nerve to put his hands on his sweet, defenseless wife, even after she damn near tried to kill him. What would his father have done?

He pulled his cell from his pocket and pressed *Dad*, and then pressed *End* all in the same second. He thought about what Pastor Tanner would have said. Is this what he would have meant by leaving is easy, but to stay takes strength?

He placed his cell on the passenger seat, and reached inside his console. Inside he found the folded pamphlet from Maxine.

He turned the wheel to the right and pulled alongside the curb, kept the engine running and placed the car in park. He turned on the overhead light and read.

His fatigued eyes fed him each and every word of each of the four panels of the domestic abuse help-line for men. It was titled, *Intimate Partner Abuse Against Men:*

If you've ever been in a violent relationship, you may have some of these feelings:

- *Afraid to tell someone.*
- *Guilt about leaving.*
- *Confused because sometimes she is loving and kind.*
- *Are you in a relationship with somebody who has anger problems?*
- *Is your mate raging about what is or isn't going on?*
- *Does she constantly accuse you of being unfaithful?*
- *Does she hit, punch, slap, push, kick or bite you?*
- *Are you shameful and worried about what people will think if they knew a woman was abusing you?*
- *Do most violent encounters end in sexual relations?*

You may not acknowledge the pain and grief of abuse to others, but it's time to acknowledge it to yourself and get help. Now.

Don't let female violence control you.

You are a victim of abuse.

Adult male survivor support groups are staring now.

Call us. Today. 1-888-7HELPLINE

His cell phone rang once. His cell phone rang again. And again. Wifey. Wifey. Wifey. He did not answer it even once. And not one time did she leave a message.

A text message sounded. It simply read, *I'm sorry.*

He deleted it.

As he put the pamphlet back, he remembered what Pastor Tanner said the previous month.

The drama has a purpose. And you will not come out of the other side the way you went in. Cease struggling and know that it will all lead to your deliverance. You may be bruised and battered, but be not weary. You will reap in due time. Anyone can leave. It takes grace to stay. There is a purpose. Waiting requires trust, so trust. Trust not in man, but trust in Him. You are not going through it, you are going to it. Humble yourself.

"Hello," he said, being snapped out of his mental reflection by the tone of his phone.

His dad spoke quickly, "Mangus, what's going on?"

"Nothing."

"You just called. I answered but the call had cut off."

"I'm fine."

"Where are you?"

"I'm in my car, Dad. I didn't want to bother you." Mangus leaned his head back and closed his eyes. His left hand was over his eyes.

"What's wrong? Are you okay?"

"I just left. Marina and I had a fight."

"What kind of fight?"

"A bad fight."

"Bad. How bad?"

Mangus thought for two seconds. "We had…we argued and I left."

"Son. I'm not exactly sure what happened, but leaving does not solve anything. This is not some woman you moved in with after you met on the street corner. This is your wife. You married Marina. And in sickness and health, the good and bad, you must stick it out and live up to your commitment. Now I know you never witnessed me leaving your mother, nor her leaving me. Unless there's something else you're not sharing with me, go home and work it out. If you two come to an agreement to part ways, then so be it. But, know this…anyone can leave. It takes grace to stay."

Mangus opened his eyes. “I hear you.”
“Go home, Mangus. Go home to your wife.”
He sat upright. “Goodnight Dad.”
“Goodnight.”
Mangus disconnected his call and pulled away.

Chapter Twenty-Nine

"She was playing hide and seek with joy."

It was Friday afternoon. Two long, slow, drawn out days had gone by. Distant days filled with silence and avoidance.

Mangus seemed to make a point to wake up earlier, leave earlier, arrive home later and go to bed earlier.

Marina made a point to stay up later, try to survive on four hours sleep, wake up too late whenever she did manage to doze off, and arrive at work later than she ever had before.

Bob Hill, Marina's co-anchor, followed Marina as they stepped down from the anchor desk after the 4 p.m. newscast. "Marina, are you okay?"

"Yeah. Why?"

"You just seem a little bit reserved lately."

Her voice dragged. "I'm sorry. I know I started out reading your copy a couple of times."

"It's not that. That happens to me all the time. But you do seem a little distant. Much more quiet than I've ever seen you before."

"I'm fine, really. Everything is fine. Just a little tired, you know."

"Yeah, I remember. I was a newlywed, too," he said as he grinned.

"Oh yeah."

He placed his ink pen in his shirt pocket and then looked up at Marina as though he had the brightest of bright ideas. "Hey, what do you say we all get together, maybe next week or next month, no rush, perhaps one Sunday night? Maybe the four of us can all go to dinner at that restaurant called *Two Urban Licks* you said you like. What do you say?"

"I'll check with Mangus and see what his schedule's like. Sometimes he works on the weekends."

"No problem, Just let me know. Anyway, I'm headed over to do a radio report. I'll see you in a little while." Bob patted her back before he departed.

"Okay."

Marina headed to her desk in her classic blouse and slacks, walking past her coworkers in the newsroom without saying a word.

"Great newscast, Marina," one of the news writers said cheerily.

A young female reporter and a male photographer looked up and gave major smiles but Marina did not notice.

"Thanks," Marina said, focusing on the stack of teleprompter pages from the show she'd just delivered. Her eyes perused the pages, but her mind was focused on her home life. She tossed them into a small trashcan along the way.

She arrived at her desk and slowly pulled off her conservative clip-on earrings as she took a cautioned seat. She still felt a little bit sore along her backside from her tumble in the kitchen. Exhaustion crept through her veins. She flipped to the current date on her calendar and was thankful that she had canceled her workout at the gym with Leah, and passed on an invitation from a middle school to speak to the sixth grade students regarding the news business.

She just needed a minute to think.

Think about what she had done to her marriage.

And think about what needed to be done about it.

She was playing hide and seek with joy.

And she was the one hiding.

Her assignment editor approached and stood over her, extending her hand. "Marina, here's the beta from last night's ride along with the new intern. I need you to write copy for it if you would. It's a voice-on-tape so just the lead-in would be fine. It shouldn't take long."

"No problem. I've got it."

"Thanks," said the editor, giving a double take to Marina's low energy as she walked away.

Marina carefully scooted her chair over to the video tape player when her office phone rang.

"This is Marina Baskerville," she said as if in autopilot.

"Mrs. Baskerville. Hello, this is Holly Hunt. I'm Naomi's foster mother."

"Oh hello."

"Do you have minute? I know you were just on the air."

"Yes, I have a second. How are you? How is Naomi?" Marina managed a teeny tiny glimmer of a pleasant face after she spoke.

"Oh we're fine. Naomi talks about you all the time. She had such a blast being with you and your husband. She really liked spending time at your job. Now, all she ever talks about is being a news anchor. She even pretends she's on the TV, flipping through papers and making up stories. But that is what Naomi is good at, making up stories."

"Yes, well, most kids are at her age."

"You know, she's only gonna be here until they find an adoptive family for her, and well, I can really only accommodate her for another six months or so. My eldest daughter graduates soon and I've always said that once she leaves the house, my foster parenting days are done. I want to travel and see the world. I knew I couldn't keep kids as young as Naomi for very long. And I'm single, you know. I just think this time in my life will make for a brand new me. I'm really excited about it."

"Good for you. Does Naomi know?"

"No. But I did tell *Melon Heart* and they're making arrangements for another home for her. They knew from the beginning."

"I see. That's a shame because I know she's adapted to your home. I'll bet Naomi would really appreciate some quality time with you until they find someone, instead of having to go back and forth too soon. You know what I mean."

"Yes, I know. It's tough on these kids. And Naomi, being parentless since she was a little baby and all, she's just had a rough time."

"Yes, she has."

"I'm calling because I wanted to ask you. Well, Mrs. Baskerville, have you and your husband ever thought about adoption?"

"Ms. Hunt, to be honest with you, we have. But also we've talked about trying to get pregnant. We're newlyweds you know. But in the meantime, I guess you could say I'm fulfilling my maternal nature with the kids from the fostering organization. I'll do anything I can to help these kids. I mean I've helped to raise about four-hundred thousand dollars with the past events, and I've hosted a couple of telethons to fund new locations for abuse shelters. I really try to do my best."

"I know you have. I was just wondering if you'd ever considered stepping in and adding to your family by giving what these kids need most. A home. It's been very fulfilling for me. I just hope I've made a difference."

"Oh, I know you have."

"Thanks. And I just know any one of those kids would be privileged to have you as a mother. I mean you just seem to be the epitome of a great woman and a loving wife. You'd make a great mother. Maybe even to Naomi."

"Naomi is a doll." Marina picked up a pencil and began tapping the eraser along her desk blotter.

"Please feel free to make arrangements to spend time with her whenever you'd like. She'd be just thrilled."

"I will make sure to do that, Miss Hunt. And thanks for asking me. I'm flattered."

"Okay, well you keep doing that great work there at the station. You're awesome."

"Thanks. Goodbye now."

Marina pressed an open line and placed an outgoing call right away.

"Hello, Connie. It's Marina Baskerville. How are you?"

"Good, and you?"

"Good. I hope you have a minute. Let me ask you a question." Marina sat back and brought the tip of the pencil to her chin. "I just got a call from little Naomi Spencer's foster mother?"

"Okay."

"She actually called to ask if I would consider adopting Naomi. I didn't know her situation was as temporary as it is."

"No, she let us know when she took her in that it wouldn't be for long. We've had such progress made through Miss Hunt parenting these kids that we figure any amount of time we can get with her is a plus."

"She seems like a nice lady."

"Yes, she is. So, why don't you adopt her? I agree that you and your husband would be an easy fit for any of these children."

"Connie, I'll be honest with you. My husband and I have some issues we need to work out. Mainly whether or not we want to have our own children first." Marina rubbed her lower back.

"I see. A lot of our adoptive parents have birth children as well as adoptive children. It's your choice though."

"We just need to take a minute to get a clear idea of if, and when."

"So, if and when you decide, just let me know. I'm sure we can make it happen."

Marina asked, "What about a single parent adoption? How easy do you think that would work?"

"What do you mean?"

"Connie." Marina twisted side to side in her tweed swivel chair.

"Marina, I surely hope that's not the case. Though just like Miss Hunt who's single, it happens all the time. I'd just say if that is a possibility, that you'd truly be single, that you take time in-between before you consider bringing a child into your life. I really do pray that it ends up being both you and your husband adopting though. Or particularly, you and your husband conceiving your own kids."

"Thanks for your understanding."

"And remember, adoption takes a long time. Sometimes six months, sometimes up to a year."

"I see."

A station intern approached and spoke to Marina's back. "Marina, can you look at the story copy I just posted on the train derailment that happened in Union City this morning?"

Marina turned around. "Sure." She smiled, held up her index finger and refocused on her call. "Connie, I'm gonna have to get some things in line for the next newscast. But I'll be in touch."

"Sounds good."

Marina hung up.

It was back to what she did best…her job.

"So, where did you post this story," Marina asked, turning her computer screen squarely and placing her hand on the mouse as the intern intently looked over her experienced shoulder.

Chapter Thirty

**"...devil starts messin,
God starts blessin."**

Daybreak had broken, and the Sunday morning light crept through the slivered space between the layered bedroom curtains. Even without much being said, Mangus and Marina both got dressed and headed out of the house at the same exact time.

"See you later," Mangus said in the garage, reaching in for a half-a-hug just as she stepped close enough.

Marina raised her chin to the other side as he caught her cheek. "Yes, I'll see you, later, Bye."

"Bye," he replied, but her eyes avoided his.

They pulled off.

Mangus, dressed up, headed in the direction of church, going west.

Marina, dressed down, headed in the direction of her mother's house, going south.

Interestingly enough for Mangus, Pastor Tanner's message was about the bitter and the sweet. Mangus' ears and mind were undivided.

"Webster defines bittersweet as pleasure alloyed with pain. With every sweet reward, there is a bitterness that precedes it. Have you ever found yourself doing what you don't want to do, or found that things end up happening exactly the way you don't want them to? You can rest assured that with every good thing that happens, before you know it, you will be in a conundrum again. Certain things in life are bittersweet. A marriage is bittersweet. Sometimes things are good and loving and oh honey, let me get that for you and oh dear you look so good, and then, in the blink of an eye, you want to scratch their eyeballs out, just put a pillowcase over her head until she stops breathing," Pastor Tanner said with his eyes squinted and with a snicker of a look, adding in all of the physical gestures as though he were acting out a scene in a stage play.

The congregation laughed out loud longer than usual.

"Even parenting is bittersweet. One minute they're so cute and the next minute they become teenagers and start telling you they want to be their own person. Excuse me. This is my house. You'll be your own person when you get your own house. But seriously, even walking with God is bittersweet. Sometimes you taste sweet victory and then other times you're suffering. Something can look beautiful and have a thorn. Even a rose has sharp thorns. Did you know that ninety-percent of flowers do not have a pleasant fragrance? Just think about that for a moment.

"You don't get anointed unless you're bleeding. You see, pressure has to come in life. Pressure is a good thing. Did you know that the point in which water boils is 212 degrees Fahrenheit? It takes pressure to make something happen. And so I say that pressure has to come in life before things can get better. We are made bitter before we are made better. Remember that, you are made bitter before you are made better. You are most vulnerable to the attack of the devil right after victory because that's when you have your guard down. You'll have your wedding day and then bam, all of the sudden the relationship is filled with bitterness. Well you have to know that when the devil starts messin, God starts blessin. Because for every testimony God gives you, the devil will come a creepin."

Mangus nodded his head and then shook it as though it were a shame. He knew all about that creepin, up close and personal.

"You cannot get out of your bad situation until you put something into it. Turn it around. You must accept the bitter with the sweet. If something dies, you can tell yourself you're gonna get out of it, or you can cling to what you have and put something into it. Refuse to run and then you can turn things around. Don't define who you are because of your experience. You are not what has happened to you. Don't attach your experience to your identity. When the root of bitterness springs up, don't attack the fruit without dealing with the root."

Sitting next to Mangus was an elderly lady wearing a wide, satin-bowed black hat. "Amen," she shouted like she had been kneed in the back, and then she looked to her left for a visual confirmation from Mangus.

He turned to her and smiled and then quickly resumed his vision upon the pastor, as though hungry for more.

"I ask you one and all to allow God to strengthen you for the journey. Prayer will change things for *you* or change *you* for it. God has positioned you for a test for a reason. As long as you have faith, when you fall down, you'll get back up. You must say all things work together for my good. Say that with me."

"All things work together for my good," Mangus said along with the other members.

"What God has done to you, he now wants to do through you. Taste and see that God is good. Get your marriage to the cross, your business to the cross, lust and pornography to the cross. The good and the evil will be sifted through. Those who are dominated by bitterness will have a sweet testimony if you only keep your head up. God is the lifter of your head. God is easy. He's easy like Sunday morning."

Mangus sat up straight, squared his shoulders and raised his chin. He kept his sights upon the wise, well-dressed man with the uplifting words. The man who had just given him a boost of faith. Enough of a boost to remind him that the lesson will reveal itself. If only he remembers that there is good after the test. And tested he was being indeed.

"Calm yourself. Dear God peace flows in this room. As we come to you this day…"

As the peaceful members of *Faithful Word* disbursed, Mangus placed his maroon bible under his arm. He stepped outside and headed to his car. He waited for a car to back out of a space and looked behind him for a moment. Porsche was walking out of the tall, glass doors of the spanking new cathedral. She looked sophisticated and proper in all white. And she was alone.

Mangus faced the direction he was heading, holding his gold key ring, and pressed the remote to summon the unlocking of the car doors, pulled on the handle, jumped inside, strapped on his seatbelt, turned the ignition and put his ride in drive all at once. As he pulled forward, Porsche took one step nearly in front of his car, wearing her painted-on dress. He pressed his foot to the brake and she appeared next to his driver side door.

He rolled down the window little-by-little. "Hello."

Her energy was undeniable. "Hi, Mangus. I called your name a few times but you must not have heard me." Her brown mane was blowing back under the command of an unusual, ever so slight wind. It was as if in slow motion. The strands were set ablaze in the sun. She shook out her neck and her hair followed, and then she readjusted her small purse to her other hand.

Mangus loosened his pale green silk tie from around his sweaty neck. "No, I didn't. You take care." He offered a quick closing.

She removed her amber shades with a slow undoing. "Where's your wife?"

"She's with her mother."

"I see." Porsche pulled open the corner pocket of her purse. She dropped her right wrist and extended her rose-colored fingernails toward him, as a few cards were revealed. "Here, I just wanted to give you a few of my cards. I do massages in my spare time and I thought maybe you could pass some of these out to people you run into."

"That's good for you." He took the cards, glanced at the sepia sight of a woman's receiving a backrub, and kept them in hand.

"Make sure you tell them I don't do happy endings." She flashed her Colgate smile, which extended from ear to ear.

He uttered a laugh. "I can only imagine what that means."

"Yes, you probably could. Though for you, I'd make an exception." She eyed him carefully after her voice bounced like a rubber ball.

He extended his hand toward her. "You know on second thought, you'd better take these. I don't want you to waste them and I'm probably not the best person to be telling people where to go to get a massage."

"Oh, I see." She looked down at the cards as she gingerly took them back, and then pointed one back at him. "Well, you could keep just one maybe."

"No thanks." His hand was on the gearshift. "I'm out of here. Enjoy your Sunday."

She took a step back and kept her eyes upon him. "You too, newlywed."

"Goodbye, Porsche."

She gave a departing nod and took a small cautioned step to walk away. "Bye, Mangus."

He lifted his foot from the brake and his car rolled slowly forward until he turned past the end of the row and then drove off and onto the roadway.

He replayed the inspirational morning message in his head and said to himself, *God will position you for a test. Just when you think you can't get something out of it, you need to put something into it.*

Chapter Thirty-One

"You are not just your childhood."

Marina's mother's house was filled with Mabel's familiar Tresor scent. The Atlanta air in the apartment was thick and still and moist, and for the most part, quiet. Quiet like a quiet storm, considering that the two occupants inside had much unspoken history between them.

Aside from the slight humming sound of a large, ancient air-conditioning unit that was perched in the front window, which blew the sheer, medium blue valances up and about, an occasional slipper wearing footstep or two could be heard along the barely padded carpet.

Marina had arrived at her mother's home nearly an hour ago. At first, Mabel took a moment to come into the living room where Marina sat, as she had just awoken when she heard the doorbell, even though Marina called the day before to confirm, and that morning to tell her she was on her way. When Marina arrived, Mabel had gone into the back to make herself presentable for her visitor.

Mabel moved at a snail's pace. She barely bent her swollen knees. She held on to a chair or a wall whenever she could. She managed to change into her light orange, pocketed, button up sundress and brushed her hair and applied a bit of makeup with coral lipstick. And she did make some sweet instant coffee and had a frozen waffle.

Marina stayed in the living room, picking up an outdated *Ebony* or *Essence* magazine, flipping through the pages, or more like looking at the pictures than putting any real effort into reading the actual words.

Wearing a Capri set and black sandals, Marina crossed and uncrossed her legs as she sat in the middle of the soft sofa cushion, trying to get comfortable. Her hip still had a faint bruise but her physical pain had diminished.

She then picked up the Philips remote and scrolled through TV channels, glancing at snippets of *That's So Raven*, and a national golf tournament. Her mind was not into any of the shows that appeared before her. Her mind was rehearsing the same script she'd been practicing for days. She could hear herself in her head, and then she heard her mother, who took a seat in her leather recliner across from Marina.

"Are you sure I can't get you anything?"

"Oh, no thanks," Marina replied.

"Did you eat this morning?" Her question had a tinge of a maternal coating.

"No."

"You've got to eat something."

"I'm fine."

"Okay." Mabel set her coffee cup upon a forest green patterned TV tray.

Marina aimed the remote at the television and pressed the power button and then turned her body and sights to Mabel. "Mabel, I really want to be a mother."

"You do?"

"I mean really, really want to be a mother."

"But why right now? Motherhood is tough as it is, and your marriage is so new."

"Because, I want my own journey of motherhood. I'm sure that based upon what it was like for you, you'll say it's a certain way and it may have been that way for you. But right now, it's about what motherhood looks like to me."

"Is that what you wanted to talk about? About you wanting to be a mother, or about me not being a mother?"

"Mabel, in all honesty, you, as a mother, didn't teach me to self-soothe when I ached. You were hands off. You didn't prepare me for the hurt. I've had to learn to prepare myself. And I'm trying to get to a point where I can handle what happened when I was young. And also handle what's happening now."

"So right now your answer is to be a parent, as if you'll get it all right all the time. Sometimes being a parent means doing it all wrong even though your intention is to do perfectly."

"It means doing it the best you can, taking the good from all you are and all you know."

"Well, hell, if it's based on all that you know from your childhood, you will do it all wrong. Why would you want to do that?" Mabel's eyes showed confusion and curiosity.

"You don't really believe that do you?"

"I do."

"That's not fair. I came through it with good grades and a college degree and a career. I am not just my childhood."

"Yeah, but I know it weighs heavily on you. Besides, you and I know I was the worst mother any child could ever ask for."

The motion of Marina's head affirmed Mabel's statement. "At times, I think you were. You were all I knew."

"What I did was all I knew."

Marina scooted again so she could totally face Mabel's position. "And you're fine with that? You don't think you had a choice."

"I'll just say I'm fine with what I did. I have to be." Mabel picked up her coffee mug.

"How is that?"

"Marina. Do you know which church I belong to?"

"No."

Mabel spoke with a bit of pride. "I belong to the African Methodist Church of Gwinnett. They pick me up every other Sunday and I attend and tithe and pray regularly."

"Okay."

"And you know what? I've been saved."

"Why is it I don't know that?"

"I didn't do it for you. I did it for me." Mabel took a slow sip.

"That's good for you. But still, why didn't you tell me?"

She swallowed and spoke. "Because God forgiving me for my sins is personal to me. My maker is my husband. And besides, I've had to just accept the fact that you see me the same way you've always seen me."

"And what way is that?"

"As an addict. I was a powder head, as you kids call it. It's been fifteen years since I snorted speed, but I'll always be an addict."

"Mabel, obviously I knew you were using. Sniffing something. But what bothered me was that I saw you as more of a user. User of something and someone."

Mabel replaced her cup to the tray. "Well, now I'm a reformed user. And I've come a long way from when you were a child. I am paid in full, Marina."

"Okay."

"But you still see me as that wild woman who raised you, or tried to raise you. The woman you had no choice but to leave." Mabel spoke as though it were so.

"I left because you neglected me."

"I didn't do it on purpose. I didn't do it because you deserved it. I did it because I was sick."

"Sick with what?"

"I was sick with an addiction, Marina. And when you have an addiction, no one and nothing comes before it. It takes over your mind, body and spirit, and, it comes before yourself, before God, and before your own children, no matter how well behaved they are, or how pretty they are. And you were both, well behaved and pretty. You deserved better than me."

Marina's voice shifted a notch. It was unsteady. "I deserved better than being witness to my father's murder. I deserved better than you pulling me along every time you went out and hit the streets like I was your forty-year-old girlfriend. I deserved better than to lose my father because some jealous man you were committing adultery with shot him in the head in cold blood right in front of me. I'm surprised I even have one bit of sanity left in my head, if I do at all. And I'm surprised I'm even sitting here." Marina blinked and released a small tear from the corner of her left eye. She wiped it immediately before it could make its journey.

Mabel gave Marina her undivided attention with full-on eyes. "Yes, so am I."

Marina sniffled. "Mom. Why?"

Mabel's ears paused. The three-letter word was almost two decades old. She replayed it and then replayed again, though her eyes did not tell on her. She simply asked, "Why what?"

Marina's hand pounded her thigh with each sentence. "Why did you bring me along? Why did you fool around? Why did you ignore me and make me have to look after myself after Dad died? Why?"

Mabel watched her daughter's every physical motion. "You and Mangus go to church, right?"

"Yes."

"God is who helped me make it this far. And if you want to make it through, you're gonna need Him. I sinned like nobody's business. I was far from perfect. But, I am your mother."

"Yes you are. But one night I watched my mother hold my dead dad in her arms. I'm angry. And I would think you'd be too."

"Angry at whom? Angry at Teddy? Teddy got his. Angry at God. No. Angry at myself? I'd lived my whole life being angry at myself. From the time I was a little girl I had an uncle who was so sick, he would allow our own German Shepard to lick him from the waist down while he stood before him getting his rocks off, and he'd make us watch. He touched my little brother Trent and me for years from the time we were eight. Trent ended up gay and hung himself before he graduated high school. I hated myself. I never told anyone what that sick man did to us. I held it inside. I medicated my mind so tough just so I wouldn't have to think about it. I even turned to sex to chase it away. And whoever could get me medicated in return for sex, I was all for it. I never even enjoyed sex. What sex I did have was out of self-hatred and necessity. I didn't think I deserved your father. And I knew I didn't deserve to be a mother."

Marina's face was flushed. She kept her sights on Mabel and said, "Well, excuse me but I can't for the life of me figure out why the sex I heard you having sounded like an old Vanessa Del Rio movie."

Mabel sat straight up and spoke. "It was an act. It was for show. It made men get it over with faster. I hated it and I gave it away because I was not worthy of monogamy, love, or life. I wanted to die a slow death. And I'm still here. You are very angry. And if you look up and find yourself at my age, still keeping all of this anger inside, you will end up raging yourself into a life that's the complete opposite of what you're living now."

"It already is." Marina came to a quick stance. "It already is the complete opposite of what you might think my life is."

"What does that mean?"

Marina spoke with a constricting sound in her throat as she walked around the other side of the sofa table. Her sights searched for her purse. "I'm sorry about what your uncle did to you and to Uncle Trent. I'm sorry I never met my uncle. I'm sorry he died. I'm sorry about the kind of life you led in trying to work through your issues. You see, I too have issues though. I'm in counseling with someone who talks to me like she's a psychologist or a psychiatrist, either one, and she sits before me and tells me this is something that I must do…talk to you. Okay, so now I did it. But I can already see that this will not be an easy fix simply by showing up here. Talking to you is not gonna make me blink and snap into a normal life. I'm not ready to be a wife. I'm not ready for me. I'm not ready for anyone."

Mabel looked up at her. "You already took a vow. Make the most of it while you're still in it. Don't look back and have regrets later. Regret can eat you up inside."

Marina picked up her purse and tossed it onto her shoulder, and took a firm grasp of her sterling key ring. She spoke down at her keys. "I can't. I don't trust. I'm insecure. And if I stay with him, something bad will happen. I can't stay." She stepped to the door and turned the knob. "And by the way, thanks for coming to my wedding. I just wanted to tell you that."

Mabel slowly arose and took one small step away from her chair, keeping her right hand along the top of it. "Marina. I saw you stand before God and say your I do's, for better or for worse. Please don't leave your husband. You need him. Remember what you said to me. You are not just your childhood. You are all that is possible for you."

"I have to." Marina opened the door fully and stepped past the threshold, holding the knob behind her.

"Marina. I love you."

Marina turned her head back but kept her body forward. "Goodbye, Mabel." She shut the door tight and left swiftly.

Chapter Thirty-Two

"I attack him on the regular."

"What else am I supposed to do but leave? I make him miserable. I can't even go a few days without giving him grief about some-thing."

That same day, as late afternoon was on the horizon, Marina sat at the new and trendy *Starbucks* on Abernathy with her best friend Leah. Outside, they'd selected a black wrought iron table for two, shaded from the rays of the high sun, under a wide green umbrella.

Marina sat up close to the table's edge, with her back perfectly straight, her rear end curved behind her, and her legs crossed.

"Girl, excuse me but, you and your posture. That's a trip. You can't say that little bit of ballet class your mother put you in didn't pay off."

"Very funny. I can't shake it."

"It's kinda sophisticated actually. In an uncomfortable looking way." Leah examined her friend's elongated spine.

"Yeah, yeah, you're just jealous." Marina placed her purse under her chair.

Leah sat back and had her ongoing legs stretched out before her, wearing bright red shorts that looked like hot pants, sipping on a Blue-berry White Iced Tea. "You know Marina, it's funny to me how you say what you can't do. You say you can't go a few days without giving Mangus grief, so you don't. I've never known you to be so negative."

"If I don't leave, I guarantee you, he will. I'm obviously just meant to be alone."

"Oh girl, please. When have you ever been alone?"

"That's just the point. Every time I get with a guy, it's usually right after a recent broken relationship, and then the new guy and I have drama, and then it ends. My answer is to always hook up with another one as fast as I can. Hell, I do need to be alone. I should never have gotten married." Marina swirled the crème of her Raspberry Mocha with her long straw. She pulled the straw out and licked along the sides, taking the crème back into her mouth and then she took a slow sip.

"You were with some real jerks who fooled around on you because...well because they could. Now, you're with a good man who loves you."

"Leah, you know what?" Marina just put it out there. "I'm with a good man, who I slap, and punch, and kick, and throw things at, and yell at, and call names. I attack him on the regular. What man is gonna love a woman through all of that?"

Leah placed her iced tea on the thick glass table. She gave Marina a crooked stare. "See, I asked you if you'd started up with your temper tantrums again and you said no."

"I didn't say no. I just didn't say anything until I knew if I could change."

"And you thought being married would change you? You thought the possibility of having a husband would calm you down. You know it's much tougher than that."

"At first he did keep me calm." Marina reached her arm around and scratched her back.

"No, you kept yourself calm until you knew you had him. You need to calm yourself, period. One day that boy is gonna bust you in your damn lip."

"Very funny. Anyway, I'm tired of living with this secret. I'm a damn fraud." Marina leaned back and again sipped her drink.

Leah gave her friend a questionable look. "So, what's your answer? Just run away from him? You push him away with your explosiveness, and then when you see he doesn't bail on you, you bail on him? What the hell is that?"

Marina's eyes flashed a hint of longing for understanding. "I just can't live with the fact that I have the capability of being volatile enough to hurt him."

"I think if Mangus wanted to leave you he would have been gone. He must love your crazy ass. He probably just wants you to get help. I thought you two were seeing a therapist anyway." Leah again picked up her tea and took a few sips.

"No, I said I was. We never got around to it."

"And?"

"And, my counselor says I have trust issues. Imagine that. She made it sound like some damn post traumatic stress thing. She told me I need to forgive my mother."

"I know you can't dismiss your childhood. None of us can. But she's not encouraging you to leave is she?" A man dressed in a dark suit, with the height and stature of a Rick Fox, stepped near them and grabbed the handle of the front door. Leah's eyes followed his trace.

Marina's eyes never indulged. "No."

He smiled at Leah just before he entered. Leah smiled back until the door closed behind him. "It sounds to me like you need your husband more than ever now. These seem to be the kind of problems you two need to go through together."

"Leah, Mangus can do better than me. There's some woman out there who will trust him. He's a good man."

Leah retuned her drink to the table and lightly banged her flat hand upon the table. "Then be that woman. Learn to trust him. Be all of those things, Marina. Don't walk out on your marriage. Some men do cheat and lust, but not all men. And yes some of them leave us, but not all of them. And obviously Mangus is not leaving you."

"Don't be so sure."

As the muted sound of the song "*Brick House*" sounded, Leah reached into her red leather hobo bag to snatch her phone. She looked at the I.D. and pressed ignore.

Marina asked, "Who was that?"

"D.J. I'll call him back in a minute." She replaced her phone.

"At least somebody's relationship is solid." Marina drank more of her mocha and shook the cup counter clockwise to release some of the whipped cream from the sides, moving her straw about to scoop and spoon-feed herself.

"It is."

Marina placed her empty cup on the table and moved her purse from under her chair to along her arm. "Well, for now, I'm gonna look for an apartment. I'm moving out."

"You are so foolish and stubborn. You just wanna leave before he does."

Marina waved her hand toward her friend as she stood up, taking one step to throw away her cup. "That man doesn't care. I don't think he has it in him to leave. So I have to do it for him. I can't be where I'm not wanted."

Leah stood as well. The extra-tall man exited the coffee shop holding his brew and nodded Leah's way. She again smiled and he proceeded. She kept her eyes on the back of him, somewhere around his rear end.

They proceeded to the parking lot.

The man then slowed down, turned and asked, "Excuse me, but aren't you Marina Maxwell. I mean Marina Baskerville?" He walked slowly next to Marina.

She looked up at him as though she forgot that she and Leah were in public. "Yes."

He showed his white bright teeth. "I thought so. It's nice to meet you."

Leah looked over and up at him and asked, "Well, what is your name?"

He smiled at her. "Larry. My name is Larry." He looked back at Marina and said, "Well, have a good day. And by the way, you're even prettier in person." He gave an obvious wink and looked back for a moment as he stepped away.

"Thank you," Marina replied, quickly refocusing her attention back to her best friend. "So, like I said…"

"Woman, you are something else. I think sometimes you forget how well known you are. Hell, I know I do."

"It means nothing. It's not even like real life. Most folks don't know me from Adam."

"Well Larry does and he's fine as hell."

Marina waved her hand in front of Leah who still looked ahead at the tall one. "Leah, D.J., remember."

Leah shook her head quickly. "Oh yeah." Still holding on to her tea, she rummaged through her purse to find her phone. She held it in her other hand as they walked. "Anyway, I'm going with you."

"Where?"

"To find a place."

"You are?"

"Yes I am."

Marina focused in on her best friend's face. "You'd really support me like that?"

Leah gave her a full look back. "Yeah. I wouldn't call it backing your decision. I'd call it helping you out because you're my friend and your ass is foolish and stubborn like I told you." She took her elbow and bumped Marina alongside her arm.

Marina laughed. "Thanks."

"Yeah. Yeah." Leah flipped open her pearl white phone and began dialing. She asked Marina, "Where do you want to live?"

"Somewhere north."

"Like Alpharetta?"

"Yes."

"Move on over Whitney Houston." Leah then spoke to her phone. "Hey baby, sorry I missed your call. I'm with Marina. We're going up near the North Point mall. I'll be home in a few hours. You too. Bye."

Marina peeked into her purse, spied her phone and noticed a couple of missed calls from Mangus. She closed her bag and proceeded on to Leah's car. She said, "Like I said, at least one of us has it like that."

"One of us chooses to. One of us refuses to."

Chapter Thirty-Three

"If I were you I wouldn't be here."

The latter part of Sunday evolved and Marina sat at the kitchen table eating leftover shrimp fried rice and orange chicken from Panda Express. She sat with her plastic fork propped before her mouth, chewing what was barely left of her scant mouthful. She looked down at her styrofoam plate and sifted through the green onions and fried eggs, checking for more shrimp, and then giving up. She grabbed a large glass of ice water, swigging down the salty taste and then coming to a stance, heading toward the trashcan to toss what was left.

Mangus had left two messages after church while Marina was at her mother's house. She'd left her phone in the car. And then he had gone to play a relaxing game of golf with Bruce while Leah and Marina were apartment hunting.

"How did it go at your mom's today?" Mangus asked as he walked in, heading straight to the refrigerator.

"Good."

"Did you guys talk?"

"A little bit."

"Good." He pulled out a cold bottle of red Gatorade. "And what else did you do?"

"Hung out with Leah."

He screwed off the cap and took a long swallow. He said, "Good." His sentences were bland. He removed his golf cap.

And as matter-of-factly as she could speak it, she said, "Mangus, I'm moving tomorrow morning."

His head darted back. "What?"

"Our stuff will not work out. I'm all screwed up in the head. There's no way this can get better. Not right now anyway."

"That's what I wanted to talk to you about."

"About what?"

He stood next to the sink and placed his bottle on the countertop. "That, today, when I sat at church, I understood something. I understand that we have a big problem. A problem that I admit, I cannot tolerate. You have issues, and I know that. You have some very serious anger issues. And I never ever would have even imagined that I would have allowed a woman, my wife or anyone else, to ever put her hands on me, much less, pull a knife on me. I've had temperamental women my whole life. I can handle temperamental. But..."

She wore great anticipation on her face, as though she already knew the next sentence. "But, what?"

"But, it's not in me to leave. I can't leave you. I still think there's a reason to see this marriage through, however it might end up. And you can't leave me."

Her surprise only lasted a second. She could once again begin to explain her reasons for leaving him for his own good. "I understand what you're saying. But it's almost like I need to look out for you because you won't look out for yourself. When it's all said and done, as cruel as this may sound, you need to find yourself a new, healthy, unbroken woman. Do yourself a favor, Mangus. Stop taking my shit and give up." She stood a few feet away from him.

"I'm not sure where this is coming from but I do know you've been seeing someone to help you through not only what we've got going on, but also, through the things you'd witnessed as a child. But as dumb as you think this is, I still want to take this thing day-by-day. I have faith enough to believe that it can be worked out."

"Why would you even want it to work out? You're married to a woman who goes completely off at the drop of a hat."

"And you're getting help for it. We'll get help for it."

She gave a full nasal exhale. "I met you, still broken and wounded, more than fifteen years after my father was murdered in front of me. You accepted me falsely, because I led you to believe that I was one way, when in reality, I have found that I'm still another way. I have to be a better woman for myself first before I can be any good to you. I can't come to you and then expect you to be a victim. I need to get myself together. And, well, I found an apartment today. Like I said, I'm leaving tomorrow. The truck will be here in the morning."

Mangus wore a look of absolute amazement. "In the morning? What are you thinking? You can't make decisions like that on your own so quickly. It's not just you anymore, it's me too."

Marina wore a look of absolute amazement back at him. "You should be the one telling me to get the hell out of here. I pulled a knife on you. Why do you put up with me?"

"Because I made a promise to God. And so did you. You can't run when the heat gets hot. It's us now. Together. Every move you make affects the both of us."

Her face showed a glimmer of a second thought, but her words were clear. "Well, Mangus, I am leaving. I'm leaving before the next time comes. Before you leave me because of it. And it will come if I'm with you. It will come if I'm with anyone."

He looked around the kitchen and raised his arms to the left and right. He also raised his voice. "How are you gonna tell me you're gonna leave me and just pack up all your things by tomorrow? Why can't you just give it a few months, even a few weeks, and let's see how it goes?"

She nodded. "I can't."

He was verbally silent, but his stare was not.

She searched his all too familiar face for any sign of a smile being hidden behind his frown, but there was no trace. And then she just had to ask, "Have you ever left any woman before?"

"No."

"Can you?"

His tone was a notch lower but he flared his nostrils and increased his frown. "I told you it's not in me, but as far as a marriage is concerned, I don't think I'm ready to end it. I married you after all these years of being single. I didn't marry you to end up single only a few months later."

"And I didn't marry you to abuse you." She turned on the water, held her hands underneath and turned it off. "I have some empty boxes and tape in my car. I'm gonna start packing tonight." She tore off a paper towel and rubbed her hands dry.

He stepped up beside her and asked, "What ever happened to you practicing your own words? Every night when you're closing your newscast you say, 'Keep the faith.' But you aren't keeping it now. You're just letting go."

She looked down at her hands. "Only because I love you. Because I love you, I'm letting go for you."

Throughout the evening, no matter what room Marina was in, Mangus occupied the room next to it, as though keeping one ear within a few feet of her.

He said not one word.

He sat and stared.

He listened and sat.

He sat and thought.

His thoughts kept him up all night, without a wink.

He never even tried to lie down.

Her packing kept her up all night, without a wink.

She never even took a seat.

He didn't stop her.

And she didn't stop herself.

She unhooked her own computer and made sure to take one of the new TV's. She taped up her own boxes and made sure her clothes were organized on hangers for when the movers brought the ward-robe boxes. She organized her many pairs of shoes, and made sure they were all in labeled plastic boxes. She had no heavy furniture and no appliances. She only had boxes, and her few cherished pieces of artwork.

She'd asked for two men and a small truck.

They'd be there at noon.

It was already 11:45 a.m.

She stood looking out of the window of the formal dining room. She heard Mangus' footsteps behind her.

She turned to face him and saw his tired eyes. Though to her they looked like the same eyes she'd seen time after time when she was deep into her ranting and raving and rousing. It was a look of being fed up, either way.

Mangus' shoulders reeked of heaviness and his words moved slowly. "You know, at yesterday's service, I just kept hearing about how I should calm myself, and get my marriage to the cross and turn it around. I realize it's true that we can't get through this without God. But also, I can't turn this marriage around without you. I'm gonna ask you one more time to stay. Marina, stay here and work this out together. We need to be more faith-filled, together. We need more than just church on Sunday. We need God in our lives, we need to walk the walk, and we need Him now. We're no saints. I'm no saint in any way. I sin everyday. I sinned every time I lied to you. But I want to be better and do better. It's killing me to watch you leave. I'm asking you to not leave. I'm your husband and I'm asking you to spend the rest of your life with me. Flawed or not. I accept you as you are." His every word exited his mouth precisely and slowly.

Marina's heart had his full attention but it was her head that stepped up to reply. "Mangus, maybe I just don't know how to calm myself. It takes two healthy people bringing all of who they are to make a whole. I'm the one slacking, not you."

"Then let me take up the slack."

"You can't."

The rough sound of a motor could be heard coming closer. The feel of a vehicle pulling into the driveway could be detected. The rapidity of two beating hearts could be seen and tasted.

Mangus licked his lips. He stepped back as Marina walked to the front door. His hands were in his pockets. His heart was in his throat. He said nothing. He just watched.

As the two men, one older and one younger, were instructed on what was to be packed and what was to stay, Mangus stood and stared.

"Aren't you the news anchor on DBC?" the younger man asked with excitement.

"Yes," was all Marina said.

Mangus looked at Marina as the men went over the estimate papers with her, and then each took an item into their hands and headed outside to begin the load.

Mangus made a basic statement. "Take whatever you want."

Marina's ears heard his first real sign of surrender loud and clear. "No thanks."

He nodded and stepped aside.

He simply watched his wife leave him.

The white paneled truck, barely one-quarter full, backed out.

Marina backed out in her packed up Acura.

Mangus stood in the garage and watched her as the truck slowed down for her to lead the way. She pulled off and peeked through her rearview. Mangus was still motionless. She turned the corner and disappeared out of sight.

Of all days, the radio station KISS 104.1, which had always been her most trusted driving companion and her welcomed distraction, played a cruel trick on her.

The first few melodic notes to the familiar song began. And then the first sentence. She knew the words almost as though she had written them herself.

Her heart thumped. "Not now," she said aloud. Yet her finger did not press the station control button. Both hands remained in place, gripping the wheel as she drove away.

As Tamia sang to her, it seemed like the song of her life. Marina had warned him if she were him, she wouldn't be there. That love and trust were not her strong suit.

And just for a moment, I drifted away
But I couldn't stay cuz
A hint of love, a bit of fear
I'm tryin' to say
If I were you I wouldn't be here
If I were you I would stay right where you are
I wouldn't come near this broken heart
Just turn around and leave here.

But it was not him who was leaving. She was again the leaver.

Like the song said, she'd warned him to find someone who wouldn't hurt him. Someone who still believed in love. Someone who wouldn't slap him. Wouldn't hit him. Someone who could and would trust him.

Marina sang along, belting out each stanza, on key. All she needed was a microphone and a backup singer. She remembered how the words had moved her when she and Mangus attended a romantic Tamia concert in the rain at Chastain when they first met. He'd brought wine and strawberries and shrimp and a votive candle. Somehow, that same song at this very moment had an entirely new meaning. The sweet song was bitter agony.

And as the truck that followed carried her life's possessions, she felt not one, but two tears upon her lips. And by the time the words, *I can't trust in love again* sounded, Marina's upper body began to jerk, and her stomach muscles contracted, and her red face spelled intense pain, and her vocal cords let out deep writhing wails.

Even trying her best to focus on the traffic light ahead of her, forcing herself to see the turning of red to green, her eyes bled water, and her heart broke in half. Not only for the fact that she knew she was in trouble by trying to live without him, but also because she knew, really knew, that he deserved better. She did it for him.

Her heart broke for the both of them.

But the tears she cried were for Mangus Baskerville more than for herself. Or so she believed.

Chapter Thirty-Four

"...her mother's raspy voice still tiptoed in her head."

Marina played with her ring finger, rubbing the area where her wedding ring used to live.

She was now able to admit it to the woman who could help her most. She was now able to call a spade a spade. She broke it down two days later. Her therapist's observant blue eyes were locked on Marina. And Marina kept it real.

"I left because I was beating him." Marina looked her dead in the eyes, too.

The therapist blinked a few times but did not break visual contact. It sounded almost like a scolding, yet it was mixed with a tinge of understanding. "Marina. In no uncertain terms is that okay. It is a violation. It is against all that we think we know about love. And with that said, the question still needs to be asked, why you did that. What was it that brought you to the point of raising your hand and striking him at any point? Were you ever beaten as a child or by anyone?"

"Never. I was never even spanked. I wish I had been."

"But what really triggers you? Is it jealousy?"

"Yes. I do know I felt hurt and fearful and very jealous."

"Did you know that the first act of domestic violence was recorded in the Bible when Cain killed his brother Abel out of jealousy? It is said that the majority of violent domestic arguments are due to some form of jealousy. That speaks volumes. But it's mainly about control. Feeling you will lose control, or lose something or someone, can cause some people to work overtime to maintain control over another person. And if we have inadequate coping skills, we're even more at risk. Can you tell me what it is that you're fearful of?"

"Of losing him."

The therapist crossed her legs and unfolded her arms. "First of all, I think you might equate your father dying to the possibility that you could lose your husband, as in that male figure again leaving you. But instead of stressing out about something that most times is only an issue that we've created in our own imaginations anyway, focus on toning down your emotions. In the big picture, it's not worth the grief. But it's all about perception. The question is, in your mind, how do you perceive what happens?"

"I guess I thought that him looking at someone else meant I was gonna lose him."

"Marina, your sense of abandonment is very real. You are very fearful inside and you have a lot of pent-up aggression. On the outside this angry monster appears. You really are this damsel in distress who needs to be protected by Prince Charming. But Prince Charming can't come to your rescue because you're so busy rescuing yourself that he doesn't recognize you. You ball up your fists and you're ready to battle at the drop of a hat. You have to ask yourself if everyone is really out to get you. Is he really evil and sneaky? See, your own thoughts control your actions. What you're thinking brings more pain than what he might really be doing. Sometimes, we trick ourselves into thinking we see things as they are, when in reality, we're only seeing them as we think they are."

"Oh Lord, that makes me stone nuts."

"You're not crazy. And I doubt that you're depressed either. I think you need to learn to make yourself feel good and not sweat the small stuff. Yes, you have survived some big tragic events. But I want you to read this." She reached to the side table and handed Marina a small yellow paperback book. "It's called *Feeling Good* by David Burns. It is an excellent source on mood therapy for how to think about what is actually happening, not what you imagine is taking place. This book can help you if you give it a chance, but you have to put serious time into reading it. It will go against the grain of a lot of what you've learned in life. Sometimes we don't want to be a fool or the punk, as they say, and we want to get on someone who may have done us wrong. Sometimes though, we set ourselves up for more pain. It's kind of like *The Secret*. It's the law of attraction. Stop attracting negativity to you. Attract peace. Calm yourself."

Marina flipped through the first few pages and then glanced at the back cover copy. "I've heard that term quite a bit recently. Calm yourself. And that sounds so simple." She looked at the therapist. "I remember trying to count to ten one day before I went off and then at that very moment, he turned his back on me and it just felt like this wave of rejection came over me. I couldn't fight it."

"You don't fight it, even when it's temporary rejection like that. People who walk away from you trigger something deep inside of you. But you're afraid it will turn into permanent rejection because that's all you knew when you were little. But as an adult, you must learn to stay calm. Even going through this separation, whether it's temporary or permanent, you must do what's right for you. You need to feel good, period."

Marina took a minute. "But why is it only like this with my intimate relationships?"

"Those are the ones who we let get close. It's usually after the honeymoon when there's an increased level of attachment. And we let our spouses around 100% of the time. We can't hide from them. They discover us. Marina, let me ask you, have you ever actually been left by a significant other?"

"No."

"See, you leave so they can't pull a daddy on you, right?"

"I guess so."

"Marina, your father is gone, but you're still here. He can't pull anything else on you. So stop pulling it on yourself. Stop being your own worst enemy. It's time to feel good."

Later that week, still emotionally spent from her confessions, Marina sat in her new, small two-bedroom apartment, amongst all of her rented furniture and electronics. She'd gone to Wal-Mart to buy knick-knacks, and kitchen and bathroom essentials. She did have her cherished royal red and ebony black and soft gold toned artwork in every room. And each bit of furniture and décor seemed to tie in. It was supposed to be home.

All that was in her refrigerator was frozen dinners and fruit. She'd suddenly found that going to the grocery store was difficult, considering all of the happy couples and families shopping together. She, once again, was back to a grocery list for one. But, it was all a result of her own doing. She'd asked for it again.

She had a new home number but it hadn't rung once. No one had knocked on her second story door. Even her cell phone seemed to be quieter than usual. It was like she was unplugged.

By midnight, the music video and reality shows had driven her up the wall. She lay in her cherry and beige queen bed, flipping channels until she found herself watching the shopping network, almost ready to call and order a way too expensive vacuum cleaner. *If it also serves as a dildo I might try it*, she joked aloud. A tinge of a whisper from her private part spoke to her but she hushed it and stayed PG rated.

But before she could pick up the phone to even begin to waste her money, her cell sounded, seeming louder than ever.

She found her hopes rising and her eyes perking up. She prayed that the name *Hubby* would appear. That maybe he too was lying up, counting sheep, wondering what she was up to. It would have at least made her feel that her misery had some company, that some of the break up pains had been kicking him in the ass too. And that their love hadn't been a big fat lie. But the I.D. read *Mabel.*

"Hello."

"Hi, Marina. Did I wake you?" The voice was even deeper than before.

"No."

"Sorry to call so late. I didn't wake Mangus, did I?"

"No. Mabel, I live alone now. I left Mangus. I have my own place."

Mabel hesitated and Marina could hear it. "I see. I can't say I'm surprised. But I am sorry."

"You and Mangus haven't been talking to each other have you? I mean, you truly didn't know?"

"No, I didn't. I haven't talked to him."

"Good." Marina pulled her top sheet away from her body. "Did you need something?"

"No. I couldn't sleep. Just doing a lot of thinking." Mabel cleared her throat.

"Join the club."

"Well, Howard keeps calling."

"Sorry. He calls and leaves messages at my job, too. I'll call him and tell him to stop calling you."

"I just don't answer."

Marina lay on her back, looking up at the ceiling. "Well, he needs to stop."

"Marina. I wanted to ask you. Do you know why I took you everywhere I went when you were young?"

"No."

"I thought maybe you needed to know. I'm sure you think even worse of me for dragging you along all the time."

"I don't know what to think anymore."

"You need to know. I took you along because I didn't trust your dad."

"Trust him?"

"I didn't trust him to be alone with you."

"You didn't trust your own husband to be with his own daughter."

"No."

"How long had that gone on?"

"I never left you alone with him. Not even while I ran to the store. Not even when I went to work. I took you to daycare and I picked you up."

"He was never home alone with me when I was sick?"

"No."

"Why?"

"Your dad knew why. And it drove him crazy."

"Please don't tell me what I think you're about to say. Please don't tell me that my own father…"

"No. No Marina. That was the whole point. I wasn't gonna take the chance that it would happen. I never let that happen. I thought I was protecting you. But what I was really doing was keeping you from the times you could have had, just father and daughter, and I'm sick about it."

"You really thought he had that in him? To be that sick?"

"I thought every man had it in him. Just like my father. Just like my uncle."

"Your father?"

"My mother caught my father masturbating over my bed when I was very young. I was asleep. She left him and never looked back. She told me about it when I was a teenager, when I was trying to locate him. But I never shared with her what her own brother had done to my brother and me. And that, mixed with what I'd been through when my brother killed himself, and having no father that I trusted or even knew, I grew up hating men. I have never trusted men. That's why I'm alone today. I wanted you to know that Marina. I took you with me to protect you. I stayed high all the time just so I could try to forget. And even high as a kite, you were wherever I was. The speed helped to keep me awake. That may not have been the best decision. I know that now. But, even with all of that, here I am today, clean, yet still most times unable to sleep just from remembering. It backfired I guess." Her mother sighed greatly.

Marina sat still, with a feeling of shock. "I am so sorry. I had no idea."

Mabel's voice became shaky and it grew a bit softer. "Marina, I'm gonna go now. I'm glad I was able to bring myself to call you."

"Wow, I'm glad you did, too." A part of Marina wanted to say more. "Well here, take my new home number please. Are you ready?"

"Yes."

"It's 404-550-5656."

Mabel was momentarily quiet. "Okay. Got it. I'm gonna check on you. I'm worried about you. I hope you two work it out. I'm sure, if you both want to, it can be healed."

"I doubt it, but thanks."

"Be positive. I'm glad we're speaking more. I'm glad you came by the other day to talk."

"Me too."

"Goodnight. And Marina, I do love you."

"I do love you, too."

Marina tossed the disconnected phone onto the other side of her big empty bed, but her mother's raspy voice still tiptoed in her head.

She lay alone and wrapped her arms around herself. What she felt was a mixture of tension and peace. A long mirror greeted her as she lay on her side. She could see herself. And she felt as though she saw her mother's reflection staring back. The look on her face was one of a woman destined to be alone. Bound by the past. As much as she denied it, their chemical makeup's matched, and a shot of truth put who she was into clear focus. Everything made sense.

She brought her legs up and curled up in her pain. Her long body was in the shape of a question mark, just as her personal life was in the same crooked shape. She couldn't stop hearing the long ago melody of her life song. That mixed with the distant bark of a neighbor's dog floated in the distance. She heard both, all night long.

Chapter Thirty-Five

"Four minutes later there was a knock."

More than one week later, Marina again found herself in bed. She was surprised that her therapist hadn't actually diagnosed her as depressed. She would have guessed that depression looked similar.

It was barely eight in the evening. Her body was exhausted and her mind was unsettled. Parts of the conversation she had with her mother were in the back of her mind, even though she tried to stay focused on the fact that their reconnection was part of the healing.

Work was going well, as usual. She'd even hosted the event on non-violence education for the organization called *ONE*. She had her weekly meetings with her therapist, as usual. Her best friend Leah had stopped by a couple of times for some real girlfriend conversation. She was giving the idea of adopting Naomi a little bit more time. But, the truth was, she was just plain old horny.

Wearing her burgundy silk pajamas, she sat back on top of the covers against the rented maple headboard of her rented maple sleigh bed. She snuggled up with the book, *Feeling Good*. But before she could get too into it, she closed it.

She clutched the book to her chest and looked up at the fancy swirls of the textured ceiling. Next thing she knew, she had dialed Mangus' number and asked what she knew was a dangerous question. But, she had to ask nonetheless.

"Mangus, can I see you?"

His voice could be heard over the sound of a Johnny Gill C.D. "What do you mean, see me?"

She spoke softly. "I need to see you. I miss you."

"Marina, why do you sound like that? Have you been drinking?"

"No. I need to see you. Please."

"Why are you asking me this now? You left a while ago, remember?" His voice echoed a different beat than the last time she had seen him.

She broke it down plain and simple, speaking what she had been imagining in her head for days and days. "I need you to make love to me."

He took a minute. "That'll only make things worse."

"Please," she whispered strongly.

"This is only about you being horny. You left me. You left me and the sex."

She sighed. Her eyes were hopeful. "I know I left. But, I need you to make love to me."

"Marina. I can't. I'm sorry."

She rubbed her thigh and moved her hand alongside her hip. "Mangus."

"I can't do that. I'm gonna go now."

"Please."

"Goodbye, Marina." He waited for her closing.

She spoke in a hurry. "Wait. Mangus, meet me at the Hilton airport in an hour. Call me when you pull up. I'll be there. Goodbye."

Marina disconnected and jumped up, running into the bathroom to shower. She whipped herself together in ten minutes flat, making sure to wear her scented body oil, and she was out the door. She reminded herself to stay optimistic, yet realistic. She breathed deeply, thought in terms of calming herself, and sped off.

A few minutes past the hour, Marina's cell rang. "Room 1424," she said.

Four minutes later there was a knock. One single knock.

She steadied her fluttering heartbeat by inhaling through her nose and exhaling through her mouth. She wore a skin-toned, ruffled baby doll and fluffy high-heel slippers. She pulled the doorknob and stepped back. She stood as though to present herself to his hopefully hungry eyes, like it was his first time ever seeing her in his life.

"Hi," she said sweetly. "Come on in."

He stepped inside and gave her a cautious look.

"Thanks for coming." She closed the door, admiring him physically. He looked even more handsome than before.

"How's everything going?" he asked, stepping straight to the leather desk chair and sitting down. He leaned forward with his elbows to his knees. He wore jean shorts and a white tee with a blue and white L.A. cap pulled down to his bushy eyebrows.

"Things could be better. And you?"

"No comment." He glanced down at his spotless white Jordans.

"Okay." She stood with her arms crossed. No radio. No TV. "I'm sorry. This is awkward."

He looked up at Marina. "We broke up. We're sitting in a hotel. In Atlanta. Not far from the house we shared as man and wife. Maybe that's why."

Her eyes darted around his sentences. She stepped to the mini-bar. "Would you like something to drink? I brought some Tequila and some Vodka."

"No thanks."

"Not even grapefruit juice?"

"No."

Marina unscrewed the Tequila cap and poured a tall fluted glass over ice cubes for herself. "I want some," she said, giving off a nervous laugh.

He let a couple of moments pass. "So where's your apartment?"

"It's in Dunwoody near Perimeter Mall. I'll give you the address."

"Why couldn't we have met at your place?"

"I just thought it would be better to keep it neutral."

"Neutral? How do you keep sex between a husband and wife neutral?"

"It's just me needing some physical attention. And I'm not ready to meet new people. I'm not ready to date."

"Maybe that's good to know. Maybe I don't need to know." He looked at her legs and then looked away.

"When two people break up, it's almost a given that they will eventually."

"And if I'm at your place I'll know for sure, right?"

"No."

"It's cool." He turned off his cell and placed it in his pocket. He slipped off his shoes and socks and stood up. He pulled off his hat and set it on the desk. He unbelted his pants and placed them over the chair. He took off his shirt and laid it over his pants. He stood in his gray Hanes and said, "Whenever you're ready."

Marina sat upon the pale yellow and royal blue covers of the queen bed. She had her drink in hand as she crossed her naked legs. "Mangus, you're not some gigolo serving a client." She again gave off a laugh.

He stepped to the right side of the bed and pulled back the covers. "I didn't say I was."

He laid back and rested his legs on the white top sheet.

She rested her eyes on his obvious manhood. She tilted her head back and drank the strong liquid deeply, standing up and setting the glass down next to his side of the bed. She turned off the lamp, leaving only the desk light.

Mangus laid still while she climbed on top of him with a lioness type approach.

His eyes went to her chest.

She straddled him and kept her head low and traced his chest with her eyes, suddenly bringing her tongue forward to graze his left nipple and then up to his neck.

He closed his eyes and his hands reached up to touch her upper arms.

She laid flat upon him and she grinded. She breathed hard and moaned.

He grinded back.

She rubbed her pubic area along his firm shaft and pressed down.

He opened his eyes and lifted her face to his with his hand. He just barely missed her lips, but instead kissed her neck.

With her one hand she pulled down his underwear and he assisted by maneuvering his legs and feet out of them.

She pulled her tiny string of a panty to the side, and sat up, making sure his dick was right where it needed to be. She wiggled him inside of her.

Mangus lay underneath the woman he was legally separated from, together, inside of her, hard and seemingly already about to blow.

He held her tight and focused on going deep the way she liked it. It felt to him like pussy galore, even more than he remembered, and he was growing with every thrust she gave him.

Marina spoke softly as she sat upon him, placing her hands on his chest. "Awwww, baby, I miss this." She stirred herself around clockwise. Her breasts bounced faster as she bucked. She leaned forward a bit and braced herself for her usual booty clap pounding. Her body banged against him. The sound and rhythm was perfection.

Her long auburn hair draped over her shoulders and he noticed it.

Her thick legs were working it. Her breaths were fast and short.

He gripped the sides of her hips as though his life depended on it.

"You took my pussy away and now you wanna tease me with it. First you leave me and then you wanna remind me of what I'm missing." His jaw was tight.

She whined, "I missed my dick. I'm the one missing out."

"You left this dick. You just threw it away like you didn't even care. You can't throw me away and then keep the dick."

She could only moan.

She bucked harder.

He felt her insides squeeze and release. "That's my girl. Get that nut like you know you need to."

She could only moan some more.

"Get it," he said loudly, squinting his eyes and tightening his ass, bracing himself for his own rush that he was about to shoot inside of his ex-pussy.

"Dammit," he said,

"Dammit," she said.

Her eyes were in the back of her head.

She made that erotic face.

His swells, one after the other, gradually faded in intensity but continued longer than he'd ever remembered before.

She was full.

He was quiet.

She climbed off and lay upon her back, wiping her forehead with her fingers.

He stood up and headed to the bathroom.

She watched his familiar, tight ass muscles along the way. She spoke aloud, "And so what happens next time? How about next week?"

"Okay," he said without hesitation.

"And the week after that?"

"Okay." He reentered the room and headed straight to his clothes.

"What happens if one of us starts to trip?" She turned her head to watch him again.

"I don't know."

She said, almost as though assuring herself, "Well, it's just sex. No strings. Just sex."

He slipped on his shirt and shorts and then sat down to tie his shoes. "You're sure?"

"Yes, I'm sure. Are you sure? Can you handle it?"

He said, "Yes."

"Fine."

"See you next week," he told her while powering up his cell and stepping to her, patting her on her leg. "Take care."

"You too," she said as he walked toward the door with his phone to his ear. He closed the door behind him.

She placed her hand in between her legs and felt his manly left-overs. She said to herself, *No strings. Just sex*, and rolled over, fluffing up two down feather pillows and curling up into her all too familiar fetal position, focusing on staying calm.

When silence finally settled in, she managed to fall into a calm, deep sleep. It was post-orgasmic, but sleep nonetheless.

Chapter Thirty-Six

"It's not my menstrual cycle..."

Marina had just attended service at a small agape church in Roswell, but wasn't quite ready to go back to *Faithful Word.* Reverend Beckwith's message was positive and all about attracting what is spoken and thought. It was spiritual but it wasn't as religious as she would have liked. They never ever opened the bible.

She drove home thinking about a topic that should have been the last thought after church. Sex.

She was actually looking forward to meeting with Mangus every week as she'd done twice already. The short time they had spent together was erotic, and it was physically satisfying, as usual. But it didn't spell reconciliation on that chapter of her life. And she convinced herself that she was fine with that. It was, after all, done all for his own good anyway.

As she entered the onramp to 285 north, her BFF called.

"Hey Oprah," Leah yelled with a giggle.

"Hey Gayle," Marina said, giggling back.

"What's up? You heard from Mangus lately?"

"Yes."

Leah spoke loudly and had the radio playing. "What's he talking about?"

"Not a whole lot."

"I can't believe that. You two broke up over a month ago and there's nothing to say?"

"Leah, I didn't leave so he would ask me back. I left so he'd be able to move on. And it looks like he has. Seems like he's adjusted just fine if you ask me."

"How long has it been since you talked to him?"

Marina didn't even have to do the math. "About five days."

"What was he talking about when you did talk to him? Did you call him or did he call you? Give me details."

"No one had to call the other. Leah, we've been meeting at the same time and the same place for a minute now."

Leah's voice jumped. "For what? Oh please, don't tell me."

"Yes. For sex."

"Bad idea, Marina. Very bad idea."

"Why?" Marina asked.

"You know why. That's how you stay bonded to a man, by letting him fuck you. And then you teach him that you're no longer virtuous. If you keep letting him in, you'll be stuck because he'll never be out of your heart but he'll jump out of your bed and go home to his bachelorhood. Are you trying to prolong your misery, woman? I thought I taught you better than that."

"How in the hell was I supposed to detox from the kind of sex we have. If I met some new guy and he couldn't screw, I'd be worse off. It takes time to get to know somebody like we do."

"Which is why your ass shouldn't have left. You two had something."

Marina accelerated to pass a slow truck in the fast lane. "What we had was a nice man who was forcing himself to deal with a woman with issues. And now he realizes that."

"I never knew that a woman could complain about a man being nice and it would be considered a bad thing. And the fact that he didn't leave first is not about him being nice. It was about him being in love. That man really loved you. He wanted to work through this as a couple."

"Okay, so are you trying to make me feel worse, or what? I don't need to hear that." Marina frowned.

"What are you really trying to do by sleeping with him? You don't ever demote yourself or downgrade your title. You don't go from a wife to a lover, you only upgrade."

"Oh please. Sex was the one thing we had that was good. I don't see anything wrong with keeping it going."

"That's what you think. Why do this to yourself?"

Marina began her merge to prepare for her exit. "I don't know. Maybe I should stop."

"At least until you two decide that it's really over."

"Leah, I'm not sitting in my new place away from my husband to play games. It's really over."

"Then here. You asked me about this before. I got this number from my boss who just went through a divorce. If you're so sure, then go ahead and file. Unless of course you're waiting for something."

"No, I'm not."

"If he's only showing up to get his rocks off then maybe he is really done."

"Hell, I don't know what he's doing." Marina took the off ramp. "It's like I've been unplugged from the life I had before. What in the hell business did I have getting married anyway? I should have known better. For me to think that the love of the right man could change me was stupid as hell. It's not my menstrual cycle and it's not my man. It's been me all along."

"At least your sessions are helping you get to know you. That's worth everything."

"True. What's the attorney's number?"

"404-459-6575."

"Okay, hold on." While at a traffic light, Marina looked at the keypad of her phone and entered the number. "Got it."

"So you're gonna do it?"

Marina's eyebrows showed her confusion. "Why does it sound all of the sudden like you want me to divorce?"

"I want you to move forward or go back. One of the two."

"Can't I just sleep with him a little longer?" Her voice begged.

Leah could be heard turning off her car and opening the door. "Marina, you know what? I'll talk to you later."

"I'll call the guy."

"Bye."

Chapter Thirty-Seven

"We're like night and day."

The next Wednesday, Marina had the day off. She'd substituted for anchor Pam Sykes a while back, so Pam filled in for her in return, which was a good thing because Marina's head felt like someone had beat her with a headache stick.

She felt her level of energy sinking. She needed to feel good, as her therapist often said. And as much as she wanted to run around the corner to buy something that was eighty proof and distilled just to bury her sorrows, she talked herself out of it, because of her mother.

She curled up in the suede club chair in her living room and sat back, again with her yellow self-help book. By now she'd gotten to chapter twelve when the section on healing anger before parenting hit home. It said if you can't control your temper, you can't keep your kids safe, and it said a parent can unknowingly destroy a child's sense of safety. But some of the theories on perception seemed unrealistic. She found her thoughts drifting, so she picked up her cordless home phone and tended to some weekday business.

"*Melon Heart*, this is Connie."

"Hi Connie. It's Marina Baskerville."

"Hello. How have you been?"

"Good. I was gonna ask if you think I can go ahead and start the adoption process for Naomi?"

"Sure we can."

"I'm gonna be honest with you. Since we last spoke, my husband and I did separate. But I want to go ahead and do this anyway. You said there are single women who adopt, like Miss Hunt. I make enough money and I have room. I'm in a two-bedroom apartment in Dunwoody. I'm so ready to do this."

"Are the two of you sure there's no reconciling? I mean a break up is tough enough but especially when there's a pending divorce, if that's what it comes to."

"It will. But, Connie, I really need to adopt Naomi."

"Marina, I'm a little concerned that you feel you need it so badly. You have to want Naomi. And maybe if not Naomi, you still might want to think about adopting a different child. But, this can't be a way to replace your feeling as though you've lost an aspect of family."

"It's not. But I'm not thinking past anyone but her right now."

"How about if we wait a little while. Just to see if you two work things out. I see these separations end up being a good thing at times."

"That's not gonna to happen. I'm filing for divorce."

"Then maybe give it another few weeks just to see. Naomi's not going anywhere that soon. Okay."

"I've thought about it hard for a while now. I'm ready." Her tone was convincing yet anxious.

"Marina, just relax."

"I'm telling you, I'll be doing this as a single woman. And I can provide a good home for her."

"I'm sure you can. Give me a buzz in a few weeks."

Marina's voice surrendered. "I understand. I'll do that. Thanks."

"Take care."

She leaned back and took a deep breath, and then resumed her reading. She read the same sentence three times and still didn't get it. The ring of her cell saved her. It read *Attorney*.

"Hello."

"Mrs. Baskerville."

"Yes."

"This is attorney Thompson. I'm returning your call regarding your divorce filing."

"Oh, yes. How are you?"

"I'm good thanks. Can you tell me a little but about what you'd need?"

Marina sounded caught off guard. "Oh, well, I was calling to find out about the process of filing, and about the cost I guess."

"We charge a minimal fee to prepare the docs. Your spouse is then served and once the papers are signed by both of you, we file them and a date will be set for the two of you to appear before a judge, if necessary."

She took it all in. "Okay."

"That is if it's a simple, no fault divorce. Is there any property involved?"

"He owns a house. I've only been married a matter of months."

"Perhaps you could come in and talk to me about it. The consultation is free. You might even be able to file for an annulment. That way, it won't count as an actual marriage, but those cases are more expensive because they involve strict adherence in the state of Georgia to make sure you fall into certain categories. But, I can schedule you for later this week if you'd like."

"No. I'll call you back once I do some more thinking. I think it would just be uncontested. Possibly just unresolved differences."

"You mean irreconcilable differences. May I ask what the main problem was?"

She fidgeted with the pages of her book, dog-earing a page every now and then for no particular reason. The silence was long. "We were just extremely different. We're like night and day."

"I can understand that. Well, let me know when you're ready and we'll get you scheduled."

"I will." Marina prepared to close the conversation when she said, "Actually, Mr. Thompson, do you have an opening today? It's my day off. Maybe I could just come by and get things started."

"Let's see, we have a late one, at five o'clock. Would that work?"

"I'll take that one."

"Okay I'll put you down. Do you know where we are? Just look up the Thompson Law Office in Buckhead. We're on Piedmont."

"Okay. I'll find you. Thanks for returning my call."

"Have a nice day."

Chapter Thirty-Eight

"Mangus didn't have to say a word."

After four weeks of regular sex-only sessions with his wife, Mangus Baskerville actually looked forward to the little bit of time they spent together.

As much as he'd gone on with his life, going through the motions as though it was business as usual, the reality of the state of his marriage always seemed to slap him in the face once he stepped through the door after a long day at work.

The house was hushed as though it was forever napping. It was not a happy home. He was not happy, and it didn't look, feel or smell like a home. He was not living his life as a husband, like he'd vowed to. And he did not have an actual, factual wife.

For the most part he stayed a good boy, not wanting his mind too cluttered with distractions. Pretty much his only escape, other than sex with Marina, was playing golf with Bruce every week.

He'd been tempted to hit the streets and let the fast life chase his troubles away. But, he wanted to feel the full intensity of what was going on at home. His wife had left him. And she said she'd done it all for him. Still, it felt like abandonment. And it felt like he was a failure.

Before she moved out, he gave himself one more time to ask her to stay, but she left anyway. And he believed that only a punk would run up after her now to ask her to come back. Since she wanted to leave, she'd need to be the one to live with her decision. But the reality was that they both had to live with it. And considering what had been going on, he kept reminding himself that he should have been glad.

His intense pride, his biggest weakness, kept him from announcing to the world what had really gone on. No one knew, or so he thought. He played it off. Even when he talked to Bruce he'd change the subject. He wasn't quite ready to tell all, and to expose himself. And, he wasn't quite ready to even begin to contemplate the possibilities of committing to anyone new, or old. He would just continue with the ex-wife sex, until that ended up not making sense to either one, or both of them.

Late in the afternoon, he noticed for the first time that the empty walls looked extra abandoned as he walked around the family room, wondering where the remote was hiding. He searched between the cushions and under the couch. Just when he was rising up from his knees with the remote in hand, the doorbell rang. He stepped up and answered the door.

"Yes.

"Mr. Baskerville?"

"Yes."

"Mangus Baskerville?"

"Yes."

"This is for you." The man handed him a flat package. "Will you please sign here?"

"What is it?"

"I don't know, sir. I just deliver the envelopes."

"Okay." Mangus took the ink pen and letter in hand, and signed on the bottom of the card. He handed it back.

The man said, "Thanks," and stepped away.

Mangus closed the door and pulled the tab along the perforation. He looked inside and saw three sets of stapled papers. He pulled them out and the top set read, *Complaint For Divorce. In the Superior Court of Gwinnett County, State of Georgia. Marina Laurinda Baskerville, Plaintiff. Mangus Allen Baskerville, Defendant.*

He dropped the envelope and the three documents onto the sofa table. Without looking down at his hand, he felt for his wedding ring and finally removed it, also placing it down on the table. And he stepped toward the front door, noticing the dent in the wall near the stairway from when Marina had thrown her glass. He exited and closed the door behind him, walked down the driveway, along the short distance of the sidewalk to the driveway next door, up his neighbor's walkway and to her entrance.

With force, he knocked on the hard dark wood of her front door.

Maxine Butler opened up for him, pulling the door wide.

She stood barefoot in a sheer, light pink negligee.

Her large breasts hung free.

Her stiff nipples were obvious.

Her eyes gave him permission to come on in.

And so he did.

He stepped inside onto the bamboo flooring.
She did not say a word.
He did not say a word.
She closed the door behind him and locked it.
And she took him in.

*   *   *

"Why?" Marina asked Mangus as she arrived home from work the next day, preparing to meet Mangus that evening as usual.

"I just can't," he told her flatly.

She spoke with speed. "But why, Mangus? We said we'd still do this. I need to do this tonight."

He spoke at a slow pace. "I have to pass on tonight."

"That doesn't make sense to me. We said same time."

"I'm not changing my mind about every week. Just tonight. I can't tonight."

"Mangus."

"Marina, stop it."

Her voice frowned. "No. Please don't make it sound like here I go again. You can't tell me to stop it anymore, because I stopped being difficult a while ago. I took myself out of your life for your benefit, not mine. And you have total freedom to do what you want, no questions asked, six days a week. All I ask is for an hour or two, one night a week. Why didn't you call me and tell me before now? You waited until I called you. Why?"

"Don't question me." His tone was low but it was clear.

"You could at least give me a reason. You just tell me after I happen to call you, and then you simply mention that you can't make it?"

"I have to work."

She popped her lips. "You do not. You just got home."

"I have to go back."

"Stop lying, Mangus. There's no need to lie anymore. If you've got someone to see just say it. It's the same old thing with you. I should be asking you to stop it. Maybe you've gone back to lying to me again. There's no risk now. The truth is not gonna get you in trouble anymore."

"Goodbye Marina."

"No. You need to stop abruptly ending conversations when you decide you can't handle me."

"There's no answer that's gonna work for you right. I can't see you tonight. Why can't you just accept that?"

"Why can't you just be honest with me?"

"Goodbye."

"Mangus. Mangus." Marina said to her phone, "Oh no he didn't."

He heard her. He just didn't reply.

Chapter Thirty-Nine

"...like he'd lost his ever-lovin mind."

A knock sounded once. A knock sounded twice. A knock sounded again. And it sounded again. Each time louder than before.

Mangus' surprised face greeted a gruff-faced Marina. "What are you doing here?" he asked as he pulled open the front door to the house she'd abandoned.

Marina wore the skirt she'd worn to work but she had slipped on a sweat jacket, which was zipped up to her neck. "Mangus, is that any way to greet your wife?" Her hands resided on her hips. She was purse-less. Her keys were in her jacket pocket. And her car was parked at an angle across the front lawn.

"My wife huh?" He'd opened the door three quarters of the way.

"Yes. I am your wife until we divorce and until everything is final."

"Well, considering that I got the papers yesterday…"

A voice in the background asked, "Mangus, who's that?"

Marina's ears perked up and her brows stood up. She pointed in the direction of the voice. "I know that's not our little Porsche. That had better not be Porsche."

He pulled the door open the other quarter of the way. Marina spied an image of her shapely, busty, and comfortable looking next-door neighbor.

Marina asked with clear amazement, "What is she doing here?"

Maxine replied with a casual tone, "What are you doing here?"

Marina took a half a step. "This is my house."

Maxine stood. Her stare was not casual at all. "You left this house and everything in it."

"Mangus, no you didn't." Marina spoke to Mangus but left her eyes on Maxine.

In the distance, Maxine leaned her tootsie-roll colored body against the kitchen doorframe, holding a cocktail glass. "You don't have a key anymore, huh?"

"You can just shut the fuck up." Marina felt her heart rising to her throat. She felt flushed. She felt that this particular perception was difficult to get wrong. This was exactly what it was. Mangus had company that he invited. And the company was holding a lead crystal cocktail glass from Marina's own wedding registry set.

Maxine peered at Marina from over the top of her eyeglass frames. She spoke up clearly, "I was invited. Obviously you were not."

Marina jumped a small jump and stepped a half step closer onto their front porch. She bit her bottom lip and blinked a mile per minute. "You…"

"Maxine, excuse us," Mangus interrupted as he spoke to Maxine without turning back. He put his hand to Marina's chest and stepped forward as she took two steps back, looking down at his hand like he'd lost his ever-lovin mind.

"Get your hand off me," she shouted.

He reached back to pull the door from behind.

She sounded panicked. "Hell no, you are not escorting me out of my own house while that…"

"Calm down."

Marina reached past him in an attempt to stretch just far enough to grab the doorknob.

Mangus placed his hand on her arm. She snatched her arm away and raised her hands in a clear surrender position.

"Don't you touch me," she told him, tilting her head slightly.

He glanced back toward the front door. "Come here." He began to step away a few feet.

She crossed her arms and took a long exhale, watching as he stepped behind her. She turned to face him and breathed out and in and out, and said, "No, I'm not coming anywhere."

"You can't just show up over here and expect to be let in, Marina."

She raised her hand and shooed it at him, shaking her head. "You know what? I don't want to come in there. You enjoy your evening with the very woman you're too ashamed to tell me you canceled our evening for. And I hope you two have fun. I know I sure will." She made an about face and stepped toward her ride.

"Where are you going?"

"Anywhere but here." She did not look back as she got in and started the car. She spoke through the window. "And since I gave you my address last week, please send me my wedding glasses and china. Thanks."

"Marina, wait."

"Goodbye Mangus," she said, backing out and pulling off and out of his life, again.

The hours passed and twelve midnight hit. And then one. And then two. And then three. Mangus lay in bed for three hours, tossing and turning, eyeing the digital alarm clock. But he wasn't in his own bed. His sugar-glazed dick was coated with remnants of his new lover, Maxine, who lay next to him in her home, in her room, in her bed. She was in after sex dreamland, curled up to the side facing him.

He looked over at her face. His heart sped up. He examined her nose, her ears, her hairline, and her mouth. As much as it wasn't fair to her, they were not the features he'd grown accustomed to for so long. Her scent was not familiar. Her skin seemed unusual to the touch. Her taste was that of a stranger. Her voice was not the same as the voice he'd shared a bed with before. Her orgasm was calm and mild and ordinary. Her kisses were passive and her tongue seemed shy. Her oral talents were not as he was used to. She didn't use two hands and she'd neglected his testicles. She didn't lick his shaft-skin like a lollipop, adding generous saliva every other minute. She didn't take time to suck his nipples. She didn't quite yet know the right spots. Maybe in time, but for now, she was still too new to fill the void.

He turned onto his back and looked up at the barren peach ceiling. He then looked to the floor to ceiling mirror and caught the nightlight sight of their bedded reflection. He closed his eyes for only a moment. He then opened them and looked around the huge room, at all of the peach frilly curtains and stuffed animals, and silk flowers and feminine scenic art. It wasn't home. It wasn't his home. It wasn't Marina's home.

He turned over to his right and again eyed the clock for the hundred and eightieth time. He then slowly reached over to retrieve his cell phone, again. He quietly dialed. He dialed again. And he dialed again. His calls went unanswered, straight to voicemail. Every single time.

His mind raced.

His chest pounded.

He sprang to his feet.

He shifted in bed.

Her rose-colored satin sheets made a soft sound as he moved.

But the movement was just enough to cause a mattress wave to interrupt her sleep.

"Hey there," she said in a half-awake voice.

"Hey. I'll be right back," he whispered.

She lifted her head, rubbing the sleepy haze from her eyes. "Where are you going? Are you going home already?"

"I'm going out for a minute." He reached over to the white wicker seat and slipped on his clothes.

"Where?"

"Actually, I'll call you later this afternoon. It's an emergency."

She sat up straight and reached for her eyeglasses. "Mangus what happened?"

"Maxine, please. I'll explain later."

She pulled the covers off and stood up, throwing on her sheer bathrobe. Her leer from above her black frames was the opposite of pleased. She tugged at her silk belt and tied it with a yank. She didn't say another word as she followed him down the stairs.

And neither did he.

She locked the door behind him.

He made a b-line to his garage, hopped in his car, and drove off in a hurry.

Chapter Forty

"Mrs. Bad Temper, violent ass?"

After pushing most of the posted speed limits, Mangus pulled up. It was a thirty-minute drive to the gated North Winds apartment complex. He entered the security gate close behind the bumper of another car. The entry arm nearly caught the back of his long truck but he accelerated.

He pulled up to building fifty-one. There was no sight of Marina's silver car. Again he dialed.

"Marina, I don't know where the hell you are, but you'd better get your slick ass home or call me from wherever you are. And I mean now."

He called again. "Marina, where are you?"

He parked, backing in to secure a full-view of her arrival and banging his hand against the steering wheel. He then hit the middle console with his right fist. "Fuck. Where is she?"

Four o'clock rolled around and he sat.

Five o'clock rolled around and he sat.

He'd reclined the seat a bit and leaned back against the black leather headrest. He pressed redial.

"I can't believe your ass has been out all night. I give you ten minutes to call me."

He hung up and called again, and again, and again. He sat and waited. Helpless.

A slight glimmer of sunlight shone upon his eyelids. He peeled his eyes open, almost forgetting where he was as the sky had changed while he dozed. He noticed a car pulling up to the right of him. As the car pulled into the space, he could see Marina's wide eyes looking toward his truck as though she was seeing things.

By the time she put her car in park, Mangus was standing at her door.

"Get the fuck inside, now," he said firmly as she opened the car door and put one leg out.

She stood. "What are you doing here?"

"Don't question me. Lock the car and get your ass upstairs."

"Mangus, what is wrong with you?"

His voice shook and it was extra deep. "What is wrong with me? What the hell is wrong with you?"

"Calm down."

"Get inside. Now." He pointed. He said not another word while they stepped in silence. She turned the key and the knob and went in. So did he. He double locked the bolt. "Turn around," he demanded.

She slid her purse and keys along the speckled bar and turned to face him. "What are you doing here?"

"Why haven't you answered your phone?"

She looked up at him. "I left it in the car on purpose. I turned it off."

He fired away his questions. "And when did you notice I called you?"

"Just before I pulled up. It said I had forty-one missed calls. What is wrong with you? Why do you have that look on your face?"

That look continued. "What is wrong with me is that you stayed out all damn night after leaving the house."

She kept her sights on him. "You were in that house with your new woman. I don't think what I did is your business anymore either."

"Oh, you don't? But who I'm with is your concern, right?"

"It hadn't been until I saw what I saw. I have not sweated you. I just wanted to see you because I needed to see you. I was looking forward to it. But you lied."

He squinted. "So who did you go see in my place?"

She rested her weight onto one leg. "No one."

"Then where have you been? And don't say it's none of my business, because I'm making it my business."

She looked down and then back up. "I was at Leah's."

"Call her. Now." Mangus took a step toward Marina's purse and reached inside, grabbing her phone. He scrolled through.

"No. Stop it."

He pulled up Leah's number, took his phone into his other hand and dialed her number from his cell. "Then I will."

Marina raised her hand toward his.

He warned, "And don't you fuckin touch me."

Marina put her hand at her side, tapping her foot.

"Leah. Hey, it Mangus. Is Marina there? She called you when? And you haven't seen her?" He cut his eyes to Marina. "No I'm sure she's fine. No, I'm sorry to bother you. Oh good. I'm glad you were up. Bye."

He shut down his phone. "Now come up with another answer about where you were. And this time, get it right." His eyes joined in on his tone.

Marina waved her hand about. "How dare you embarrass me like that? That is not right. I have never called your friends and brought them into our crap." She took a small step back.

He moved in on her. "No, you don't, do you? Because you never want people to think you're any less charming a news anchor than the one they see on TV. You don't bring outsiders in because you have an image to uphold. But I'll tell you one thing, I'm not worried about upholding a damn thing right now. Now I give you one minute to tell me where the fuck you've been." He took her upper arm into his hand and squeezed.

She looked down at his hand and jerked but it did not help. "Mangus, stop."

"I am not playing with you. Who were you with? Answer me." His eyes agreed with his words.

"No one, Mangus."

He pulled her closer with a yank. "Marina, you had the fuckin nerve to have me served divorce papers yesterday, and then your ass gets a damn attitude when I cancel our sex meeting, and then you show up at the house unannounced to sneak up on me and confront me. You've taken my kindness for weakness for way too long. Now you get the asshole side of me. How does it feel?"

She blinked like the wind. Her back stiffened. Her breaths accelerated. "Mangus, I saw you with someone and I walked away. But when I pull up by myself, you're acting like you've lost your mind."

He yelled at the top of his lungs. His windpipe worked overtime. "Yes, I've lost my damn mind thanks to you fuckin with me. Your ass is always in somebody's face, talking shit like you're gonna hurt somebody. Well how does it feel now to have it given right back to you, when all my anger is up your ass for a change? What'cha gonna do now, Mrs. Bad Temper, violent ass? I'll tell you what you can do. You can tell me right now where the fuck you were." Mangus' eyes begged her to defy him.

She raised her shoulders in a cringing fashion and said lowly, "I was with Howard."

"Howard who?"

"The guy I told you about from high school. The one Mom said wanted to see me."

"You left my house and went to see that nigga?"

"You were with Maxine…"

"Don't you say another fuckin word." His stare pointed at her.

"Mangus, stop."

"Shut the hell up." He took both of her shoulders into his hands and shook her torso up and back. His nose was nearly touching hers.

"Mangus, stop," she demanded again, squinting her eyes.

"Did you fuck him? Huh? Did you fuck him?" He squeezed her tighter and backed her up against the wall. "How are you just gonna leave a brotha who stuck by you when you were beating his ass, and in his face confronting him on every damn thing, and then have the nerve to move out, and then serve him with papers, only to come by and have a damn attitude with him and then run to someone else. Are you trying to make me fuckin snap? Do you need me to beat the fuckin life out of you?"

Marina's home phone rang three times in a row. She stared at Mangus who looked over near the phone on the bar next to them. Then he looked back again.

"How long have you been in touch with Howard? How long?"

She looked down and tried to move her body away from him.

He held on tight. "What's the damn answer?"

She spoke rapidly. "I wasn't. I called him when I left your house and asked him to talk. I needed to talk, that's all. We talked all night long. We just talked."

Her phone rang again. He continued to grip her shoulders, looking as though he had ten million other questions brewing.

"Maybe that's his ass now. Does he have your home number?"

"That's probably Leah." Marina forced herself to aim her chin over to the caller I.D. of her cordless.

He attempted to grip her even tighter when she said loudly, "Oh my God, it's Grady Memorial Hospital. Move." She squirmed and yanked her arms away from him as he opened his hands and took a step back.

She snatched the phone from the cradle and rubbed her left shoulder. "Hello. Yes. Who is this? Yes, this is Marina Baskerville. Why? I just got to a phone. My phone was turned off. What happened? What? How did she just collapse? Tell me then. She what? No. Please, no. Ma'am, please tell me no. She wasn't even sick. Oh my God," Marina said, letting go of the receiver as it dropped onto the top of the bar and bounced onto the carpet.

Mangus stepped toward it and scooped it up. "Hello. This is Marina's husband. You told her what? Mabel Maxwell died? When? We'll be right there."

Marina collapsed onto the floor and curled up into a ball. She cried like a newborn baby. And Mangus knelt down to hold her, hugging her and brushing her hair back from her face, saying, "I'm so sorry."

Chapter Forty-One

"...wisdom is earned in the trials of life."

The African Methodist Church of Gwinnett was beautiful, with colorful stained glass windows that stretched up high and mahogany pews that went on forever. The full choir was dressed in dark red robes, and the elder pastor was dressed in all white.

He directed most of his glances to Marina and Mangus in the front row, as he spoke profoundly about life and death, about how God is the author of life, about how the spirit never dies, and about how he knows for a fact that Mabel Maxwell is in heaven.

He closed the eulogy by saying, "The young are strong but the old know the way, and that wisdom is earned in the trials of life."

The viewing that followed was only for the immediate family. Just as Marina and Mangus stood to enter the side area, mourners lined up to meet them, in honor of the life of Marina's mother. Some of them knew Mabel well, much better than Marina even knew her own mother. But one thing was for sure, they all knew who Marina was.

One woman said, "Mrs. Baskerville, we're so sorry. Your mother was a great woman and she was so proud of your broadcasting career. She talked about you all the time and we'd all watch you and think of her."

Marina, wearing all black with her hair gelled straight back, dabbed her eyes with an embroidered handkerchief that Mangus' mother had given her. 'Thank you." Mangus stood right by her side.

Another woman stepped up. "Marina, I'm an old friend of your mother's, My name is Edwina."

Marina's memory provided a flashback. "Hello. I remember you from when I was young. Thanks for coming. How did you two end up not staying in touch?"

The lady was thin and pretty, and she was the epitome of class. "We just went our separate ways, both with our own lives to lead. But when I heard, I just had to come and pay my respects. She was a good friend when we were young."

"You're still young. My mom was young, too." Marina offered her hand and a smile.

Edwina took her hand and squeezed. "Well, I'll tell you, lifetimes can't be measured by years. They're measured by growth and by the love in your heart for the Lord. It looks like your mother loved the Lord."

"Yes, she did." They released hands and Marina touched Mangus' forearm. "This is my husband, Mangus, and those are my in-laws over there, Mr. and Mrs. Baskerville, and next to them is my best friend, Leah." Marina pointed nearby.

Edwina looked over at them and then back at Mangus. She nodded. "Nice to meet you Mangus."

"Nice to meet you, too, Edwina," he said with warmth.

"Marina, I see you married into a very influential family. I'm happy for your happiness. You take care now."

"You too. Goodbye."

Marina quickly spoke to Mangus before the next person stepped up. "That might be the only person my mom has known for any length of time. It's like she had no family, other than us."

The pastor was all smiles. "Mr. and Mrs. Baskerville, we have a repast next door with all the food you can eat. It's what we do here for our church family. Our celebration of Sister Maxwell's life will continue this morning so I hope you can stay for a while. And I hope you enjoyed the service."

Mangus said, "We did."

"Please feel free to visit any time in the future. We do have a service that follows today at eleven. We have a special guest, Pastor Jeffrey Willis and his lovely wife Kristina." He pointed to the couple.

Marina looked over at their cruise buddies Jeff and Kristina who were talking to Mangus' parents and Leah. Mangus took Marina by the waist and hugged her.

Dressed in her fitted, violet colored, Sunday best, Kristina looked over at Marina with her hazel eyes and smiled warmly, and then spread her eyes to Mangus, with the same type of below the waist look she was known for.

Mangus cleared his suddenly dry throat.

Marina immediately looked back at the elder pastor.

"We won't be able to stay for that, but thanks."

"No problem. But we'll see you next door, right?"

"Yes."

"Very good," he said, looking pleased.

Marina dabbed the tip of her sweaty nose.

As the elder pastor stepped away, Mangus said, "Wow. Let's go on inside the viewing room. That is if you're up for it."

"Do you mind if I go in alone first?" Marina asked facing him, holding on to his forearms.

"Are you sure you'll be okay?"

She looked up at him. "Yes."

"Sure. I'll go check on my parents."

Marina nodded. "Thanks honey."

Marina entered the small, quaint room with the tranquil sounding waterfall, warm lighting, and vibrant flower spray arrangements all around. She gracefully approached the shiny silver casket, generously adorned with sprays of ivory calla lilies. She saw her mother's long body, dressed in a classic blazer. She had an orange scarf around her neck, and she was all made up, with her gray hair looking pressed and curled. Her lips were coral.

Marina stood before her birth mother. She saw that her face was at peace. And surprisingly, it brought a feeling of rest to Marina's heart. She placed her hand along the edge of the casket. Her fingers grazed the white satin lining. And she spoke.

"Hey there, Mom. Funny how all the things that matter when someone is alive, suddenly don't seem as big when they pass on.

"You made your peace with God. You believed with your heart and confessed with your mouth. Good for you. You even cleared your mind of what was on your heart with me. Your life was painful in many ways. But you worked with what you were given. You gave me life, and you stayed by my side in spite of it all."

She choked back a sensation to sob and straightened her back, holding her head up high.

"I left you, as I've become so good at for so long. And I'm sorry. I'm simply sorry. Sorry for how I treated you at times. Sorry for being resentful.

"I know that where you are now, none of this matters. But you, being my mom, will always matter.

"I love you. And as you asked me to do, I'll do better. I'll be positive. I'll be a better woman. I'll be a better wife. Because if I didn't know it before, I know it now. Life is short. And I am not my childhood.

"Goodbye, Mom"

And Marina leaned down and kissed her mother on the lips. Twice.

Chapter Forty-Two

"It did hurt to see her in my home."

Marina and Mangus' honeymoon cruise portrait once again lived proudly upon the fireplace mantel. And for the first time in a long while the house smelled of a home cooked meal. Specifically, it was Mangus' mom's pot roast, red potatoes and cabbage. Marina had called Mrs. Baskerville to ask for the recipe. Marina figured out that Mangus had not even told his parents about the break up. They acted like it was business as usual. And so did she.

The aroma of the simmering dish and the sound of Marina clanging pots and pans together reminded Mangus that she was back home where she belonged. He had personally sent all of her temporary furniture back to Abbey Rents, and he packed up Marina's belongings while she was at work on his day off. He'd paid the leasing company for the remaining four months due after breaking the lease, less the full security deposit. But it was a small price to pay to have a chance to get his wife back so they could make a go of it. Especially since it took the high price of Marina's mother's life to prompt their reunion.

Mangus approached Marina while she stood near the kitchen counter.

Her eyes lit up at the sight of him. He was her family.

He handed her a tubular vase of two-dozen red Ecuadorian roses.

She brought her head back in girlie surprise and her eyes grew as big as her smile. "Thank you, honey."

"Just a little something to show you how happy I am to have you back home." He placed a peck on her cheek.

She took the vase with both hands. "They are simply beautiful."

"Glad you like 'em. You know I have my special florist who hooks me up."

"Yeah, right. *Krogers*. You ain't foolin me, Mangus."

"Okay, you found me out. But I do have this little honey up there who makes up my arrangements especially for me."

"You tell her to keep on making 'em. As long as they're for me, I'm happy you two found each other."

He looked totally shocked. "Damn, you're not gonna ask me what she looks like?"

"Not." Marina turned and headed to the kitchen table to set down her arrangement. She adjusted a few stems just right. "But I hope she's not the one whose long strands of jet-black hair I found in the downstairs bathroom."

"Strands of hair?"

"Please, I'm not even going there. I don't even wanna know."

He gave her a look like she had to be kidding. "Marina, please."

"I don't dare for a second think that you were sitting here twiddling your thumbs after I left. As a matter of fact, we both know that you weren't."

He stood silent.

Marina half sounded like she was joking. "First you men get all excited once you realize the break up means you can have all the pussy you want without having to explain. It spells freedom for a while. But most times, if you still care, that only lasts a month or two, and then you start missin all of the good things about us, as if the memories of the bad stuff fade away. Lastly, you start thinking somebody else might be enjoying your good stuff. Don't get me started on your crazy butt, showing up at my place."

His eyes played it off. "Who me?"

She managed a laugh. "And Mangus, will you please do me a favor now that I'm back. Clean the bathrooms if you don't mind. Especially the floors."

"Yes, ma'am." He headed toward the back porch and said, "Yeah, she's back all right."

"And I'm not messin with your crazy ass, with your hidden temper. Anyway, I'm making your favorite meal to show just how glad I am."

He said from behind the door, "I knew what that smell was the minute I pulled into the garage."

She opened the oven as she spoke. "Maybe we can play scrabble and watch a movie later. How about if we just light the fireplace and cuddle, like we used to do?"

He stepped out with a mop and bucket. "I'm there. In the meantime, I'll be on bathroom duty." He reached under the sink and grabbed a bottle of Pine Sol.

She closed the oven door and looked at him. "Thanks, Mangus."

"You are more than welcome."

Suddenly the doorbell rang. Mangus put his gear down and headed to the front door.

"Who's that?" Marina asked, looking toward the front door from the kitchen.

"I have no idea." He opened the door and said, "Yes."

"Oh, I'm sorry. I'm looking for Maxine Butler. Does she live here?" A tall young man with cornrows asked.

"No."

"My apologies." He glanced down at a small piece of paper. "I must have written down the wrong address. I'll just call her and get it straight. I'm sorry."

"Well, Maxine lives right next door. On that side." Mangus pointed.

"Oh okay. Thanks, dude. I'll move my car."

"No problem."

The man stepped away and Mangus closed the door, heading upstairs after getting his cleaning supplies.

Marina had been watching closely.

Less than a half-hour later, Marina called, "Mangus," as she walked upstairs to check on him. Mangus was standing at the bedroom window, looking outside. "What's out there?" she asked.

"Oh, nothing. I just heard someone outside. Just making sure that guy is cool. You can never tell what people are up to nowadays."

"He's still out there? I thought he was looking for your, I mean, Maxine." Marina stepped up to the window as well.

Mangus walked away, back toward the bathroom, but Marina separated the sepia silk drapes and looked out of the wooden shutters, while the man walked back to his car, holding hands with Maxine.

"She looks all dressed up." The man held the car door open for Maxine who had on a tight, black, short number, and then he ran around and jumped inside.

"Yeah."

"Looks like she's got herself a stud muffin for a date. Thank God," Marina said as they pulled off in his midnight blue Mazda.

Mangus did not reply.

Marina walked to the bathroom door as he was rinsing down the double sinks with a sponge. The room smelled of fresh pine. "Mangus, we didn't talk about the fact that she's still our next door neighbor. I won't begin to tell you what ran through my mind that night. It did hurt to see her in my home."

Mangus turned off the water and approached her. "I know it did. And I'm sorry." He kissed her on the tip of her nose.

"And because I did go and see my friend from high school, and, well, as you know I sat up all night talking with him, I'm gonna cut you some slack. Nothing happened between him and me. But because Maxine lives right next door, and yes that is a little close for comfort, I'm gonna ask you whether or not she was ever in my bed."

"No."

Marina took a deep breath. "I'm trying to change. I'm trying not to panic. I'm trying to not let my mind run away with me. And most of all, I'm trying to trust you. Will you help me please?"

"I will."

"Thank you. Dinner is almost ready, so whenever you're done up here, I'll serve you."

"Oh you will, huh? I'll be right down."

She said as she stepped away, "And the bathroom looks good."

"Thanks."

He smiled at the sight of his new woman as she went back downstairs. The new and improved her made him feel good.

Chapter Forty-Three

"...the sweet scent of Tresor."

"No, Connie, we're back together."

"Marina, what's going on with you two?"

"We've reconciled," Marina said into her cell from the passenger seat of Mangus' car as he drove them to church.

"I was hoping so. I'm happy for you both. I've just been trying to make sure these children are placed in the best environment for their own well-being and proper development. I'm sure you'd want that for Naomi, too."

"I do understand that."

"Then maybe you can wait a little longer and see how things go. I know you two need to get resituated."

"But I don't want Naomi to be with another family. Whether or not I'd gotten back together with my husband, I was gonna adopt her. I just needed to get myself settled in either way. But now that my husband and I have worked things out, that's even more of a reason for her to be with me and Mangus, as a family."

"I know. I'll talk it over with our director."

"Who is that? Mrs. Pearlman?" Marina asked.

"Yes."

"Oh, I know her. She knows how important this is to me."

"Marina, we make decisions like this based upon many factors. And the final decision is from a judge and as I told you before, that could take a long time."

"I'm fine with that. I just don't want her being tossed around in the meantime."

"How about if for now, we schedule an in-home interview and in the meantime, I'll talk to Mrs. Pearlman. I promise I'll get back to you within the next couple of weeks. Now I have an appointment open next month. You'll have to excuse me. I'm in my home office and things are not quite as organized."

"No problem. I appreciate you for giving me your cell number. Sorry to call on a Sunday."

"Oh no, that's fine. How's the sixteenth of next month at eleven in the morning. It's a Saturday. Would that work for you?"

"Any time is fine with me. I can make it work."

"Great. The caseworker will be in touch. And so will I."

"Have a blessed day, Connie."

"You too Marina."

"Thanks." Marina looked to Mangus as she turned off her phone and filed it away in her two-tone brown Coach bag. She pulled out her small note pad and wrote down the date and time. "I told her before that we separated so, she just wants to be cautious."

"I can understand that. I'm excited about getting the adoption going." He turned off the engine and opened the door, and then came around to get his wife.

The two entered the Faithful World mega-plex, greeted members along the way and then found their regular seats.

Both sat still for a moment with their hands folded in their laps, heads down and eyes closed. They said their own individual silent prayers while the organist played.

Marina could be heard saying, "Amen," as she opened her eyes and looked out amongst the many people. Mangus gave the sign of the cross to symbolize the ending of his prayer. They held hands and sat still. Mangus played twirl and spin with the diamond ring on Marina's finger. She patted his knee with her fingertips.

The message was about love. It was called *To Love is to Risk Not Being Loved in Return.*

After a couple of hours, the Pastor was deep into his closing, and the majority of people were on their feet, including Mangus and Marina. Some stood still. Some were screaming and shouting, some were dancing in the isleways, some were speaking in tongue. The band was heavy on the percussions.

Mangus applauded and pumped his fist in the air.

Marina held her hands out in front of her, and wept silently.

"Greatness is always on the other side of inconvenience. Surely somebody out there has been inconvenienced."

"Yes, Lord," said Marina, looking down at the floor as she held her left hand up high.

"It's not what people call you, it's what you answer to that matters. You are not the person today that you were yesterday, and you will not be the person tomorrow that you are today. There's no growing without knowing. Give birth to something now that is greater than the pain of your past. And so you need to ask yourself, what do you know today? Do you know what it's like to come into the light? Do you know what it's like to see joy in the morning? Do you know what its like to be healed, to be delivered, to be made better? Then tell somebody. Praise the Lord. Thank God. Get on your feet. Stand before God and give Him the praise. God is the reason you woke up this morning. Come up and kneel in praise. Now." The Pastor spoke one level above yelling. He was plain old shouting.

Marina let go of Mangus' hand and took hold of her bible and purse. She excused herself to the person on her right and took small steps to exit the row until she got to the isle and walked forward. She heard applause bounce off the walls of the newly designed auditorium as she walked, looked ahead and saw a female greeter with arms open wide, who placed her hand on Marina's back and guided her to the altar steps. Dozens of other churchgoers joined in and Marina fell to her knees.

"If you don't know Jesus as your own personal savior and wonder that if you were to die now, would you be sure you'd go to heaven, then rise up your hands for God. We want to pray for you. And we want you as a member of *Faithful Word*, today."

She buried her face into her hands and an older woman next to her put her head on Marina's shoulder. The lady found Marina's hand, interlocked her fingers and gave a soft squeeze. Marina felt her own breathing grow shallow just as she looked over at the woman's brown face. The lady, who was obviously wearing the sweet scent of Tresor, lifted her hand and Marina's hand up high, and then raised her head to the ceiling. Marina did the same. And Marina's teary eyes were cleansed with the waters her own tears. She looked up at her hand and felt a loving touch.

"I'm proud of you."

"Thanks," Marina said as Mangus drove them home. She'd pulled out her bible and slid the day's program inside, along with a few pieces of literature that the new member's coordinator had given her. She tore of a sheet from her tiny note pad and began to write.

"And I know you've been the main focus between the two of us, but we've both sinned, we've both had issues in our lives. I just don't want you to feel like you were the bad seed."

"I know."

He looked straight ahead. "My mother yelled morning noon and night. Did you know that?"

She looked at him and placed her hand on his for a moment. "It doesn't matter."

"It mattered to us. My father and me."

"Your mother is a strong woman."

"Strong or not, my father believed in showing respect for the woman. That's how he was raised."

"It looks like it worked for them," Marina said, again looking down at her handwriting.

"Mom's cool. She'd give the shirt off her back. She's a lot like you."

"I'll tell you one thing, her positivity is what got her through her cancer scare."

"I agree."

She looked away from her notes and eyed him. "Your dad never lost control?"

Mangus still kept his eyes on the road. "One time he literally hit a hole in the wall. I was about eleven."

Marina said, "Wow. Well, one thing I know is that men feel, too."

"I'm just telling you, sometimes the silent ones have more issues than the ones who tend to shout."

"Maybe." She folded up the paper and leaned over to hug his right arm as he drove. She cuddled closely.

He told her as she pressed her chest to his side, "You are a blessing. We made it through." He turned his head toward her and kissed her on the forehead.

She grinned big. "Yes, we did. I feel good. Life is good." She put on her shades and snuggled back in her seat.

Mangus' cell phone vibrated once in his pocket. He ignored it.

Marina looked out of the car window, proud of herself, watching the city sights change.

Chapter Forty-Four

"I just wanted to give you something you could feel."

Marina called to say that she had just left work and would be home soon. She wanted the two of them to go to the local ice cream shop after dinner. Mangus agreed. It was early evening on a Thursday. Things seemed to be going well.

But when Mangus disconnected the phone, pulled into the garage and exited his car, to his surprise there she stood. She being Maxine Butler. Out of the corner of his eyes, Mangus saw her not so friendly face.

Without even a greeting, she spoke what was on her mind. "I've called but you don't answer. I can't believe you took her back."

Mangus nodded and kept aiming his body toward the door. "Don't do this."

"What am I doing? You're the one who went against your word."

"I didn't give you my word."

"I think you used the word never."

Mangus faced her and spoke clearly. "This is none of your business."

"Your business is my business. I care about you. You are me, actually. I was you, I told you that. Believe me, it doesn't get any better. It can only get worse."

He glared past her, keeping one eye out for Marina's arrival, and explained, "In your situation, maybe. But this is my marriage."

She removed her eyeglasses. Her eyes were red. Her cheeks were redder. "So what about me? You two act like you snapped your fingers and became new people. What am I supposed to do, turn my feelings off like a light switch so you can go back to your quaint little fairytale life? What about the next time I hear her yelling at you, going upside your head? Am I supposed to just turn over and go back to sleep when she's abusing someone I care about? Was I just your little side piece, good enough to be the jump off but not the wifey?"

Mangus found himself standing a little bit closer to her, if only to make it clearer. "Maxine, I came over a couple of times. We got caught up in the heat of the moment. I thought my marriage was over. But it's not. I'm sorry that you got caught in the middle of that."

"Caught in the middle? We're neighbors. I've been moved from the middle to the side of you two, right next door to witness your little reunion. How do you think that feels?" She pounded over where her heart lived with her right hand.

"We both have to witness each other's lives."

She dismissed his intentions. "Oh please, you could care less. Maybe I'll just move and spare us all."

"Or maybe we'll move."

"Well somebody should. I don't want to be reminded of what I could have had every time I step outside." Her eyes were possessive.

He looked away again and then back. "And honestly, I don't want my wife to have to wonder every time she sees you."

She shoved her finger in the direction of his crotch. "Then you should have kept your dick in your pants if you still cared that much. You used me. And I, of all people, was here to help you. I was glad you'd no longer be a victim. And now you just want to run back to your life. No, you two stay."

"Fine."

She eyed him squarely. "Mangus, I think you're making a huge mistake. Women who abuse have serious issues. One day, you're gonna go off on her, and I promise you, you'll be the one to go to jail, not her."

"I know what can happen."

"You'll be sorry."

"Keep your advice to yourself from now on. Goodbye." He did an about face and walked.

"You're headed into a lifetime of drama. It's a losing situation."

He spoke toward the door. "People change."

"No they don't. By the way, does she know you had your ex-girlfriend Melanie over here?" She stood as though waiting for a reply.

"Goodbye, Maxine." He pressed the garage door button as bit-by-bit, the door slowly trundled down before her.

Bruster's Ice Cream on Peachtree Industrial was the place they'd chosen as they pulled up and got out, stepping up to the window. The night air was warm yet comfortable. It was what they used to do back when they were dating.

They held hands. "What kind do you want?" Mangus asked, perusing the menu overhead.

Marina told Mangus and the young employee, "I'll have the single Graham Central Station ice cream in a cup. Make it a double."

"And I'll have the large Oreo Blast."

"Got it," he said from the other side of the window.

As usual, it was the youngsters who were middle school and high school age congregating outside of the ice cream shop. They were laughing and being playful, living their carefree lives, or so it would seem.

"Oh, to be young again," said Mangus, watching them laugh and be silly.

Marina waved her hands. "No thanks."

He laughed along with her. "Let's sit while we wait."

He led the way to a table off to the side and they sat on the red aluminum bench next to each other, facing the front.

A thirty-something blonde woman wearing khaki shorts walked up to the window and stood, waiting her turn.

Mangus stared down at his feet. And Marina noticed.

She poked him on his shoulder, "What are you doing?"

He looked up at Marina. "What?"

Marina pointed toward the woman. "She's pretty, huh?"

He looked around, anywhere but the right direction. "Who?"

"Mangus, it's okay."

He caught a glimpse of the woman and then he sat up. "Oh no you are not."

Marina still stared. "Mangus, please tell me that lady does not have a butt like a black girl."

He again played dumb. "What?"

"It's okay."

"Since when?" he asked.

She hugged her upper arms and smiled. "Since now. It's okay to look."

He still looked away.

She asked again, trying to keep her voice down, this time pointing with her eyes. "So, does she?"

Mangus did end up looking squarely at the lady's enormous booty. "She's okay."

"Well, I think she has a ghetto butt. I wonder if she works out. Her waist is so tiny."

"Probably so." He looked over at the window to see if the man had finished.

"I'll bet you she's got herself a black man at home," Marina joked.

"Probably so."

"Sir, your order is ready," the man yelled over to Mangus.

"Oh, okay." He quickly stepped up as the woman stepped back, giving him room and a smile.

He smiled too and paid for their ice cream, coming back over to sit down next to Marina, placing the cups on the table. "Do you want to eat it here or go home."

"Here is fine. That way we can do some more people watching."

Mangus focused on grabbing his long spoon, dipping it inside of his tall cup to find the big chunks of Oreos, and he occupied himself by eating one scoop after the other.

Marina giggled. "I love you, Mangus."

"Yes, you do. I think that therapist brainwashed you into someone else."

"Not even." She licked her spoon.

Another woman walked up and Marina elbowed Mangus again just as the woman headed away from the trashcan.

He glanced over at the lady who looked like she was headed to her night job at the strip club and said, "My nerves are shot. Let's go home."

Marina stood up and said, "Chicken."

"That, I am."

A collage of grape votive aromatherapy candles flickered in the fireplace in their sanctuary of a bedroom just after midnight. Marina had climbed into bed, after slathering on a layer of beauty cream, ready to doze off and ready to get her beauty sleep. But Mangus approached her side of the bed with another thought in mind.

He moved the covers over and down. She wore one of his fresh white wife-beaters and black lace panties, which he pulled down with his curious fingers.

She looked at him and gave him the eye. From the bottom of her heart to the pit of her soul, she loved even his bad side.

His twinkle in his eye said he loved even her bad side equally. "You glad to be back fulfilling your wifely duties where you belong?"

"Yes, I am."

"I'm glad to be able to fulfill my husbandly duties where I belong."

He climbed on top of her and lay on his stomach, between her legs. He lightly kissed her thighs and her knees, and raised his face to her middle. His goatee exacted the location and the shape of her opening. He gradually inserted two fingers.

She grinded and moaned sexily, enjoying his stage of toying with it first, as he always did.

He kept his fingers inside and kissed her pussy. He pecked his lips against her pussy. He made smacking sounds upon her pussy. And then he licked her pussy. She melted in his mouth.

He tasted her moist honey with his stiff tongue. "You missed me going down on you in our own bed, didn't you?"

"Uh-huh."

He removed his fingers and reached his arms up toward her. He took her right hand with his left hand. "You see I put my ring back on."

"Yes," she said, feeling his ring finger.

He took her left hand with his right hand, feeling her triple diamond.

"Don't you ever take that ring off again."

"Yes sir." She was in complete surrender.

He allowed his tongue to wiggle its way inside of her.

She rubbed her vagina against his face.

He brought his mouth two inches higher and found her upright peak. He took it into his mouth and flicked his tongue across it with fast motion.

She moaned.

He pulled on it and kept it between his tongue and top teeth, and gently sucked, bobbing his head.

She jerked. "Ohhhhh, that feels good."

He felt his dick stiffen below him as he readjusted to make room in his shorts.

He released her hands and again entered her with his middle fingers.

She stretched her arms above her head. Her slender fingers clutched the bedpost. She was grinding faster and moaning louder. Her eyes shut tight. She was disappearing in the darkness of lust.

He could feel her muscular waves building with more intensity. He curled his fingers upward as he felt her about to cum, and secured a steady oral grip on her clit.

She raised her rear end and froze, and said intensely, "Oh Mangus. Oh. Oh. Oh."

She spewed her silken syrup onto his fingers and her clit throbbed until it came to rest, still in his mouth. A pool of juice had been delivered from her pleased pussy.

She opened her eyes, squirmed, and reached down to push him away. The sensitivity was too much to bare.

He removed his fingers and inserted them in his mouth to taste, sucking them gently. His lips looked wet as he retreated. "That's the real deal there. Ain't nothin fake about that."

She released the headboard and tried to control her breathing.

Mangus positioned his lips to blow her lower skin dry. "That's for putting up with me and all that I put you through. That's just my little way of saying, thank you. I just wanted you give you something you could feel."

"No. Thank you." Marina smiled down at him and then he stood, replacing the covers over his wife, and tucking her in.

"Now, you can go to sleep. Goodnight." He kissed her on the lips.

She kissed him back. "Goodnight," she said, just as she found the right spot and closed her eyes in satisfaction.

This time, her curled up position was one of comfort and content. She was back home where she belonged.

He blew out the candles and joined her.

They slept through the night in peace.

Chapter Forty-Five

"She had a glow about her."

It was a week or so later, and Marina had finally contacted the foster agency to allow Naomi to spend another weekend with them. Naomi was dropped off on a Friday night. They had a slumber party again and stayed up late, baking cookies and making up silly bedtime stories.

It was now the next morning and Mangus had to work. Leah made sure to stop by just to see the happy family with her own eyes. Plus, she wanted to finally meet Naomi.

Leah joked with Mangus, while giving a wink to Marina. "I can't believe you took her back."

Marina popped her tongue and shot him a dry look.

"Yeah, and she took me back, too," Mangus said.

"Oh how sweet," Leah said. She then asked Marina, "So what do you and Naomi have planned for the day?"

"We're going to the bookstore," Naomi answered for Marina. She had a face of wonder and innocence. She was on Marina's laptop playing a game of junior scrabble.

"I love books," said Leah.

Naomi smiled.

Mangus had his jacket and gun belt in hand while he walked up to Naomi. "Hey Naomi, I'll see you later, little lady. You two have fun today, okay?"

"Okay. Bye, sir," Naomi said, keeping her sights on the computer screen.

Mangus hugged Marina and said, "Bye, sweetheart. I'll call you in a little while."

Leah said, "You gonna stop at the donut shop on your way?"

"Very funny," Mangus replied, heading toward the door.

"I'm just saying." Leah's eyes laughed.

"Anyway, I'm out. I love you, baby," he said loudly with the sound of a kiss.

Marina yelled out with the kitchen wall between them, "Baby, don't forget that we're going out with Bob Hill and his wife tomorrow night, okay?"

"Got it. No worries."

"Love you back," she said.

"I love you, too, baby," Leah yelled to Mangus.

He could be heard laughing as he closed the door.

"Life looks good over here, girl," Leah told Marina.

"Hey, why don't you come with Naomi and me and we can make it a girls morning."

"I wish I could. D.J. left last night for the weekend and I'm headed up there now to meet him."

"Meet him where?"

"His family reunion at Lake Lanier. They've been there since yesterday."

"Uh oh, I guess this thing you two have going is serious."

"About as serious as I'm gonna let it get. You won't see me running around with a husband ever again."

"Oh Leah, you are not doomed to be single unless you choose to be."

"Well, I choose to be. If it's not broke, don't fix it."

"Very good Naomi. You're so smart," Marina said, looking over as she scored a triple point word.

"Okay, Marina, you know what? I'm about to go because your way of speaking and quaint little family life talk is making me nauseous."

Naomi said, "My foster mom told me my name means pure and sweet. Did you know that?"

"No, I didn't," said Marina, smiling.

Leah whispered near Marina, "I guess Naomi Campbell didn't get the memo."

"Leah. Stop that." Marina then said to Naomi, "I think you have a very beautiful name. And it fits you."

"Gag, I'll call you later."

"You do that."

"Naomi, it was nice meeting you. I'll see you again soon."

"Okay, ma'am. Bye."

"She's so polite," Leah said to Marina, looking impressed.

Marina stepped up and hugged Leah as she stood at the front door.

Leah said, “I love you.”

“Love you back.”

Marina closed the door and spoke to Naomi with a smile, “Okay, after we eat, how about if we head out to Barnes and Noble and then to Pizza Hut for lunch? Would you like that?”

“That would be cool.”

“I’ll be in the kitchen if you need me.”

Marina had a pep in her step. She had a glow about her. This was Marina’s idea of true calm.

Chapter Forty-Six

"...must be writing fiction books nowadays..."

Mangus and Ronnie stood near their pale gray side-by-side lockers in the sterile police precinct locker room.

Ronnie adjusted his gun belt while he spoke. "Hey dude, what's up?

"Everything's everything. How about with you?"

"Just hanging in there."

"That's all you can do," Mangus said, sitting on the long bench, buttoning his shirt.

"I'm hoping today is peaceful. Just wanting to get out of here so I can get the day over with and enjoy what little bit of whatever's left of the weekend."

"What's on your list?"

Ronnie opened his locker and adjusted the mirror to face him. "Probably church tomorrow."

"Me too," Mangus said.

"Funny how so many cops seem to find church."

"If those rookies don't think they need it when they first get here, they'll find out soon enough. So, you all still looking to buy a new house?"

Ronnie replied, "Yeah, but probably south of Atlanta. The prices are better."

"Oh, I was gonna see if you wanted to check out my house."

"You two are selling? Didn't you just buy that place not long ago?" Ronnie ran a black comb through his curly hair.

"Yeah, but, I'm thinking about it."

"Man, it's too pricey for us in Sugar Hill. You've got you one of those Mc Mansions."

Mangus stood up. "I do not."

"But hey, if you don't have a realtor yet, a buddy of mine, this brother named Jerome Butler is the best. He owns Butler Realty."

"Jerome Butler sounds familiar. Hey, he wouldn't happen to have a sister named Maxine would he?"

"You know her?"

"Do I know her? She lives right next door to us."

Ronnie reached deep inside his locker and removed his watch and badge. "We met her at a fourth of July barbeque not long ago at Jerome's house in Peachtree City. Fine as hell."

"I'll just say it's a long story about her. She's been through a lot. Apparently she had a crazy ex-husband. But to be honest, she's the reason I'm thinking about moving." Mangus opened his locker, too.

Ronnie gave him that look. "Man, no you didn't. What was she your little cut buddy?"

"Like I said, it's a long story."

"Dang, I never would have thought. When did that…? I don't even wanna know. I'll tell you one thing, Maxine must be writing fiction books nowadays because he was not the crazy one. And from what Jerome told me she's never been married. What I know is she served some time for sweating some brotha in Chicago a few years ago. She said it was self-defense, but it turns out he'd called the police on her a dozen times."

Mangus paused from sorting his belt into the first loop. "Are you sure this is the same person. She lived in Los Angeles, right?"

"Big tittie girl with dark skin?"

"Yeah."

"See, he said she served time in Chicago where her ex-boyfriend lived. She went to where this dude relocated to and stalked him even after he filed a restraining order against her, and then she tried to break in while he was banging his new woman. She had a gun and threatened to kill him. She did less than a year on harassment and terrorist threats." Ronnie closed his locker.

Mangus kept his focus while his eyes showed puzzlement. "You are shittin me. Are you sure about this?"

"Man, one thing I don't have a problem with is my memory. What's your trip anyway? You've forgotten to check folks out around here before you get to know 'em? Surely before you hit it, bro. You broke the cardinal background check rule. I think you're smart to move. It's a small ass world, huh?"

Mangus closed his locker and said, "Yeah. Hey, I'll check you in a minute," as he stepped away in a hurry.

Chapter Forty-Seven

"...the test I took came back positive."

"Naomi, oh pure and sweet one," Marina said happily later that afternoon when they returned from their girlie day.

"Yes, ma'am."

"Let's go check and see if we have any mail."

"Okay."

Naomi did her best to pull Marina along from the front door to the sidewalk and then ran ahead of her. Marina laughed and kept her feet moving, making sure not to step on anything as she was barefoot.

Marina said as she pulled the mailbox cover forward and down, "Here, you can reach inside and get it."

Naomi stuck her thin arm deep inside the box and pulled out a stack of letters and handed them to Marina.

"Thanks."

Naomi instantly ran back to the front door and darted inside.

Marina admired her energy, walked slowly, and looked through each of the letters, most of them bills. She had a light green notice from the post office indicating that a package was left at a neighbor's residence for the Baskerville household. She made note of the house number. The address was that of Maxine's. She glanced over at the front of Maxine's house and then looked back, continuing to check the mail.

She headed back into the house and tossed the mail onto the large coffee table, next to her cell phone and keys.

"Naomi, I'll be right back, I'm going right next door to get some more mail. You stay right where you are, okay?"

"Yes, ma'am." Naomi sat on the floor watching a Disney movie.

Marina took the notice and stepped down the driveway, along the sidewalk, and up the long driveway to Maxine's home.

She could see that the great care Maxine had given to her garden paid off. The plentiful bunches of gold annuals, white perennials, and pink bulbs were thriving. There was a thick, straw doormat with a big round, yellow happy face, and there was a dainty, silver door chime that hung from the porch light in the shape of blue butterflies. The chime was silent as the air was still. The temperature was in the 90's.

Marina pressed the round doorbell. It was more of a buzz than a ring. She adjusted the fabric under her arms as she could feel sweat beginning to build up. The heated summer concrete met her bare feet as she stood, even though she was standing under the shade of the white awning.

The door opened and Maxine stood in the entryway, wide jugs and all, with her hand still on the shiny brass doorknob. She dropped her hand and said, "Hello." She pressed the frame of her eyeglasses closer to her face.

Marina's eyes automatically traveled the length of Maxine's womanly body, to her long, plum acrylic nails and then to her dark, oval face. "Hi. Sorry to bother you. I have this notice that you signed for a package for us. I just wanted to come by pick it up." Marina held up the paper.

"Oh yes. It was UPS, I think. Just one second. You can come in."

"Oh no, I'll wait right here."

Maxine did a slow step away, wearing shorts, as usual, and a flowered blue and red peasant top. "Okay, it's in the den back here. Just a second."

Marina folded the paper and put it in her pocket. She turned her back and peered down the street, and then looked over at the view of her own property from Maxine's doorway.

"So how are things going?" Maxine asked, though Marina could not see her.

"Good."

"Great. I really am glad to see you back here. I mean back with your husband that is."

Marina looked down at her bare feet. The toes of her right foot wiggled up and back. "Thanks."

Maxine's voice still carried from the other room. "You know, I have to apologize for coming by unannounced the other day. Mangus really didn't know I was stopping by."

"No problem." As much as she avoided it, Marina gave a slight peek into Maxine's yellow-gold painted living room, with bright colored decorations, wooden native figurines, child-like, stuffed animals, and wide-eyed collectible dolls. It looked cluttered and cramped. Marina denied her mind the opportunity to imagine…imagine her husband as a private visitor.

Maxine appeared. “Are you guys still selling your house?” Her hands were empty.

“No. No, we’re not.”

She stood squarely in the doorway. “Oh. Maybe that’s just something Mangus was thinking of. You know what? I wanted to try to call Mangus if it’s okay.”

“For what?”

“I need to talk to him. But of course, I don’t want to piss you off.”

“I don’t get pissed off.”

“Oh, I see.”

Marina looked past Maxine’s glasses and into her eyes, sounding impatient. “Maxine, where’s the package?”

“Oh, I have it upstairs actually.” She turned and looked up toward the stairway and then turned back around. “When the guy came to the door, I had just gotten out of the shower and I ran down in my robe and then ran back up. You can come in while I go upstairs.”

“You know what? When you find it, just leave it on your porch, please. I’ll come back and get it later.” Marina turned her torso.

“So, can I call him?”

“Yes, you can.”

“Well, I guess it’s just as well that I go ahead and tell you. Maybe you could tell him for me.”

Marina turned back to face her neighbor. “Tell him what?”

“See, I left my house early this morning to get…well the test I took came back positive. Please tell Mangus.” Maxine motioned her hand as though Marina could now be excused.

Marina’s voice dropped. “What?”

“Yes, I’m so excited.”

“Excited? You’re telling me you’re pregnant? And you want me to believe you’re pregnant by a married man who lives right next door and you’re excited?” Disbelief took over Marina’s stare. It was as if a match had been struck in the recesses of her belly.

“Well I know you didn’t think I would have an abortion. That’s not what you’re thinking is it?”

Marina spoke quickly. “I’m thinking I can’t believe you want me to believe you slept with my husband. And unprotected at that.”

Maxine spewed her words and wore a smug smile. "Oh we did. And usually we were in your house. In your bed."

Marina's heart thundered in her chest. She could hear herself breathing. "Maxine, you really need to back off and cut this out. If you're trying to get to me, it's not working. You need to see a doctor and make sure you're really pregnant before you come telling me."

"These at-home tests are very accurate. But I guess you wouldn't know about that."

Marina's stare was deep. "You know, I'm gonna tell you once and one time only. Cut out the remarks. It's obvious you're trying to pull out every stop to get my husband. He made a mistake. Actually, I made a mistake by leaving and rejecting him. I have to live with the fact that he turned to you. And that's not gonna be easy. But you are not gonna get any closer to him by insulting me or using lies to try and get me upset. I have a family and I'm looking forward to living a peaceful life. And if we do end up having to put that house up for sale, we will."

"Oh that won't change the future as far as Mangus being a father in about eight months. You can't control that." The look on Maxine's face was soap opera-like.

"No I can't. Maxine, where's the package?" Marina held her hand out.

"I'm trying to go upstairs, but you won't let me."

She took her hand back and her chin dropped. "I won't let you?"

"Oops, now don't go off on me just because I don't have the package as quickly as you want me to."

"Maxine, you are one crazy broad. Goodbye. Screw the package." Marina commanded her legs to step. She waved her hand in surrender and headed down the walkway.

Maxine raised her voice and her brow. "Screw you bitch."

Marina's mind rewound. Her legs locked.

"You came onto my property. And you know what? You should be trying to keep your man because he can fuck like a damn porno star."

Marina moonwalked and jerked her body around. "What?" Her fiery mind was ripped in half, between being called the stabbing, memory jerking B word, and the unsolicited review of her husband's supreme bedroom performance. She felt a heaviness in her chest.

"Tell me, Marina, are you the one who taught him that little trick with the Timberlands? I came three times in a row, you know?" On that note, Maxine backed up as though ready to walk away.

The heat whipped up throughout Marina's body. Her voice cracked. "You…you have lost your damn mind." She stepped one big step onto the bamboo hardwood flooring inside of Maxine's home, and then another.

Maxine stood still. "So, did Mangus tell you that, uh, I think her name was Melanie? All I know is she had long black hair. That she came by one night, too?"

As if automatic, Marina drew her hand back and squeezed her fist tight, aiming it into position, preparing to stretch her arm out into the direction of Maxine's trash talking jaw. Marina shouted, "Woman, you know what?"

Maxine took a few steps back.

Marina took a few steps forward. And then she stopped, fighting to breathe, her mind racing, suddenly…allowing…her hand…to lower. "Okay, I don't even believe a word you've said. I know…"

Maxine's neck rolled like cubie-doll. Her words moved fast. "What you need to know is that you have met your damn match. I can fuck your ass up." She reached back behind her back and then gave a quick look in the direction of the fireplace. She took a couple more slow steps back and by touch, gripped the head of the solid brass poker. She pulled it to her side and scrunched up her face. "You need to know that I can break your ass in two."

Marina looked down at Maxine's side. "You need to put that down."

"You're in my house. You threatened me remember?" Maxine's voice bounced against the bright walls.

"Maxine, I did not…No," Marina yelled sharply at the top of her lungs.

And in the time it took to say that one, two letter word, Maxine lifted the poker and flung it back, raising it over her head just as Marina pivoted back toward the door and lifted her foot to step forward. Marina's neck sank and her shoulders raised, and the downward momentum from the tip of the pointed edge met the very top of Marina's skull with a dull thud. Marina's eyes flared with a straining flash. Her mouth gaped open and her tightly clenched hands sprang forward while her body unfolded onto the surface of the hardwood floor.

Maxine, with searing rage flickering in her eyes, stood over Marina's helpless body. Her eyeglasses seemed to fog up. And then, as though she had been suddenly awakened from a deep, nightmarish sleep, she dropped the poker. It hit the floor with a reverberating clang.

Marina lay on her back and stared straight up, directly into Maxine's blank face. A fading look of shock shown in Marina's half-open eyes. But with each slow-motioned second that passed, her eyes closed more and more. Her long strands of her ruby hair were mussed about. Her fists, which were braced tightly, had opened flatly and were still.

Finally, Marina's mouth closed for a moment, and it looked as though she swallowed. Her eyes opened again and she gave a faint whimper. Her head dropped limp to her left, with bright red blood tricking from her raised, busted scalp, while the bloody poker lay just a few feet away.

"Ma'am!" Naomi hollered, standing in the middle of the doorway with her wide, dark eyes. She screamed piercingly at the top of her lungs. Her young, slender body froze and she instantaneously dropped Marina's cell phone, which bounced near her bare feet along the threshold. It landed straight up.

Marina had twenty-three missed calls. All from Mangus.

* * *

Downtrodden-faced anchorman Bob Hill made a low-keyed announcement during the late news that evening, broadcast to the station's faithful Atlanta viewers.

His voice was deep. "A member of our family, local DBC news anchor Marina Maxwell Baskerville, died today from what has been reported as an undisclosed fatal injury. Authorities have arrested Maxine Butler, a neighbor of Mrs. Baskerville, on suspicion of murder."

Bob sat at the news desk alone. The cameraman had a close, tight shot on his impassioned face.

"Marina Baskerville has been an anchor here for over five years, and originally began her career in Atlanta out of college. She also worked as a news reporter in Miami, Florida and then in New Orleans, Louisiana.

"Marina's husband, Mangus Baskerville, a local police officer in Gwinnett County, along with his parents, retired City Council President William Baskerville, and his wife, Camille Baskerville, who runs the United Way here in Atlanta, issued a family statement calling this is a tragic loss and saying that Marina Baskerville was a woman of great courage and undying generosity."

He gave a quick sigh and continued, "On a personal note, I grew to know and love Marina. Even though she was very young, we were colleagues, and dear friends. My wife and I had plans to have dinner with the Baskervilles tomorrow evening. This is a big loss for the world of journalism, for the numerous organizations Marina supported throughout her lifetime, and obviously a tremendous loss for her family and friends.

"Funeral services will be held early next week at the *Faithful Word Church*, though no specific date has been set at this time, pending further investigation and a coroner's results.

"A fund has been set up in her name at Sun Trust Bank by her friend Leah Hyatt-Mitchell. All donations will benefit the *Melon Heart Foster Care Agency*.

"In the immortal words of Marina Maxwell Baskerville, 'Keep the Faith.' Goodnight my dear friend."

Epilogue

One year later

"...feeling a large lump snowballing in his throat."

The scarlet and mustard colored leaves stirred slightly, depending upon the random suggestion of the wind. Fall had arrived and the large Duluth home was ready for a special celebration. The familiar smell of clean linen was comforting.

While closing the front door behind them, Mrs. Baskerville extended her greetings just as Mangus and Naomi pulled off their shoes. "Hey, son, come on in. Hey, Naomi. How are you sweetie?"

"Hi Grandma. Hi Grandpa," Naomi said excitedly, stepping up to Mangus' father who stood next to his wife, hugging him tightly.

He laughed with his arms open wide and bent down for the sweet embrace. "Hey Naomi. Happy birthday."

"Thanks, sir." Naomi stepped across the rooms and into the kitchen with her grandpa. She wore a yellow and pale blue party dress with a big bow in the back. Her hair was pushed back with a baby yellow headband. The fine hairs of her bangs aligned her forehead.

Mrs. Baskerville spoke as she and Mangus stood in the middle of the living room. "She looks so pretty. Seems like she's doing better."

Mangus kept an eye on Naomi. He could see his birthday girl beyond the kitchen doorway. He nodded. "Today's been good. She's coming along."

"I know it's been tough."

"Even harder than I ever imagined." He narrowed his eyes.

"I'm proud of you for being there and for going ahead with the adoption."

"She's a good kid. She's been through a lot."

Mrs. Baskerville examined the tiny new lines forming under her young son's eyes. "Naomi's got a good father." They took a few steps into the family room. "Is Maxine still trying to communicate with you from her forty year cell?"

"Not lately."

Wearing a short-sleeved tunic, Mangus' mother rubbed her upper arms up and down and looked up at her son. "As tragic of a story as this is, you've stepped up and that's a good thing. Mangus, if you ever need to get away, you know we're here. Seems you haven't really had time alone to grieve."

"I'm fine."

"Good."

"If only Marina was far enough along for our baby to have been born, I could have had a part of her forever. I know she didn't know she was pregnant."

"Well, let's just thank God Maxine wasn't expecting. Even though she tried to tell the police Marina was jealous because she thought she was. Self defense my foot. That unborn child is why they doubled her sentence. Thank God."

Mangus stayed in thought.

"Son, it doesn't matter to us that you two separated and we didn't know. Some things are sacred between a husband and a wife. Parents just know, no matter what our kids say or don't say. Your father and I understand every decision you made."

"Thanks."

"Have you been to church lately?"

"Yes. Naomi enjoys it. She's made a new friend or two in Sunday School."

"Maybe we can go with you next week?"

He managed a smile directly at his mother. "I'd like that."

They casually stepped closer toward the kitchen again. She saw his smile fade quickly. "Mangus, I know we talked about this before, but you are not to blame for what happened."

"Like I told you, I should have been there. I should have known."

"You did all you could do."

His tone decreased, almost to a whisper. "I let Maxine into my life on a personal level. I never should have done that."

"You're only human. The Lord took Marina home when He wanted to, the way he wanted her to go. You can't live with regrets."

"It was still a triangle, and I made it one."

She assured him with a look of nurture. "It was her time to go. We miss her too. She had a good heart. And son, remember it'll never be okay, but it'll be all right." She placed her hand on his forearm as they stood.

"Thanks, Mom."

She chose to say at an energetic level, "Well, this is no mood to be in for an eleventh birthday party." She spoke toward the kitchen. "It's the birthday girl's day, right Naomi?"

Naomi walked up to her father while smiling at her grandma. "Yes, Grandma." She gave Mangus her china doll eyes. "Daddy, can I have my cake now?"

He looked down as they locked hands. "No, baby. We need to wait until everyone gets here. We'll cut the cake after we eat."

Mrs. Baskerville said, "Oh that reminds me. Leah called. She and her husband D.J. are on their way. They were just leaving home about ten minutes ago."

"Good. She's been great."

Naomi glanced up at Mangus again. "Auntie Leah's coming?"

"Yes."

Naomi's eyes lit up. "Can I have some gum, please?"

"Sure."

Mangus released her hands. Her lips broke a smile. He grinned in appreciation of having her, and in acknowledgement of her bubbly nature, which was the total opposite of her so-so mood the day before. Her resilience was motivating, even if it was all because of the magic that a birthday can bring.

He dug into his right pants pocket and his fingertips detected the shape of a single, foil-wrapped stick of cinnamon gum. As he pulled it out, a tiny sheet of white paper fell out onto the Oriental rug. It was folded into eighths.

He bent down to pick it up.

"Here you go," he said to Naomi.

"Thanks." She hurried back into the kitchen with her grandma behind her. "Did you see my cake, Grandma?" she asked in the distance.

"Yes, Naomi. I saw it," her grandma laughed as she replied. She looked at her son. "Oh, I love that word. Grandma."

Mangus smiled and turned his back, walking to the other side of the family room. He checked out the piece of paper and peeled it open, noticing the neat, fancy script that brought familiarity. It was dated the day that Marina joined the church, the morning she'd come forward for the alter call. Mangus realized he was wearing the same black dress pants he'd worn that day.

The letter read:

Honey,

I'm so glad to be back home where I belong. Lord knows I love you.

I vow to be a better wife for life. A better woman. And soon, I hope, a loving mother. I've accepted all of me and this much I know. I've found peace.

I've asked God to forgive my sins and I have accepted Jesus Christ as my Lord and Savior. Thanks for being there for that. Now I know I'll have eternal life. I am grateful for the journey. My reward is greater because of the pain. I cherish the lesson. I've kept the faith. And I am here. And so it is.

Until death, do us part.

You and I, you and I, you and I.

Signed, Mrs. Marina Laurinda Baskerville

P.S. Thank you for letting me tell my story. My drama had a purpose. And God tells me that my healing will bring healing to others.

Mangus took a deep breath. His eyes darted back and forth to see if anyone detected his swift change in demeanor. While refolding the never-to-be-lost paper and replacing it into his pocket, he found his way back through the room and down the hall, heading to his mom and dad's guest bathroom, all the while feeling a large lump snowballing in his throat.

He closed the door.

And he leaned against the wall.

And he crossed his arms along his pounding chest.

And his left hand met his weighted eyelids.

And he lowered his thought-filled head.

And Mangus Baskerville…cried.

There's no such thing as a happy ending,
only a story that hasn't ended yet.

Marissa Monteilh

MAIL TO:
PO Box 423
Brandywine, MD 20613
301-362-6508

FAX TO:
301-579-9913

ORDER FORM

Date:
Phone:
E-mail:

Ship to:	
Address:	
City & State:	Zip:
Attention:	

Make all checks and money orders payable to: **Life Changing Books**

Qty.	ISBN	Title	Release Date	Price
	0-9741394-0-8	A Life To Remember by Azarel	Aug-03	$ 15.00
	0-9741394-1-6	Double Life by Tyrone Wallace	Nov-04	$ 15.00
	0-9741394-5-9	Nothin Personal by Tyrone Wallace	Jul-06	$ 15.00
	0-9741394-2-4	Bruised by Azarel	Jul-05	$ 15.00
	0-9741394-7-5	Bruised 2: The Ultimate Revenge by Azarel	Oct-06	$ 15.00
	0-9741394-3-2	Secrets of a Housewife by J. Tremble	Feb-06	$ 15.00
	0-9724003-5-4	I Shoulda Seen It Comin by Danette Majette	Jan-06	$ 15.00
	0-9741394-4-0	The Take Over by Tonya Ridley	Apr-06	$ 15.00
	0-9741394-6-7	The Millionaire Mistress by Tiphani	Nov-06	$ 15.00
	1-934230-99-5	More Secrets More Lies by J. Tremble	Feb-07	$ 15.00
	1-934230-98-7	Young Assassin by Mike G.	Mar-07	$ 15.00
	1-934230-95-2	A Private Affair by Mike Warren	May-07	$ 15.00
	1-934230-94-4	All That Glitters by Ericka M. Williams	Jul-07	$ 15.00
	1-934230-93-6	Deep by Danette Majette	Jul-07	$ 15.00
	1-934230-96-0	Flexin & Sexin by K'wan, Anna J. & Others	Jun-07	$ 15.00
	1-934230-92-8	Talk of the Town by Tonya Ridley	Jul-07	$ 15.00
	1-934230-89-8	Still a Mistress by Tiphani	Nov-07	$ 15.00
	1-934230-91-X	Daddy's House by Azarel	Nov-07	$ 15.00
	1-934230-87-1-	Reign of a Hustler by Nissa A. Showell	Jan-08	$ 15.00
	1-934230-86-3	Something He Can Feel by Marissa Montelih	Feb-08	$ 15.00
	1-934230-88-X	Naughty Little Angel by J. Tremble	Feb-08	$ 15.00
	0-9741394-9-1	Teenage Bluez	Jan-06	$ 10.99
	0-9741394-8-3	Teenage Bluez II	Dec-06	$ 10.99
			Total for Books	**$**

Shipping Charges (add $4.25 for 1-4 books*) $

Total Enclosed (add lines) $

*** Prison Orders- Please allow up to three (3) weeks for delivery.**

For credit card orders and orders over 25 books, please contact us at orders@lifechaningbooks.net (Cheaper rates for COD orders)

***Shipping and Handling of 5-10 books is $6.25, please contact us if your order is more than 10 books. (301)362-6508**